THE CARDIST

A NOVEL OF HEARTH AND HOME

DEREK KENNEY

To Britt, who I refused to let read this book until it was done but still nodded along in understanding whenever I'd excitedly describe a random idea for the story she knew nothing about.

To Finn, who made finishing this book infinitely more difficult by running up to me every time I sat at my desk saying "No, dada! Don't work!"

To Me, my target audience. Even if no one else enjoys it, you got hours of enjoyment writing, editing, and sharing it.

CONTENTS

PART THREE

PART ONE

"Our life is frittered away by detail... simplify, simplify"
- Henry David Thoreau

~~~

"In the presence of profound wisdom, even the most confident find
themselves humbled and compelled to reevaluate their own lives."
- Plato

~~~

"Big, big booty, what you got? A big booty."
- Jennifer Lopez

I

THAT BUTT THOUGH

"I HOPE YOU KNOW WHAT YOU'RE DOING."

The corgi didn't move a muscle, the only evidence that it wasn't a statue were a determined "Boof" sound and flinch of its snout.

Its gaze remained locked on the sliding door of the van, reminding Ethan of regal knights from old fairy tales. Its bark, if it could even be called a bark, seemed weak compared to the slobbery, menacing growls coming from outside, making the van feel like a to-go tray filled with a tasty, greasy dinner.

And yet, the small dog looked entirely unbothered.

"Well, alright then," Ethan grunted as he swung the door open, hoping to catch the wolves off guard.

Before the door was even half way open, the corgi launched itself out of the van like a cannon, vaulting over the closest of the three wolves and landing on the ground facing away from all of them. Ethan for some reason felt afraid for the dog's safety, as though the dog had been a close friend for years.

Don't expose your back to wolves!

He was about to yell for the corgi to turn around when it

moved. But it didn't turn around; it started... twerking? Dancing? Whatever it was doing required a lot of butt and hip movement.

All three of the wolves stopped growling, their heads turned to the side like they were working on a particularly difficult puzzle. Ethan could only stare, his mouth open.

After a few moments of silence, he threw his hands up in frustration.

"... the hell?!"

The corgi glanced back with a look on its face that said "Come on man, I can't keep this up forever." Anger and confusion vanished as Ethan realized the dog was purposefully providing a distraction.

Chambering a round in his hand gun, he crept out of the van.

The closest wolf, whose fur had a distinct red tinge to it, didn't even notice as he stopped beside it. Aiming his pistol at the back of the wolf's head, execution style, Ethan took a deep breath. At the bottom of his exhale he pulled the trigger.

The explosion sent his ears ringing as the wolf collapsed like a bag of bricks, catching a glimpse of whatever bits of skull and brain matter blew out the front before forcing his eyes away.

Growling resumed as the remaining two wolves lost all interest in the corgi and turned toward Ethan, ready to pounce like a dog ready to play, but not nearly as adorable.

The closest of the two, this one with blue fur, launched itself at Ethan. Mid-air, it gathered a faint blue light into its claw. On instinct, Ethan lifted his hand and fired three quick shots, the weight of the wolf barreling into him right as he fired. A slight cold pain numbed his left arm, which probably wasn't a good sign. The wolf wasn't moving, which was a better sign.

Dizzy from the ringing in his ears, Ethan decided to hold off on any more shooting if he could help it. Better to conserve his ammo, anyway.

What had happened to the last wolf?

Ethan strained his ears from beneath the weight of the freshly killed wolf, but everything sounded muffled. He couldn't hear anything other than his own racing heartbeat.

Rolling to the side and shoving the wolf off him, he jumped to his feet, almost falling over as the dizziness settled. With a shake of his head, he looked around. A green furred wolf lay on the ground beside the passenger door of the van, its spine folded backwards. Lying on top of the wolf was the corgi, who looked like it had belly flopped onto the wolf's back and decided that was a comfortable place to relax.

The yet-unnamed corgi angled its head toward Ethan with a smug look on its face, like Spongebob when he realized Squidward liked Krabby Patties.

"Yes, yes," Ethan said, breathing out a sigh of relief. "You're a good girl."

2

THE NIGHT BEFORE

"There's nothing quite like a good poop."

A new man walked out of the rest area bathroom. That's how he felt anyway — a proverbial weight lifted from his shoulders. Or abdomen, in this case. Ethan reached his hands up to the sky, giving his back a much needed stretch, then headed back to his van.

The particular rest area where Ethan stopped was as good a place as any to get some sleep. He'd driven about ten hours through Texas and was somehow *still* in Texas. Neither New Mexico or Arizona were going to be much better. It didn't seem to matter, though, as he felt more excited and lighter than he had in a long time.

Not just because of his successful trip to the bathroom.

Friends and family had begun to notice the slump in his shoulders, the bags under his eyes, and general lack of relentless enthusiasm they were used to seeing.

You'd think that someone who'd dreamt his whole life of being in the military would finally find where he belonged; a place where he'd thrive. Turned out four years in the Army had been more than enough for him. Two years would have been the sweet spot. For now, at his wife's suggestion, Ethan intended on making the most of his newfound freedom.

Plans for the upcoming week filled his head as he climbed into the back of the van, eager to set up his sleep system. With fuel top offs, bathroom breaks, and food stops, he expected to make it to California in two days, right on time for his 30th birthday. He'd hang out with his family and get in as much home cooked food as he could before he set out on his adventure.

What kind of adventure? A backpacking trip across the Pacific Crest Trail. Twenty-six hundred miles of California, Oregon, and Washington wilderness were calling his name, a hike he figured would take him about five months.

'That's a long hike,' they'd said.

'No way! For real? A couple thousand miles is a long hike? Thanks mom, thanks dad. I never would have realized,' he'd replied, except not out loud. Only in his head. Whatever, it was fine.

Sarcasm could be therapeutic, sometimes.

Eventually everyone realized he wasn't joking and started asking real questions. Yes, Rebecca is on board. No, it was her idea in the first place. Yes, they could afford it. No, she and Jack would be staying with her folks. It was as though they assumed zero planning and forethought had been put into the trip.

Ugh, parents. He was a grown man!

To be fair, he understood the skepticism. The most difficult part of this whole trip was that he'd be away from his son for so long. Being in the Army, he was used to not seeing his wife, but his son was still young. It was hard to miss the toddler years.

But they both agreed he needed this. Ethan wasn't dumb, he knew Rebecca needed it too. He'd become progressively more difficult to live with, so this was as much a break for her as it was for him. Besides, they'd video chat as often as possible and he could fly back to spend time with them as often as needed.

So... in theory, Ethan wasn't in too much of a hurry.

After four years of being told what to do, he was eager to take his time and go at his own pace. They'd saved up enough money over the past year to not need to work for a while, his recent deployment making it much easier. It was amazing what he could do with a year of tax free income.

Before starting the hike, Ethan looked forward to spending time with his nephews. They were *huge* Pokémon nerds, especially the trading cards. He and his brother, their dad, had grown up playing and collecting them, so he was technically a nerd too.

Ethan had promised he'd battle them in the trading card game, even though he hadn't owned any cards since the prior Christmas when he'd sent them all to the boys as a gift. After a while, he kinda wished he had kept his cards from when he was a kid. Oh well. Most of the fun came from opening the packs anyway; the excitement that came from the potential in each unopened pack could be addicting.

The plan was to stop at a comic book store the following day to buy a starter deck and maybe a box of booster packs. He'd settle for a Target if he couldn't find one nearby. Again, technically, he wasn't in a rush.

Plenty-o-time.

Not quite tired enough to fall asleep, Ethan unrolled his sleeping bag, then opened the tough box in the back of the van. Inside were a few dozen MREs (Meal Ready to Eat) that he had "tactically acquired" from the training room before signing out of his unit on his last day in the Army. They were intended to be used on the hike, but he didn't feel like stopping for food out in the middle of Texas.

MREs. Bleh.

Still a better option than vending machine food, though he may have been willing to part with a stack of quarters if any of the machines had a Reese's Snack Cake. Those things were basically crack cocaine.

Ethan grabbed two of the MREs, looking over the names.

One was "Pork Sausage Patty, Maple Flavored". He mentally gagged as he tossed it back in the tough box. That MRE was the bane of his existence and he wouldn't wish it upon his worst enemy. Although, he would be happy to trade it to a new soldier who didn't know any better. That was the kind of harmless hazing he could get behind.

The other was labeled "Chicken, Noodles and Vegetables, in Sauce" which happened to be his favorite.

He tore open the MRE bag and separated the package's contents. The entree and flameless heater pouch were placed to his left. The small pouches of peanut butter and apple jelly were set to his right, while the applesauce with raspberry puree and bag of Skittles were left next to the accessory packet where he'd dumped everything. The accessory pack was the catch-all for little luxuries a soldier may appreciate: instant coffee, creamer, salt, sugar, matches, moist towelettes, and gum that may or may not be laced with laxative.

Once he had everything out and ready, Ethan took in a

mouthful of water from a one liter bottle, then spat it into the MRE's flameless heater system. A single mouthful happened to be just the right amount of water to activate whatever ridiculously unsafe chemicals were inside to heat his meal. He slide entrée pouch into the hear and stood it upright against the tough box, knowing it would take about ten minutes to properly cook.

That was ingenuity folks. Tricks of the trade.

While he waited, Ethan pulled a manila folder and a pencil from inside the tough box. Holding them in one hand, he closed the lid, then set the folder down on top of the box. He pulled a piece of paper with nine blank playing card sized outlines printed on one side. The boys *loved* drawing out their own custom Pokémon cards, so he'd had the idea to go overboard with his own.

The next ten minutes were spent drawing animals on the cards. Each animal was based on pets he'd had throughout his life, which meant they were mostly dogs. Ethan firmly believed there weren't enough dogs represented in Pokémon, and games in general, and would fight anyone who argued otherwise.

After finishing each drawing, he wrote names for the creature at the top left corner of the cards. It was all for fun, so Ethan didn't spend more than a moment on each name. Figuring he'd have plenty of time to fill in the rest of the information later, he left the "attack" sections for most of the cards blank. He did take the time to come up with a few stupid puns.

Who didn't have time for a quality pun?

When the ten minutes were up, he set aside the paper and pencil and smirked. The kind of smirk that says "Uncle Ethan is crazy".

"The boys are gonna love these," he thought as he opened the

pouch and scooped a spoonful of noodles, appreciating the work he'd done in the short time it took his food to cook.

Ethan fell asleep that night feeling calm and relaxed, knowing exactly what tomorrow held in store for him because *he* was the one who had chosen it.

Tomorrow was a new day.

3

HIM? REALLY?

"HIM? REALLY? YOU'RE SURE THIS IS THE ALTERNATE YOU WANT TO choose?"

The voice was old and grizzled, unconvinced that this was their best choice. There were an infinite number of more qualified Alternates.

"Yes, Father," responded a younger, confident voice. "You said we need to shake things up with as little direct involvement as possible. Sure, he's a bit naive and will likely cause himself no end of grief, but he has a perspective I think would have a ripple effect in Aidland."

The Father chuckled as he looked down at the man's white cargo van. It was parked at a rest stop along I-20 and was barely wide enough to fit a queen size bed in the back, but long enough to create a small living area or kitchen between the bed and front seats. Not that the man owned any of those things.

Instead of a bed, the man slept in a sleeping bag laid across a thin inflatable backpacking mattress. That in turn was placed on top of a foldable foam sleep mat, which was also meant for backpacking. The only other items in the van were a black plastic tough box, a green backpacking pack, and a large green Army duffle bag that was one extra pair of socks away from bursting.

"Very well, my son," said the Father. "Give him a bit of a head start, so he'll be less likely to get himself killed, and pick a place to drop him where he'll have time to acclimate."

"Yes, Father."

The Son thought for a moment, a couple locations in mind, but ultimately he'd already made his decision.

The ground around the van shook as the transition took effect, measuring on the low end of the Richter scale, but the man inside didn't stir. Still deep asleep, he only grumbled and rolled over. Noticing where the van had been placed, the Father bellowed with laughter.

"Ahhh, I see now why you've chosen him. This will be interesting. If nothing else, he'll get the time alone he's been desperately grasping for."

"Thank you, Father. I'm glad you like my choice," a grin spread across the Son's face. He peered into the van, his brow furrowed as he considered the challenges the Alternate would face.

"Show us what kind of man you are, Ethan Farris."

4
A NEW DAY

ETHAN WOKE WITH AN INTENSE NEED TO PEE.

Forcing his way out of his sleeping bag with a groan, he grabbed an empty Gatorade from the front seat cup holder and twisted off the cap. Relief flooded him as he emptied his bladder into the bottle.

No point getting out of the van if he didn't have to.

A strange dream had woken him and his mind worked overtime to process it before he had time to forget it. There was an earthquake, but he was young and in elementary school back in California. He was under his desk, the only place he felt safe. Those desks were basically indestructible, like a cockroach in a nuclear apocalypse.

He crawled back into his sleeping bag and fell asleep to the sounds of nature, way more nature than there should have been at the rest stop.

A while later, Ethan woke up groaning with a massive headache. He felt like a dehydrated noodle, which was strange considering all the fluids he drank the day before. No way the caffeine from a single energy drink would have dried him out *that* much.

Ethan sat up slowly, feeling some pain in his joints, then opened the tough box and searched through a sandwich baggie filled with a variety of pills. Three ibuprofen —part painkiller and part anti-inflammatory— were a surefire solution. He grabbed the pills and tossed them into his mouth, then chugged the rest of his water left over from the night before. He then ripped into an energy bar from an MRE he hadn't finished, his stomach growling at him like a dog left outside in the yard for a week.

Peeling away the rest of his sleeping bag, the cold air inside the van was bracing. No heater or air conditioning necessary.

He put on a clean pair of socks, followed by his driving shoes, which were just a pair of running shoes. As he finished getting ready for the day, he realized he didn't hear any sounds of cars driving past on the interstate. He stopped to listen, but didn't hear anything he would have expected to hear. Not even any people coming and going from the rest stop bathrooms.

Frowning, he looked down at his watch. The hour and minute hands read 6:37am. Hmm... There should have been some people out on the road already.

Strange, but not impossible.

With a shrug, Ethan pulled open the sliding door on the passenger side of his van and stepped out into the crisp morning air. He'd intended to make use of the bathroom and vending machines before getting back on the road, but instead of parking lot asphalt, Ethan's foot found grass.

Hmm... Grass? That wasn't right. He hadn't parked next to any grass. Ethan rubbed his eyes, then looked around.

He was in a small clearing surrounded by trees, but didn't recognize anything. The trees and grass didn't even look like they belonged in West Texas. There wasn't much underbrush and the trees were not close together, so he had a decent line of sight. Walking around the clearing, Ethan picked at the inside of his lips with his teeth as he took it all in, then went to the other side of the van.

Same on that side.

The trees were different. The grass was different. There was no rest stop. There wasn't a parking lot. There wasn't even any evidence that his van had driven into the clearing. No tire tracks. No footprints, other than the ones he'd just made.

"Uhh... Where am I?"

Ethan walked back to the sliding door, reaching in the van to grab his phone. It wouldn't turn on, black screen staring back at him. He held down the power button, thinking maybe he'd turned it off before bed to save battery. The phone still wouldn't turn on.

'What in the world...' he thought as he set the phone down and reached further into the van.

He grabbed his green ultralight backpacking bag and pulled it to the door. On the left shoulder strap was a small orange and black gps, attached by a small carabiner. It didn't respond to anything he did. No power, no noises of any kind. He knew for a fact that he charged the gps before driving west. Even if he'd left it on the whole time, which he hadn't, it shouldn't have died. The battery would have lasted at least a week.

Had the electronics all died somehow? Sometimes electronics were known to die from colder temperatures. But his watch still worked, right? He looked back at his wrist, the watch still reading 6:37am. It had definitely been longer than a minute since he last checked.

Well... that was dead too apparently.

Climbing into the van, Ethan moved into the driver's seat and grabbed his key from the cup holder in the center console. After a deep breath and a prayer he stuck it in the ignition, then turned.

Nothing. Not a single click. He took out the key and dropped it back in the cupholder, sighing in frustration.

Ethan climbed back out the side of the van, placing his hands on his hips as he took another look around.

"What in the world is happening?"

He let out a groan and dragged his hands down his face.

"Okay, Ethan. You can figure this out," he took a another deep breath in an attempt to calm himself. "Remember the Hitchhiker's Guide. Don't panic."

5

ETHAN PANICKED

"No! No! No!"

Ethan's heart thumped hard as he paced beside the van, like it might leap out of his chest at any moment.

The increased heart rate in turn raised his body temperature. A thin line of sweat dropped down his back, his forehead felt damp, and his lungs felt compressed like a Victorian age noblewoman in a too-tight corset. Struggling to breathe, he was only able to take in short breaths and was on the verge of hyperventilating.

Or... he supposed that meant he'd already started.

Pacing around the clearing for a few minutes, Ethan shook his hands at a tempo that would impress even world renowned drummers. Like when he needed to dry his hands in a public restroom, but they were out of paper towels and he refused to use the air dryers.

Ethan abruptly stopped his pacing.

"Breathe, man. Just breathe," he encouraged himself. "Breathe first, plan second."

He closed his eyes, taking a deep breath in, and counted to

five. Hold for another count of five, exhale for a count of five, then a few normal breaths. Heart rate still elevated, he did the breathing exercise two more times.

The shaking in his hands slowed and his lungs didn't feel quite as compressed. Ethan mumbled a thanks to his community college psychology professor for teaching the exercise to the class. Maybe it hadn't been as random as he thought it was back then. Ten years since he took that class and he still used it regularly.

With step one of *'calming the hell down'* complete, Ethan moved on to step two: planning. He scurried back over to his van. Although he wasn't as panicky as before, he still made a mess of the van as he searched for his notebook and a pen.

"Three phase plan."

He repeated it like a mantra until he had the notebook and pen in hand, then sat down in the doorway of the sliding door. His handwriting was more firm and shaky than usual, but he wrote out a three phase plan.

1. Get the hell out of here.
2. Get to California.
3. See a neurologist.

Ethan stopped writing and chuckled to himself, then took another deep breath in and out. The list wasn't particularly actionable at the moment, but the goofy exaggeration did help him feel a bit less frantic. If there was one thing he learned while in the Army, it was gallows humor. Acknowledge the stupidity, laugh, and then move forward.

"Alright, actionable steps this time. Improvise, adapt, overcome."

Reading over his new plan, Ethan then broke down step

one, 'Get the hell out of here', into smaller steps he could actually act on.

1. Pee and/or poop
2. Eat breakfast and drink water
3. Find some high ground to get a look around.

Looking over his list, he nodded.

"I can do this."

His stomach gurgled. Time to complete step one. He reached into the van, once again pulling his pack close, thankful that he had already prepared some of his backpacking stuff. He pulled a gallon sized ziplock bag from an outer mesh lining of the pack. In it was a small orange plastic shovel, a flattened roll of toilet paper, some flushable wet wipes, and a roll of doggie bags. At least he could relieve himself without having to find a public restroom.

"Small victories."

~~~

After scarfing down an MRE, Ethan crossed off both step one and two of his three phase plan. He was starting to feel more confident in figuring out his situation, so it was a good time to take a look around.

Crazy what a full stomach and empty bowels can do for a man's mental state.

While eating, he came up with a simple idea on how to find some high ground. He moved around to the back of the van where a thin metal ladder was attached to the rear door on the passenger side, then climbed up to the roof.

The clearing turned out to be a pretty nice setup for a

campground. Trees provided decent shade in a way that looked like it would stay shaded throughout the day. Standing on the van didn't allow him to see much beyond the clearing, but he did catch a glimpse of what was either a range of large hills or small mountains off to the east.

As he stared off at the hill-mountains, Ethan pressed his thumbs into his palms, switching back and forth between each hand. The motions had always had a calming affect on him. After a few minutes his breathing settled, as did his fidgeting.

Now that he wasn't panicking anymore, the sound of running water off to the west grabbed his attention. He knew it was west because of his Army issued compass. Technically, he had turned in the one the Army issued him, but he'd loved it so much that he bought one for himself.

"I can do this," he coached himself, already formulating new three phase plan. "One step at a time."

6

GET MY STEPS IN

FINALLY! ETHAN CRESTED THE TOP OF THE HILL.

The hike had been a step above breaking a sweat, although the lack of humidity had been a huge relief. After spending almost a year near the Persian Gulf and a smattering of years in the Southern United States, he'd be happy to never live in a humid climate ever again.

Ethan shifted a bead along a small length of paracord tied to the shoulder strap of his pack. A trick he'd learned in the Army, how to track his distance while in the wilderness. Pulling his small notebook and pen out of his pocket, he did some basic math.

Each of the ten beads had moved seven times and, because he had just finished another ten beads, he moved one bead over on a second length of paracord. Each bead on the second cord counted as ten beads on the first cord. Easier to keep track beads rather than steps when hiking longer distances.

Based on the length of Ethan's strides, he'd learned during Basic Training that he could walk fifty meters in seventy steps.

The math looked something like this:

- 70 Steps = 1 Bead
- 1 Bead = 50 Meters
- 70 Beads = 3,500 Meters
- 3,500 Meters = 3.5 km (Hurray Metric System)

So he'd hiked three and half kilometers from the van to the top of the hill.

Flipping to a new page of his notebook, which had a dotted grid design, he drew a small dot in the center of the page to represent his current position and labeled it **"The Hill"**. Why overcomplicate a hand drawn map?

Looking back the way he'd hiked, he could just barely make out the white of his van through the trees. Ethan grabbed his compass from his pocket, aimed toward the clearing, and saw that he was directly east from where he'd started.

Through the trees he could see a river running from north to south. There were less trees to the northwest, allowing him to get a better look of the river, but he couldn't be sure of the width of its width at this distance. It reminded him of the Savannah River, on the border of Georgia and South Carolina.

So... narrow enough that he could probably throw a stone across if he really put some strength into it.

He marked another small dot three and a half grid squares west of the hill and labeled it **"Van"**. The river was only a short distance past the van, so he drew a line four grid squares west of the hill and labeled it **"Ye Olde North to South River"**, because it was his map and he could name stuff whatever the hell he wanted.

At least until he found someone to correct him.

Ethan then looked north and squinted his eyes. Either the horizon was too far away and the sun was playing tricks on him or there was a huge body of water off in the distance. It'd have to be either an ocean or something similar to the Great Lakes because he couldn't see an end to it in either direction.

He drew a line and labeled it **"Ocean?"**.

To the east was the string of tall hills... or very small mountains. It reminded Ethan of the Altamont Hills west of where he grew up in California. Definitely not impassable, but not an easy hike either. He half expected to see a smattering of windmills across the hills, that's how similar it looked with the beautiful rolling hills of Spanish grass. If he squinted, he could see what looked like deer roaming the hillsides. Well, he hoped they were deer.

"Damn, I shouldn't have gotten rid of those trash Army glasses."

On his map, he drew a crude line of hills east of the hill going north to south. Since he couldn't tell what was on the other side, he put a few question marks east of the hills. Eyes turned south, he saw an endless forest other than a gap in the trees to the Southwest. South of **"Van"**, but closer to **"Ye Olde North to South River"**.

With his less than twenty-twenty vision, Ethan was pretty sure he could make out a church-like steeple amidst the trees. Once again he wished he had kept his glasses. Actually, did he have an extra pair in his duffel bag? He'd have to check when he got back to the van.

"Okay... So there might be a town over there. Progress," he drew a small dot and labeled it **"Town?"**.

A calm settled over Ethan once he'd gotten a the lay of the land, so he took off his pack and pulled out an MRE. Time to eat and come up with a new three phase plan.

7

WELCOME

Ethan sat on the flattest rock he could find, zoned out while he ate his MRE. As the food was heating up, he'd written out a new plan that he felt was reasonable.

1. Inventory the van
2. Sleep
3. Check out the town

In his zoned out state, he became aware of a small flashing symbol in the upper right corner of his vision, positive it hadn't been there before. He only caught sight of it at all because he wasn't actually focusing on anything.

Turning his attention to the symbol, Ethan noticed it was translucent, only partially blocking his vision since he could still see through it. The symbol looked like a blank black and white trading card, like a template the Pokémon company might use to brainstorm new card ideas.

"Symbols that follow my eyes... probably only I can see," he pondered aloud. "Am I in a video game? Maybe a portal fantasy novel? Am I gently touching the fourth wall?"

If that was his situation, this was exactly how he would expect the story to start. He'd get a character sheet and would be able to level up, his body and mind becoming superhuman. Maybe his Army service-connected knee pain would finally go away.

"Or maybe I'm in a coma and am only dreaming about being in a fantasy world," he muttered.

Ethan sighed, considering the possibility. Each option could explain why none of his electronics worked. No matter what, he needed to treat it like it was real and not a coma induced hallucination.

His mind began a downward spiral of fear and worst case scenarios. His heart beat faster, his right leg bounced, and he was suddenly on his feet pacing around the hilltop as he imagined what usually happened in those types of stories.

Violence. Monsters. Magic. Greedy overpowered people who would go into a rage and snap your neck just for looking at them funny. Or they'd bide their time, then literally stab you in the back.

With a concerted effort, Ethan forced his body to be still, if only for a moment. Deep breath in, deep breath out.

"Breathe, Ethan. Breathe," he reminded himself, going through his breathing exercise.

Finally his heart rate dropped back to almost normal, low enough that it wouldn't leap out of his chest at any moment. While he did feel more calm, the downward spiral had left a stamp of pessimism in his gut.

It was time for a different mental exercise.

Memories of his resiliency training in the Army came flooding back to him. Unfortunately, most of the lectures were miserable "Death By Powerpoint" presentations that he could only vaguely remember.

One specific training sprang into memory, led by Sergeant First Class Bloom. It was about catastrophizing, though he couldn't remember the exact name of the exercise. Something like '*Worst, Best, Most Likely*', if he had to guess, but he only remembered it because she had been purposefully obnoxious with her use of personal examples.

The concept was simple. First, you think of the worst possible outcome of the scenario. Like... he could be captured by a band of orcs, become a slave, be forced to breed with the women in order to create half-orc warriors, and never see his wife and son ever again.

"Dear God, please don't let the orcs get me!" he thought.

Second, you think about the best possible outcome. SFC Bloom's examples always ended with her stumbling upon a pot of gold. The point was for it to be an exaggerated positive outcome.

For Ethan, the best outcome... He honestly didn't know. Happening upon a dragon's hoard would be cool, assuming he didn't have to fight the dragon. Sudden and unearned wealth would ensure he could afford whatever he'd need to survive. Thrive, rather than survive, while he figured out how to get home.

Oh, and in that hoard of wealth would be a teleportation scroll or something that could send him home whenever he was ready to leave the fantasy world.

Though, Ethan didn't need that much money. He'd never struggled to make do with whatever he has available. Hauling around a dragon's hoard would be more trouble than it was worth, though he'd figure out how to make good use of it if he did happen upon one. He started thinking of all the little orphans or outcasts he could help become powerhouses. It was a common trope in these kinds of stories and he'd be lying if he said he didn't feel excitement at the possibilities.

Last, but not least, you think of what's *most likely* to happen.

Well, there was likely to be some sort of tutorial or easy quest line to get him started and he'd get to go on a cool once in a lifetime adventure. Most roleplaying games required a lot of time away from towns or cities, which was a big plus for Ethan. People were cool and all, but they were exhausting. Crowds could be overwhelming and he preferred to only go into cities for day trips or on holidays.

Such were the dangers of having an overdeveloped sense of sonder. Each person lived their own complex life and humans weren't mentally equipped to handle that in large numbers. It's not a sustainable state of mind.

Shoveling a handful of MRE trail mix into his mouth, Ethan focused back on the floating symbol. As soon as he gave it his full attention, a screen popped up in the middle of his vision, causing him to flinch backward in surprise. He'd known it was coming, but it still took a few coughs to dislodge the peanut stuck in his throat.

On the screen was black text with an off white background. The font of the text was pixelated, exactly like some Gameboy games he played as a kid.

The 90s were a magical time.

Ethan read the notification on the screen, his eyebrows scrunched together in concentration.

WELCOME: ETHAN FARRIS

You've been chosen to participate in a once in a lifetime

opportunity. Prove yourself worthy and continue down the path of a Cardist.

Some of your equipment has been deemed compatible with the local system. Adaptation to local guidelines has been initiated.

Congratulations and welcome to your new world!

Ethan stood up from his boulder seat, his hands on his hips.

"Uhh... what... uhh... huh?"

He leaned forward, face scrunched up and eyes squinted, as though it would help him read the screen better.

"What the hell is a Cardist?"

8
QUESTS

ETHAN WAS UPSET.

Not because he was been taken from his world or that his plans had been derailed. He was already coming to terms with that, more or less. What pissed him off was how little information he was given. Three things he did learn was that there was something called a 'Cardist', there was a 'local system', and that this system was messing with his stuff.

"There better be more notifications. Give me at least a hint of what to do!"

A right facing arrow blinked just below the screen, which Ethan assumed was a "next" button. As he focused on the arrow, the text changed inside the notification box.

New Quest: The Very Best

Defeat your first monster in battle.
Reward: 1x Blank Monster Card

Progress: 0/1

"Alright. Okay. So this world uses cards for monsters? That's interesting, at least."

Ethan pulled out his notebook and pen from his pack, then flipped to an open page and started a list titled *"Stuff I Figured Out So Far"*. There are few things as nice as a good list; it helped him more easily keep track of his scattered thoughts.

"I wonder what a blank monster card is," he tapped his lower lip with his pen and hummed. "Maybe they're used to catch monsters, like a Pokéball in Pokémon. Weaken the monster, then you can try to catch it. Okay, that's helpful to know."

After scribbling a few notes on his list, Ethan then focused on the 'next' arrow, eager to learn more. This time, a second box appeared below the first.

New Quest: Collect Them All

Collect your first monster card.
Reward: 1x Starter Item Booster Pack

Progress: 9/1

∾

Congratulations!

You have completed this quest. Hold out your hand and focus on the accept button to receive your reward.

ACCEPT

ETHAN TURNED his head to the side like a curious dog, the screen moving to match. Logically, he understood what the notification said. He was meant to collect one monster card, but had already somehow collected nine, which had triggered a reward.

"But... I only just got here. How would I already have nine monster cards when I haven't even seen a single monster?"

How he finished the quest or had earned a reward, he didn't know. But he wasn't about to turn down free stuff either. Holding his notebook and pen in his left hand, he held out his right, then focused on the ACCEPT button. A small thin package appeared in his palm, labeled *"Starter Item Booster"* in cursive on the face of whatever paper the pack was wrapped in.

For a moment, Ethan simply stared at it. It's one thing to know things may start to magically appear out of nowhere. Totally different to experience for real life.

A pang of nostalgia grabbed at his chest as he thought of his time at Basic Combat Training. He'd tried to mentally prepare himself for what to expect, but it wasn't something you could truly understand until you had drill sergeants yelling in your face or making you drop to do pushups alongside a couple hundred other people.

Shaking off the memories, Ethan decided to hold off on opening the "Booster Pack" until he got back to the van, so he slipped it into his backpack. He made a bullet point in his notebook for "Item cards", then focused again on the arrow to go to the next notification.

He felt starved for more information and was excited when another pair of text boxes appeared on the screen.

New Quest: Collect Them All II

Collect five monster cards.
(NOTE: Duplicates do not count toward total)
Reward: 2x Common Item Booster Pack

Progress: 9/5

～

Congratulations!

You have completed this quest. Hold out your hand and focus on the accept button to receive your reward.

ACCEPT

"Hell yeah!"

Ethan immediately moved his pen to his left hand, held out his right, and focused on the accept button. Two small paper packages appeared in his hand, these ones labeled *"Common Item Booster Pack"*. If there were common cards, that implied there were a variety of rarities.

This time he didn't stop to stare, sliding the booster packs into his pack without a second thought, then focused on the "next" arrow.

A single text box appeared.

New Quest: Collect Them All III

Collect ten monster cards.
(NOTE: Duplicates do not count toward total)
Reward: 2x Uncommon Item Booster Pack

Progress: 9/10

Forcing himself to sit back on his flat boulder, Ethan thought over all that he'd read so far. He made a few additional notes in his notebook, then looked over the list.

- *Monsters exist (what qualifies as a monster?)*
- *They can be caught/collected*
- *There are quests with rewards*
- *There are item cards, awarded in packs*
- *There are levels of rarity (at least 3: starter, common, uncommon)*
- *You can collect duplicates of cards, but they don't count toward at least some quests*
- *Somehow I collected nine monster cards and completed two quests*

Top notch list. Helped him remain somewhat calm, knowing at least he wouldn't be wandering around, aimless and ignorant.

Ethan took a deep breath, then turned his attention back to the text box and focused on the next arrow.

<u>*Adaption Complete*</u>

Your monster cards have finished adapting to the local system.

Cards Adapted:
9x - Unique Monster Cards
450x - Blank Monster Cards

"Four hundred and fifty blank cards?" he muttered under his breath.

Ethan was suddenly back on his feet, pacing around the hilltop, considering the ramifications of what the text said.

Did that mean he could collect four hundred and fifty monsters?! And he had nine Unique monsters, whatever that meant. Was unique the highest rarity, like in some games?

He knew one thing: there was no way this was standard 'Cardist' procedure. He was an overpowered main character! A smile split across his face, a maniacal laugh taking shape in his throat. He stopped pacing and bellowed across the valley.

"DRAGON'S HOARD, BAYBAY!"

The words echoed across the hills, muffled by the trees. His shout made his throat sore, but he didn't care. This was good news, something he desperately needed. As the echoes of his voice died down, a new sound took its place.

Howls, scattered across the valley. Some sounded close to his van.

"Oh, biscuits!" he grunted through clenched teeth. All joy and mirth was gone from his face in an instant. "I gotta get back to the van!"

The straps of his pack barely made it over his shoulders as he rushed down the hill.

9

MONSTER MASH

SWEAT DRENCHED ETHAN'S CLOTHES AS HE REACHED THE VAN. Jumping in as soon as the sliding door was open enough to fit through, he slammed it shut behind him.

Moving to the tough-box, he pushed everything off the lid, then opened it. Papers scattered toward the driver's seat as he reached into the box, pushing aside MREs until his hands found what they were looking for. A small hard plastic case in his grasp, he let out a sigh of relief, then set the case on the floor in front of him.

With practiced ease, Ethan undid the two latches on the front, then opened the case.

Inside was a handgun, tucked into a holster meant to be attached to his pants or belt. Two magazines filled with nine millimeter bullets, one magazine longer than the other, allowing extra grip space and a few additional shots.

Ethan grabbed the larger of the two, pulled the handgun out of its holster, then slid the magazine into the handle of the gun. His shoulders relaxed as it clicked into place and he slid it back into its holster. The chamber he left empty, something he wouldn't normally do, but this particular gun didn't have a safety latch. Why risk accidentally shooting himself?

With the handgun holstered and the second magazine stashed in his pocket, Ethan snapped the case shut, tossed it back into the tough box, then closed the lid.

Time to wait.

His haunches ached from the long day of hiking, but he kept silent and listened for sounds outside the van. After a minute passed without a sound, he let out a breath he one hundred percent knew he had been holding. At least there weren't any howls. Whether that was a good thing or not had yet to be decided.

"It'd be nice if the system considered the van a safe zone," he muttered to himself.

Not likely. He didn't know enough about this world to assume safe zones were even a thing, so it was better to prepare for the worst and hope for the best.

Ethan took a look around his van, sighing at the mess he'd made. Why did clutter make it feel like breathing took more effort? One more thing to add to the next three phase plan.

He closed his eyes and ran through his breathing exercise, steading his heart rate. His eyes shot open at the end of an exhale as he remembered his last notification.

Monster cards.

Nine unique monster cards and four hundred and fifty blank cards. That could only have been from the sheets of blank trading cards he'd printed on card-stock for his nephews. At the time he almost felt bad using the office printer on his last day of work, but now was overjoyed he hadn't let the guilt stop him.

Instead, it turned out to be a stroke of genius. Or at least good fortune.

Ethan gathered up the papers he'd scattered when getting his gun. One sheet wasn't empty, the one he'd drawn on the night before. He set that one on top of the stack, then sat back down, criss-cross-applesauce style.

The cards on the paper looked more filled out and official than the simple pictures he'd drawn. The system took his simple pencil sketches and turned them into thoughtful pieces of art. Each picture took over the entire card, reminding him of those new "Illustration Rare" Pokémon cards with a subdued shine to them. They looked pretty life-like, as though the creatures could leap out of the cards any moment.

A smile crossed Ethan's face as his eyes scanned over the cards. He had no idea what kinds of cards the locals of this world possessed, but he had a feeling they didn't look like these.

Something large scraped against the outside of the van. Ethan went silent, his face a shade more pale.

Taking his time, he turned around while trying not to rock the van. Sun visors covered the windows, so he could sleep better, now making it impossible to see outside. He got to his knees facing the sliding door, hand reaching for his gun. There was a sniffing outside the door, like the sound a dog makes searching around the dinner table at Thanksgiving. One turned into two, which became three. There were three wolves sniffing around the van.

Three, at least.

Of course it was a wolf pack. Couldn't have been a lone wolf for his first monster encounter. Just his luck.

Something thudded hard against the sliding door and Ethan was launched back into the tough box, grunting as his arm slammed into a latch. That seemed to confirm to the wolves that he was in there, the van rocking back and forth as they took turns attacking.

The sounds of their bodies crunching metal — combined with the vomit inducing motions — made it difficult for Ethan to think.

What he wouldn't do for some Dramamine right then. While steadying himself on his knees, a wolf slammed into the back doors, pitching Ethan forward to the driver's seat. He was able to stabilize himself with his left hand on a messy stack of papers, causing a new notification to appear in his vision.

Activate Monster Card

You have chosen to activate the Unique Monster Card: Colby-Jack

The monster "Colby-Jack" will be bound to you.
This action is permanent and cannot be undone.

Do you wish to continue?

CONTINUE

"*What*?!" A surge of hope spread through Ethan as he yelled. "Yes! Yes! Continue!"

The sheet of cards, the one he'd drawn on, began to glow. The left card of the middle row detached itself and floated in the air in front of him. A grin split across Ethan's face as he imagined the unique beasts he'd drawn that would soon be at his command.

"Oh, hell yeah! These wolves won't know what hit 'em!"

The glow of the card began to expand as it lowered itself to the floor. The motions of the van settled as a small white and orange dog stepped out of the card, sat down facing the sliding door, and lifted its snout into the air with regal flare. It glanced sideways at Ethan with an unconcerned look in its eyes.

"Whaaa..." he stared at the small dog, his voice increasing in volume. "I chose the corgi?! That was meant to be a joke card!"

The corgi lost interest in Ethan, turning its gaze to the door and standing to its feet, letting out a single confident bark.

Ethan watched the dog in confusion. Did this little corgi think it could take on a bunch of wolves? The dog looked at him, then rolled its eyes. Could dogs roll their eyes?

It barked once, turned its head back to the door, then barked again.

Low growls came from the other side of the door, which didn't seem to concern the corgi in the slightest. Not knowing what else to do, Ethan finally pulled his handgun from its holster and moved beside the door. Left hand on the door handle, right with the weapon pointed at the floor, he looked back at the dog.

A small, orange and white corgi was about to save Ethan's life. Somehow. Hopefully.

Oh no... was he about to die?

"I hope you know what you're doing, little dude."

10

COLLECT THEM ALL

THE CLEARING WAS SURPRISINGLY TIDY, CONSIDERING TWO WOLVES had just been killed by a small dog and one basically executed by a man with a nine millimeter handgun.

Looking around, Ethan tried to figure out what he was supposed to do with the wolves. Based on their unusual fur colors, he assumed they were some of the monsters referred to in his quest notifications. Maybe the color showed what element the beast controlled? Red could be for fire, blue for water, and green for grass or something plant based.

Was there a way to loot monsters?

He touched the red furred wolf, expecting a text box or something to pop up and ask if he wanted to loot it. Nothing but coarse fur. Should he cut them up for parts that crafters could use?

Gross.

Could they still be captured if they were dead?

As he stood there contemplating his options, the corgi shuffled over from the second wolf it'd killed and trotted to the van. Despite its small stature, the dog had no difficulty jumping inside and quickly came back out with a card in its mouth, held it up to Ethan, and waited.

As he took it, the corgi stepped over to the red furred wolf, booped it with its nose, then looked back at Ethan like it had just explained how to calculate two plus two. When he didn't move, the dog sighed.

Do dogs sigh?

It moved back to the card, booped it a second time, then moved back to the wolf and booped it as well. The dog turned its head to Ethan and gave a "boof" sound with an extra bit of attitude.

Ethan had initially been lost in thought, but saw what the dog did on its second try. He immediately understood what it was telling him and crouched down next to the wolf. When he touched the paper to its body, a text box filled his vision.

Collect Monster: Fire Wolf

This action will expend 1x Blank Monster Card.
This action is permanent and cannot be undone.

Press CONFIRM to active the Blank Monster Card.

CONFIRM

"A fire wolf, eh? Red fur, I was right!"

Hitting the confirm button, he watched as the wolf dissolved into a whirlpool of red lights that swirled into the blank card like water flowing down a funnel. When the process was complete, Ethan held the card up to analyze it.

The corgi nudged his leg.

Once it had his attention, it walked to the other two wolves and booped them with its nose. The dog clearly understood more of how this stuff worked than him, and it hadn't steered him wrong yet, so after grabbing two more blank cards from the van, Ethan repeated the process with the remaining wolves. Probably safe to assume there was a time limit on when you could collect a defeated monster.

Moving back to the van, Ethan sat down with his legs hanging out the doorway. Three cards rested in his hand, like simplified versions of trading cards from back home.

Each one had a picture of its respective wolf in the upper half of the card, except they looked alive instead of the lifeless corpses they had been just a minute ago. Above each photo was the name of the beast, beside which was a small pen looking symbol.

An edit button for if he wanted to change its name?

These three were named Fire Wolf, Water Wolf, and Plant Wolf. Pretty basic, straight forward names. The body of each card was colored to match the element types of the monster: red, blue, and green. Under each photo was a line of text describing a basic attack of each monster: **Fire Fang**, **Glacier Claw**, and **Roots of Restoration**.

Ethan wasn't sure what he should have expected, but this all seemed overly simple. Perhaps the wolves were more common monsters.

Scanning further down the first card, he noticed two little blank cards overlaying each other like holding a hand of cards in poker. He wondered what those meant, but his guess was it represented the value or rarity of the card. Maybe it was worth two common cards? If that was the case, then these wolves were rare or uncommon.

Probably a bit too weak to be rare.

The corgi climbed into the van, then sat beside Ethan and

watched as he continued analyzing the cards. A minute later, it turned its casual gaze toward the dark forest like the trees were more interesting than magic. Noting the change, Ethan reached over to scratch its head. This earned him a sideways glanced, but the dog made no effort to stop the scratches.

"You're a good dog... uhh," Ethan realized he didn't know if the dog had a name... or if it was a boy or girl dog. "Do you have a name? Or am I supposed to name you?"

The dog gave him a different kind of side glance, made a combined sigh/boof sound, then turned toward the inside of the van. Stopping at the pile of paper on the floor, it grabbed a single card off the floor with its mouth, then turned and held it out to Ethan.

He grabbed it and set it on top of the stack in his hands. The card looked like the wolves' cards, but the picture section was empty. Was it because the card was active and the corgi was sitting next to him? Something to experiment with later. There was a name above where the photo should be, but it didn't say what type of monster it was. It had an actual dog's name, with a female symbol beside it.

"Colby-Jack, aye? That's a fun name for a girl dog," he smirked, impressed with himself and his naming abilities. "I guess I am pretty clever."

Colby-Jack gave another boof, then turned back to watch the forest. Ethan thought back to the night before when he'd come up with the name, which was based on a corgi from TV named "Cheddar". He'd chosen "Colby-Jack" because it seemed like a more fitting color scheme for a corgi, their common color scheme being a mix of white and orange.

Ethan read over the attack section of the card and sighed at the text. Two attack moves were listed, ones he'd hoped would have changed with whatever adaptation the cards went through.

Alas, it wasn't meant to be.

Booty Booty Booty
Confuses and distracts an opponent through masterful gyrations.

Belly Flop
Like the more common "Body Slam", but with all the grace of a charging toddler.

Ethan sighed, chuckled as he remembered a line from the TV corgi's owner, then looked at Colby-Jack.

"You're definitely not some common bitch."

Colby-Jack responded with her now trademarked "boof", which Ethan chose to interpret as a sassy "Boy, I know it."

II

MORE QUESTS

THE BLINKING CARD IN THE CORNER OF ETHAN'S VISION WAS DRIVING him nuts. Now that danger wasn't imminent, he took the time to go through them with the hopes of understanding his situation better.

Quest Completed: The Very Best

Defeat your first monster in battle.
Progress: 3/1

Receive Reward: 1x - Blank Monster Card

ACCEPT

Ethan hit accept and moved to the next notification.

New Quest: The Very Best II

Defeat ten monsters in battle.

Reward: 1x - Blank Monster Card

Progress: 3/10

"Okay, so the first quest is kind of a gimme," Ethan looked at Colby-Jack. "Probably to help people get the ball rolling."

She didn't react at all, so he moved on to the next notification.

Quest Completed: Collect Them All III

Collect ten monster cards.
(NOTE: Duplicates do not count toward total)
Receive Reward: 2x - Uncommon Item Booster Pack

Progress: 12/10

ACCEPT

"Alright... so different types of wolves don't count as duplicates. Good to know."

Ethan held out his hand and hit accept, already reading the next message.

New Quest: Collect Them All IV

Collect Twenty monster cards.
(NOTE: Duplicates do not count toward total)
Reward: 1x Rare Item Booster Pack

Progress: 12/20

"This one doubled from the last one," he glanced at the corgi with a raised eyebrow. "How much you wanna bet the next one will be to collect forty monsters?"

Colby-Jack glanced back up at Ethan, then went back to watching the area just outside of the van. Thinking that was all of the notifications, Ethan closed the window. The flashing card symbol remained.

Oops. Not done yet.

He focused again on the symbol until a new text box appeared.

New Quest: I'm On An Adventure

Explore the area. Find five notable locations.
Reward: A clue about how to get back where you belong.

Progress: 0/5

Ethan stared at the text.

"Son of a bi—" He stopped himself, looking over at Colby-Jack. "Sorry, probably not a great word to use?"

She gave the dog equivalent of a shrug, but didn't look at him. He shrugged in return.

"I see what they're doing. They're giving me hope that I can get home, using goals with actionable steps to keep me moving forward instead of panicking or falling into crippling depression. I'm not _that_ fickle, am I?"

Colby-Jack gave a condescending "boof", which he decided to ignore.

"Either way, it's a smart move. People tend to have a hard time getting started again once they lose momentum," Ethan sighed. Getting to his feet outside the van, he turned to look at the mess he made. "For now, let's clean up and get some rest."

Colby-Jack got to her feet and leapt at Ethan, knocking all of the cards he had been holding to the ground.

"Hey! I said 'clean up the mess', not make more mess!"

The dog stood over the cards and unopened packs, nudging them around until her card was visible. She gave a firm "boof", then tapped the card with her nose. Her small body transformed into motes of light covering the full spectrum of the rainbow. Though the light show was more unique and impressive than the wolves, the light funneled down into her card all the same.

Ethan placed his hands on his hips in classic disappointed-dad fashion while he watched.

With an exaggerated sigh he bent down and picked up the cards, putting Colby-Jack's on top. There was now a picture of a corgi on the card that looked like she'd belly flopped away from a camera, then turned her head back when the photographer said "cheese".

"I suppose *I'll* clean up, then get some rest."

He stored the cards and packs in his pocket, then turned back to the mess in his van. Time passed quickly as he cleaned and inventoried each item in his notebook before packing them away. Once that was done, he stood outside the van and wrote out another three phase plan in his notebook.

1. Take a break and eat an MRE
2. Change into Army uniform (to help mentally "embrace the suck" and make use of extra pockets)
3. Explore around the river

He looked at his list, then looked at the uniform and boots he'd laid out on the floor just inside the van.

"I can do this," Ethan muttered under his breath. "Hooah..."

12

COLBY-JACK

Her newly bound Cardist was capable and brave, but Colby-Jack was astounded by his ignorance.

Not only was he unaware of her abilities before picking a fight with three uncommon wolves, but he didn't know about the five minute time limit on capturing a fallen monster. On top of that, she had to remind the Cardist how to use his own Blank Monster Cards.

Her Cardist, Ethan, was fortunate that he had chosen to bind himself to her first. Though he was not entirely useless, considering his skilled use of the incredibly loud projectile weapon, he would most certainly need looking after in this world if he were to survive the next month.

Resting in the comfort of her card, Colby-Jack considered how best to help her Cardist stay alive. Being a powerful creature herself, there was a lot of risk that she could mitigate. Still, the strength and attentiveness of one companion could only solve so many problems.

For now, she'd observe the man to determine his greatest

strengths and shortcomings. When it became clear her prowess was no longer sufficient, she'd direct him to a fellow unique companion appropriate for the situation.

Couldn't have the fool bind himself to any old monster. Not if Colby-Jack had anything to say about it.

13

EXPLORATION

ETHAN, AND BY EXTENSION COLBY-JACK, FELL INTO A ROUTINE.

In the mornings, he'd pick out a couple MREs to put into his pack. This would be included with anything he may need for the day, like a stack of blank monster cards.

Before heading out, Ethan worked through the Army warm up drills and hip stability drills, making sure he didn't get unnecessarily injured while exploring and/or be ripe pickings for roaming orc breeders. The few backpacking trips he'd gone on over the past year had taught him one thing, his knee did not take kindly to the constant ups and downs of hiking.

After his warm up and some stretches, he'd eat something, then finally head out to explore.

Using his hand drawn map, he followed a rough kilometer based search grid of the area. Better to avoid backtracking, if at all possible. Hiking along the river, he found what turned out to be an ocean. Or at least he assumed it was an ocean, since he couldn't see any land beyond the water.

The Cardist and his dog ran into a handful of monsters along the way. Mostly water types like otters, fish, and alligators, which he and Colby-Jack fought and collected without much trouble. The fish were the most difficult to deal with, since they couldn't swim on land.

Frustrating fights, but they made it work.

Other than that, they had a pretty easy time of it. Colby-Jack was a beast at taking out monsters. Her booty was mesmerizing and her belly flops were destructive.

Ethan didn't even need to use his gun, though he kept it on hand just in case.

Within a couple days they found a cave with an earth-type wolf living inside. Dirt and pebbles actually crumbled out of its fur as it moved. That particular battle took longer than usual, but they beat it and collected it with a blank card.

The wolf turned out to be the first rare monster Ethan had encountered, the battle confirming rarity had a lot to do with the strength of a monster. It also explained why Colby-Jack had dominated everything so far, being a unique card and all. They tested the theory more as time passed, noticing a distinct difference in strength and ability between the common, uncommon, and rare monsters he fought.

Hurray for the Scientific Method!

14

BEAR WITH ME

Karhu rather enjoyed her new cave.

Her favorite part was the bed she'd made out of burnt fur gathered from the family of plant-type bears. She'd driven them away the day before. Best night of sleep she'd had since manifesting in this world.

What had the bears been thinking, trying to fight a fierce bear of flame such as her? Fire beats plant, every time.

Even a young and uncommon ranked bear like herself knew that plant creatures belonged in the trees, not in caves. Fear had surrounded the plant bears, palpable to her strong sense of smell, and initially she thought it was directed at her. The way they fought to stay in the cave implied maybe they were more afraid of something else than they were of her.

Lying in the comfort of her burnt fur bed after a long night of rest, her mind felt better able to tackle the concern that she'd pushed to the back of her mind.

What had those bears been afraid of, exactly?

As she considered the question, a nearby scent caught her attention. Her head rose sharply from where it had been resting on her massive paws. Silhouetted at the mouth of the cave was a small, wolf-like creature. Rather than appearing fierce and dangerous, like a normal wolf, this one was short and chunky with stubby legs, its white and orange fur looking rather soft and fluffy.

The creature directed its glare at her, unflinching in resolve.

How had the wolf-runt snuck up on her? She should have been able to smell it from at least a day's walk away. And why was it not afraid of her? Now that she was fully awake and taking in smells, she noted another creature coming up behind the wolf-runt. It held something in its hand with a peculiar fire-like scent.

Lifting herself up to a ready position, Karhu faced the opening of the cave. Whatever they wanted, they'd better not mess up her bed.

15

GET A CLUE

After several weeks of exploring, Ethan had visited four of the five notable locations from his quest.

One location was another cave, which had been unusually warm. Inside was a younger bear, this one being a fire type. Not a cub, but not full grown either. The fight was easier than anticipated, so he wasn't surprised when the bear turned out to be uncommon instead of rare.

Was there was a way to upgrade cards to the next level? Something to keep an eye out for.

The other three locations didn't have monsters, but he did find some wild fruit trees and bushes, helping to stretch out his food supplies. The town he had seen was more than likely the last notable location, as it was the only obviously important thing nearby, so he'd decided to save it for last.

One reason was because he had enough food that he hadn't needed to go there yet. Mostly, though, it was because he was anxious to meet the people of this world. He didn't know what to expect. Would they be human or a mix of races, like in fantasy stories? Maybe humanoid animals? Would he have to deal with uptight elves who are prejudiced against humans? Would they be welcoming or hostile to outsiders?

Turned out his anxiety was unnecessary. When he visited the town, it had been abandoned for a long time. Probably decades, if he had to guess.

To even call it a town would be inaccurate, as it was more of a small village surrounded by a wooden palisade wall. A wide dirt road ran south through the town out what used to be a gate. The town looked like a modern version of Viking era architecture, like something he'd expect to see in scenic Scandinavian towns.

Mangled slabs of wood were everywhere, splintered and thrown about. Buildings were marred with giant claw marks and damage from rocks thrown about the area. One dog-sized rock had broken through the wall of what looked like a longhouse. All signs pointed to the town being overrun by monsters.

Potentially raided by people with monster companions.

The town itself looked pretty cool to Ethan. If he had more people with him, he could see turning this place into a thriving town. He had no interest in leading any large group of people, but he could imagine setting himself up in the town. Maybe he'd claim it if he couldn't figure out a way to get home.

Though there was the reward hint from the quest about finding a way to get home, so he didn't foresee that happening.

Once he'd thoroughly inspected the town, Ethan decided to stroll along the river on his way back to the van. He'd just made it down to the bank when he stopped to listen to the water. The sounds of running water usually provided Ethan with a measure of peace but, on that day, the peace was broken by a new sound.

Drum beats. Deep and consistent.

Before there was even time to process the noise, Ethan sprinted to the tree-line, got behind a tree, and hid himself in the underbrush. The drum hadn't been especially aggressive or loud, but it was the first man-made noise he'd heard since this whole thing started.

It made him cautious.

Minutes passed as he waited, the drums slowly getting louder as they drew near.

A wooden boat came into view that looked like a stereotypical Viking Era ship, an intimidating creature carved into the front. Some sort of bird that Ethan didn't recognize. The boat was weather worn, so it was hard to tell what it was.

Round shields lined the sides of the boat and eight oars stuck out between the shields, rowing in sync to the steady beat of the drum. With eight oars on either side, Ethan guessed there were twenty to thirty people aboard, assuming they had enough people to take turns rowing. It was only guess though, as the shields made it difficult to see more than a few people's heads.

"Wow, there are actual Vikings here?"

At the front of the boat stood a woman roughly Ethan's age, maybe a little younger. Mid to late twenties, at least. Short red hair and an overall thin, yet athletic body type covered in some sort of leather armor with a cloak over her shoulders. Based on how she stood at the front instead of rowing, he could tell she wasn't a grunt, but she also didn't give off *"Aggressive Leader of Viking Raiders"* vibes.

As the boat pulled even with Ethan's hiding spot, a red bird about the size of a bald eagle came into view flying wide circles above the boat. The red-headed woman brought the fingers of her right hand to her lips, then blew a kiss to the circling bird.

As though waiting for that exact signal, the bird flew off in the direction the boat was traveling. The man drumming at the back seemed to pick up the same cue as the bird and increased his tempo, the boat picking up speed as the rowers pulled harder to match the beat.

Ethan watched in silence as the boat continued on, moving only once it was out of sight.

It looked exactly how he'd expect a boat of viking raiders to look, though the woman didn't give him the typical impression of wanton violence his favorite movies and TV shows had portrayed. Either way, it seemed there was civilization of some sort further south and north, he supposed.

If he followed the road south out of the abandoned town, he may reach another town. A flashing card appeared in the upper corner of Ethan's vision as soon as the thought occurred to him. He must have completed a quest!

He pulled up the notification, excited at what he may find out.

Quest Completed: I'm On An Adventure

Explore the area. Find five notable locations.

Progress: 5/5

Receive Reward: Clue of how to get home has already been given.

"WHAT?!" He shouted, "How do I already have the clue?" He held a hand out in the direction the boat had gone. "The only thing that has happened since I left the town was hiding from the boat!"

Realization dawned on him and he smacked his palm to his forehead

"Duh! The boat, the bird, and probably the woman were the clue!"

He sighed, resting his hands on his hips in standard disappointed-dad fashion. Sometimes Ethan could be an idiot. Fortunately, Colby-Jack was resting in her card and wasn't there to agree with him.

Ethan felt a rise of panic as he thought about having to maneuver through the complexities of civilization. Crowds were suffocating. He took a deep breath and stood to his feet, looking down the river where he'd lost sight of the ship.

"One step at a time, Ethan," he said to himself. "No point in pre-suffering. Suffer once when it's time to suffer, not a moment sooner."

Thinking back to his supplies at the van, Ethan started formulating a new plan.

He was down to his last box of MREs, which he could make last another week or two if he rationed. Maybe gather more of the fruits he'd found. Eventually he'd need a new source of food and he had little hunting or gathering experience. Probably better to catch monsters, rather than eat them. If they were duplicates, maybe, but the idea still didn't feel quite right.

As much as he was enjoying his time alone in the wild, he did miss having some human contact.

An image formed in his mind of finding a Viking style coffee shop, with him sitting with a drink and enjoying the general atmosphere. A tavern would be more realistic, he supposed.

Bleh.

Maybe he could find a bookstore. Did they even have

books? What did they use for currency here? Hopefully his monster cards were worth enough to trade for food, shelter, and information.

Turning away from the river, he walked with purpose back toward the van.

"I need to pack."

16
THE BOY

THE BOY RAN.

Though, at that point it was more accurate to say he stumbled forward with urgency, the sounds of monsters crashing through the underbrush followed behind him. Why had he thought he could be out here on his own?

Stupid, stupid, stupid!

Bjorn's lungs burned as he pushed himself forward. If he could get back to the road, maybe he'd come across a patrol. He'd be in a lot of trouble for leaving town by himself, but at least he'd be alive.

Moving past another pair of trees, the boy burst through the tree-line and into a small open meadow where he came to an abrupt stop. His momentum caused him to lose his balance, faceplanting him into the dirt. He looked up to see a man with a surprised look on his face sitting on a boulder next to a campfire.

The man had the distinct feel of a soldier to Bjorn, but he wasn't dressed like the town guard.

His clothes were... odd. No armor, no visible weapons. His

boots were the color of an Earth Coyote's fur, pants and a jacket a green and brown blotchy pattern with a lot of pockets. The shirt under his jacket had a strange pattern to it, like a finely woven fishing net similar in color to the boots. The jacket had some patches that didn't look sewn on, almost as if they were floating above the fabric. One said "US ARMY" and the other said "FARRIS". The letters seemed similar to his own language, but Bjorn had no idea what any of it meant. Maybe it was his name? The third patch was a square bit of fabric between the two longer ones. Centered on the patch was a solid black shield, not quite a heater, but also not quite a kite.

Surrounding the man were two dogs and a very large cat. One dog, medium sized with long golden fur, lay across the man's feet. The other, a small dog with orange and white fur and stubby legs, sat between the man and where Bjorn had fallen. It just sat there, watching the trees.

Bjorn's breath caught as the cat, with reddish white fur and only one eye, stalked toward him with curiosity.

Two monsters crashed through the underbrush behind him as the large cat drew close. The creatures paused, analyzing the unexpected company. Bjorn gulped, but lay as still as he could.

With a sigh and a grunt, the man stood up and brushed his hands down his pant legs.

He spoke to the dog at his feet in a language Bjorn had never heard before, then pointed at him. The dog got up and trotted over to Bjorn, sniffing all over him as if searching for something.

The man called out to the small dog and the cat, then walked with a noticeable limp past Bjorn toward the monsters. The cat circled wide to the side, eyeing the tree-line as it moved, while the small dog gave a firm "boof" sound before catching up to the man. Its swaying hips seemed to mesmerize the monsters that chased Bjorn.

What in the world had he stumbled upon?

~~~

Ethan pulled a blank card from his right pants pocket, activating it on a large blue rodent dead on the ground in front of him. Colby-Jack's belly flop made quick work of the creature and it was a bit of a mess.

As he finished collecting the monster, his companions finished up their jobs. Goldy, Ethan's golden retriever like companion, worked on healing the boy's scrapes and bruises.

Zuko, a large one-eyed house cat and Ethan's newest card companion, dragged the red creature out of the tree-line by its hind leg. He'd used Hunt Prey on what turned out to be a small fire-type mountain lion, which had run off after seeing the destructive force of Colby-Jack's belly flop. Fortunately, Zuko was a skilled hunter and had snagged it before it got too far. The cat dragged the lion to the group and dropped it like a trophy, then brushed himself against Ethan's pant leg.

"You're such a good kitty, Zuko," Ethan smiled and bent down to scratch the base of his tail. "Who's my little deadly hunter? Yes, you are!"

He looked proud of himself, enjoying the scratches for approximately two seconds, then sauntered off toward the campfire.

Colby-Jack sat beside Ethan, watching the tree-line. She gave him a muttered "boof", which Ethan interpreted as "All clear, hurry up."

"Yes, yes, we all know you're the best girl ever. So jealous."

Ethan grabbed another blank card from his pocket, then

collected the lion cub. Pushing himself up from a squat, he stretched his back, then headed for the campfire with a hitch in his step. Even with Goldy's passive healing ability, Ethan's right knee was still giving him trouble. He pulled up short when he saw the kid staring at him in shock, Goldy resting his head in the boy's lap.

"What?" Ethan brushed the back of his fingers across his cheeks. "Have I got something on my face?"

17

BABY BJORN

Bjorn had never seen monsters killed so quickly before.

A few trained soldiers might be able to handle monsters, but not one man camping out in the woods with his pets. He'd been running for his life, certain he was gonna die. Instead, he sat safely by a campfire petting a dog with beautiful golden fur as it rested its head in his lap.

More amazing than any of that was how casually the man had used two blank cards on the monsters he'd killed. *Two*! Like it wasn't a big deal at all. Just another day at the market, picking out a few potatoes for the dinner stew.

How many blank cards did this guy have?

The man had spoken to his dogs before, but Bjorn was so distracted, he hadn't paid attention to the words. The man spoke again, a questioning tone in his voice as he brushed his cheeks with the back of his fingers. Bjorn didn't recognize a single word the man spoke.

Whatever he was speaking, it wasn't Aidish.

"I'm sorry, I don't understand what you're saying," Bjorn paused. "But... uh... thank you for saving me."

The man listened, a frown building on his face. Uh oh, don't make the scary man upset, Bjorn. New tactic.

"Thank you," he said again, this time placing the tips of his fingers to his chin, then lowering his hand to stop in front of him, palm facing up.

The man's face lit up, head nodding in excitement as he returned the gesture. He even attempted to say "thank you" in Aidish, though choppy, heavy accent that didn't quite flow off the tongue. Bjorn's eyebrows arched upwards, surprised that had actually worked.

How would this stranger know a gesture taught to babies and toddlers at the orphanage?

The man turned in his seat and reached into his pack, grimacing with the movement, then pulled out a strange clear container filled with water. He removed a small lid by twisting it, took a drink, then held the container out to Bjorn and said another unrecognizable word. Bjorn shook his head and removed a small canteen attached to his belt by a thin rope, suddenly grateful he hadn't lost it running through the trees. The man nodded and shrugged, took another drink, then twisted the lid back onto the container.

A silence settled over the campsite.

What should Bjorn do next? He was starting to feel uncomfortable when he noticed the man had a far away look in his eyes, a look common to the Cardists in town. The man was reading a system message of some sort. Bjorn didn't want to rush the man, but he did need to get back to town before dark, so he made an exaggerated cough noise trying to get the man's attention. The man didn't even flinch. They sat quietly for another minute before Bjorn couldn't take it anymore.

"Is your name Farris?"

The man's eyes refocused, a wild glare trained on Bjorn in

an instant, asking a question with a low growl in his voice. More like a command than a question. His hand moved slowly to his waist, as if grabbing a concealed weapon.

Bjorn flinched back, not sure what he'd done wrong. He pointed to his own chest, then pointed to the patch on the man's chest.

"Farris?" Bjorn asked again, desperately. "Your name is Farris?"

The man looked down at his patch, realization spreading across his face as he burst into laughter and moved his hand away from his waist. The sudden movement caused Bjorn to flinch again, but the man didn't seem to notice.

Bjorn chuckled in response, but with a nervous and confused edge to it.

The man turned to his small dog, as though he was having a good laugh with an old friend. The dog looked up at the man and made a small noise that could be interpreted as a chuckle combined with a sigh, then returned its casual attention back to the tree-line.

That only seemed to reignite the man's laughter.

He rocked his head back, laughing to the sky, then leaned forward and smacked his right knee. The laughter abruptly became a light chuckle, a grimace stretched across his face as he massaged the knee he'd just smacked. Noticing the lines creased around the man's eyes, Bjorn realized this man must laugh often. In contrast, he also had heavy frown lines on his brow that implied regular intense focus.

Bjorn still wasn't sure what had made the man angry, but it seemed to have been cleared up. A misunderstanding? He pointed at the man, repeated what he assumed was his name.

"Farris?"

The man nodded, continuing to massage his knee.

"Bjorn," he said, patting his own chest with both hands. "My name is Bjorn."

The man looked up, his brow raised in surprise. Somehow he recognized the name. How could the man not speak Aidish but still recognize his name? And also know the sign for thank you?

What a strange man.

~~~

"Your name is Bjorn?"

Ethan was surprised to hear a familiar word. Also, the boy somehow knew how to say 'thank you' in American Sign Language. Assuming the gesture meant the same thing here. Maybe he and the boy had actually insulted each other.

Bjorn was a Scandinavian word for bear, Ethan knew that, but he couldn't remember if it was Danish or from a specific dialect at all. It was a common Viking era name, though. Bjorn Ironside being the most well known. There was also the whole Baby Bjorn brand of baby supplies, which was obviously more modern and less violent.

"Bjorn, as in bear?" Ethan continued.

The boy patted his chest and repeated the name. Remembering that the boy couldn't understand him, Ethan raised his arms in the air, stretching his fingers out like claws, and made an exaggerated growl in mock representation of a bear.

"Bjorn?" He asked again, doing the impression a second time to make his point.

The boy grew excited, nodding and bouncing in his seat as he repeated a word that probably meant "yes".

Ethan smiled at the boy's enthusiasm, feeling rather excited himself. He'd learned some Spanish in high school and was pretty good at it, but hadn't used it enough for it to stick. Languages came naturally to him, he just never had a practical need to use anything other than English.

Use it or lose it, as they say.

When Ethan looked at Bjorn, what he saw wasn't a bear. A lean, less aggressive cub, if he was being generous. The boy had light strawberry blond hair and a baby smooth face. If he had to guess, Ethan would say the boy was around ten to twelve years old. Somehow both overconfident and insecure.

Classic pre-teen.

The boy patted his chest and repeated his name, then pointed at Ethan and said "Farris". Well, he mostly said it, but his pronunciation was off and his vowels sounded like they do in Spanish. "Fair-iss" turned into "Far-ees". Honestly, it was impressive that the boy was able to read at all since Viking era people were more likely to be illiterate, unless they were monks. The peoples that were typical referred to as Vikings had symbols, but not an actual alphabet for their spoken language.

Ethan pointed at himself and said his name, but with the correct pronunciation.

"Ahh," the boy nodded.

He sounded it out, then repeated it a few more times. Once he had it down, Ethan gave him a thumbs up, then repeated the boy's word for "Yes" and nodded. The boy smile wide and Ethan suppressed an ache of longing in his chest, forcing himself to smile in return.

He missed his son, but tried to stay focused on the present rather than on whether he'd ever see his family again.

Ethan watched the boy for a moment, seeing a happy yet timid boy who desperately needed a morale boost of some kind. It just so happened that he had the means to provide a significant morale boost. After ten seconds of thinking, he'd come to a decision and stuck his hand into his right leg cargo pocket, pulling out a small stack of cards.

The boy stared at the cards like a deer in headlights, not daring to move as Ethan looked for something specific.

The stack wasn't in any particular order, which made it difficult to find the one he was looking for. He'd meant to organize them, but hadn't gotten around to it yet. Probably a good idea to get to that soon, since regularly pulling out a stack of cards could draw unwanted attention.

The stacks were separated into different pockets by rarity, this one being his uncommon cards. He passed over his first catches, the three wolves, then an otter, a mountain lion, a coyote, and a couple types of large fish. Ethan hadn't tested it yet, but he wondered if the card magic allowed fish to fight outside of water. He'd fought them while bathing in the river, which had turned out to be exactly as dangerous as you'd expect.

"Ah, here it is."

Moving the previous cards to the back of the stack, he held onto the card he'd picked in his left hand as he put the rest of the stack away with his right. With a final look at the hard earned card, he held it out to Bjorn.

"Bear," he pointed at the picture of the bear, then to the boy. "Bjorn."

The boy squinted at the card, but didn't immediately move to grab it.

Slowly, he reached for the card, watching Ethan as though this was some kind of trap. Curiosity won him over and he gently grabbed the card with both hands like it was a delicate bird. Ethan had tested out their sturdiness a few times, finding them to be unbreakable — or at least he hadn't figured out how to break one — so the boy must have thought it was quite valuable. He examined the card with an intense glare, like he wanted to memorize every detail.

The boy smiled, pointing at the card.

"Bear," he said in English, then pointed at himself and repeated the word.

After a full minute of analyzing the card, Bjorn let out a long sigh. There was a lot of emotion in that exhale, written all over the boy's face and in his body language. Sadness and grief mixed with longing. Using one hand to wipe away building tears in the corners his eyes, Bjorn reached out with the other to give the card back.

"No, no, no," Ethan shook his head and chuckled, then held his hands out as if to push the card back to the boy. "You keep it."

The boy pulled the card back, but looked confused.

"Gift," Ethan said. The boy was still confused. "Hmm..."

How could he help the boy understand? He pointed at Colby-Jack, at himself, then intertwined his fingers in front of himself. Next, he pointed at the card, to Bjorn, then meshed his fingers together again.

Confusion became realization, which became understanding, which became shock. The shock turned into outright refusal as the boy pushed the card away from his chest. He said a long string of words Ethan didn't understand, but the boy's body language made it clear.

He thinks he shouldn't take the card.

Ahh, so the boy either had integrity out the wazoo or he's afraid to take it for some reason. Maybe a combination of the two. In response, Ethan ignored the card as though it no longer existed and started packing up his gear.

The boy said Ethan's name a few times to get his attention,

but he ignored it and continued packing. Once finished, he squatted next to the fire, wincing at the pain in his knee, and used an orange plastic poop shovel to scoop dirt onto the fire. The fire was out after a few scoops, so he put the shovel back into the mesh lining on the back of his pack and stood up, putting most of his weight on his left knee.

The boy stared at the card, lost in another world... which was fair. Depending on how valuable an uncommon card was locally, it probably was a whole new world opening up for him.

"Bjorn," The boy didn't look up.

Ethan waved a hand and repeated himself, a bit louder than before. The boy flinched back and looked up.

"I need somewhere to eat, drink, and sleep."

As he spoke, Ethan pretended to eat a sandwich, drink from a cup, then rest his head on his hands like a pillow. The boy nodded, then stood to his feet, absentmindedly pointing toward the tree-line opposite of where he'd burst through the trees. Ethan smiled, then patted the boy on the shoulder as he walked past him toward the trees.

"He'll figure it out," he mumbled to himself as he crossed over the tree-line.

~~~

Bjorn's jaw was locked, his mouth wide open.

He stood still, staring at the card in his hand. A young fire bear. Not a cub, but not fully grown either. The man gave him an uncommon-tiered monster card. *Gave* it to him.

Like... for *free*.

It wasn't high ranking enough to be bound to him; only rare or higher could do that. The man didn't seem to know that's how it worked, but Bjorn knew. The card was valuable beyond anything he'd ever seen, let alone held in his hand.

Both of Bjorn's parents had bound rare bear-type monster cards before they'd died a few years prior, fighting off a monster horde. They'd loved bears, obviously naming their son after them. Bjorn felt a tightness in his chest, a welling up behind his eyes. He'd gotten used to the grief, but it was still there.

There was no way he could take this gift for free. He'd find a way to pay the man back, even if he had no idea how to go about it.

Bjorn gingerly put the card in his shirt's breast pocket, then turned and ran after the man named Farris.

18

GATE GUARD

Ethan was, in a word, underwhelmed.

The gate to town was not as impressive as he had expected it to be. Shouldn't the walls be lined with archers and flying companions ready to fight off monsters hordes? What he saw instead were three surprisingly clean viking-esque looking guards. And they were all human, thank God!

No orcs today, bay-bay!

Wait, weren't vikings supposed to be dirty, violent savages? Or... was that an inaccurate historical stereotype?

The three warriors stood outside an open gate, one on either side and one blocking the entrance. Two of the guards each had a small monster standing beside them. The guard on the right had a blue reptile of some sort, like a bearded dragon except it was the size of a chihuahua. The man Bjorn was talking to, the one blocking the entrance, had a young brown coyote. Probably an earth-type based on its color.

The creatures were small and not at all intimidating.

Did the town's soldiers only have common cards? If so, Ethan could understand now why Bjorn had been reluctant to take the uncommon bear. The third guard didn't have a monster at all, or at least not one that was visible, and looked unhappy to be there. He occasionally glanced down at the monsters, his mouth turned down like he had just tasted something unexpectedly sour.

The boy waved to get his attention, gesturing for Ethan to follow him into town. The lizard guard seemed to care more about watching the tree-line than Ethan, while the guard without the monster had been listening to whatever Bjorn had said, eyeing him with a squint.

Best to tread carefully with that one.

With a nod to the guards, and making the "thank you" sign as he passed, they entered the town. The guard Bjorn had spoken to nodded back, but watched them with interest as they started down the street.

"Well, that went smoother than I expected," Ethan mumbled to himself. "Didn't even have to bribe anyone."

The pair walked into a sort of modern looking town. Not 20th century modern, but more modern than the sixth century Viking era Ethan expected. The main street gave off downtown western movie vibes, but with a Scandinavian flare. Some buildings shared walls while others didn't, creating some shaded alleyways.

Closer to the gate, Ethan had seen evidence of monster attacks on the buildings. Scorch marks, claw marks, broken awnings, stuff like that. As they walked further from the gate, the damage became less visible.

After a few minutes of walking, the boy stopped in front of a two story building and said a word that hopefully meant tavern or inn. Ethan gave the building a once over, wondering how he'd communicate with these people if they all spoke the same language as the boy.

He needed a dictionary... or a translator.

Neither were likely to be available, but a dragon's hoard hadn't been likely either, and that happened. So, there was a chance. Ethan thanked Bjorn, then stepped up to the front door.

The boy didn't immediately run off as he pushed the door open and walked across the threshold, but he heard a distinct scurrying of steps as the door closed.

Inside was exactly what Ethan expected from a medieval tavern: a bar with stools running along the right side of the open room, tables filled most of the space, and a circular hearth in the center of the room with a decent sized fire to combat the evening chill. On the left side of the space was a wooden staircase leading upstairs, load bearing stone pillars scattered through the main dining area to handle the weight of a second floor.

The tavern was busy.

Most tables were full and half of the bar stools were occupied, but the general commotion died down slightly as Ethan walked in. People scrutinized him with curiosity, but soon went back to their food, drink, and/or socializing. Some snickers could be heard from a particularly rowdy table across the room. Ethan didn't mind; he must have looked ridiculous to these people, most of whom wore various bits of armor and carried at least one weapon.

He caught glimpses of axes, knives, and a few swords, but mostly blunt weapons like batons. Working class folk making sure they had some protection, if he had to guess.

Ethan moved to an empty stool at the bar, his back as close to a wall as he could with an easy view of the exit. Best to have his back to as few people as possible. Old habits die hard, he supposed. A young man — too young to legally drink back in the States — walked up from the other side of the bar with a rag across his shoulder and asked him something in the local language.

"I need food, drink, and a place to sleep," Ethan said.

As he spoke he made the same basic hand gestures he'd made with Bjorn, hoping his point came across. The people sitting near him smirked as he spoke.

The young bartender simply nodded, not at all put off by the language barrier, and rubbed his thumb across the tips of his fingers in the universal sign for money. Foreign travelers must be common, especially with the river nearby. Ethan thought his arrival would cause a bigger fuss, but everyone acted like it was any other day.

A relief, really, since he was trying not to stand out as much as possible while he got his bearings.

Ethan nodded, then pulled out a common monster card he'd prepared. This one was a small fire lizard. A duplicate, so he wasn't worried about giving it up. When he set it on the counter, the entire bar area fell silent, followed shortly by some murmuring from the rowdy table. Even they quieted down as the young bartender called back to the kitchen, his eyes not turning from Ethan even for a moment.

Aaaand there was the fuss he had expected.

The murmuring picked back up at one table, but everyone else was quiet. Hopefully just trying to figure out what was going on. Ethan wasn't sure what was going on himself, but the young bartender moved out of the way as a large bald man with skin darker than most people present appeared out of the kitchen.

He loomed over Ethan.

"Uhh..." was all Ethan could get out before the large man spoke, pointed at the card, then Ethan, then the door. The man's meaning was clear, although disappointing. Time to go. Ethan pocketed the card, stood up, and grabbed a strap of his pack that he'd placed beside his stool. He was about to move toward the door when a woman's voice cut through the silence.

It was her, the red-headed woman from the boat was speaking to the large tavern owner. The man made an attempt at arguing with the woman and they went back and forth for a minute, but in the end he walked back to the kitchen with a grunt and an unhappy look on his face.

The young bartender hurriedly filled a pint from a barrel behind the bar, then set it in front of the seat beside the woman. She made eye contact with Ethan, pointed at him, then at the stool beside her.

"Come soldier. Sit," she said in English. "Eat and drink with me."

19

YOU-ESS ARE-ME

"How do you speak English?" The man sat on the stool stool, cautiously eyeing the pint in front of him. "And what makes you think I'm a soldier?"

"That's a strange way to say thank you," Aino pointed at the name tapes on his jacket, ignoring the open suspicion in the man's voice. "Or should I call you 'Farris' of the 'You-Ess Are-me'?"

The man sighed, shoulders loosening a little bit.

"My name is Ethan Farris, so Ethan or Farris is fine," the man paused. "Though I've recently gotten out of the Army, so technically I'm not a soldier anymore."

"I'm not sure one ever stops being a soldier. A change of job doesn't change who we are," Aino shrugged, then nodded toward the stool where he'd previously sat. "And to answer your question about how I knew, that's easy guesswork. Soldiers tend to sit where they can see the exit."

"Good point, it's a hard habit to break," Ethan nodded. "So, you know my name. What should I call you?

"I am Aino Kaisdatter. You may call me Aino."

"It's nice to meet you, Aino. Especially since you're the first person I've been able to have an actual conversation with for the past few weeks."

Aino snorted.

"You may want to learn to speak Aidish soon, Mr. Farris."

The man nodded as he grabbed the wooden cup in front of him. He took a sip, made a surprised face, then took a longer drink.

"I suppose it shouldn't surprise me that you all drink mead here. The town gives strong 'viking' vibes," he took another sip, "Refreshing."

"Sometimes, yes," Aino chuckled. "The monks do their best."

"By the way, thanks for whatever you did to get the big guy to back off."

"Anker?" she waved a dismissive hand toward the kitchen. "Nah, he's harmless. Don't tell him I said that. He's an old friend of my father, kind of like an uncle to me."

"Well, thanks anyway. I doubt I would have had better luck anywhere else. Why'd he get so upset anyway? The whole place looked about ready to throw down," he lowered his voice, in case anyone else spoke English. "Is having monster cards illegal?"

Before Aino could respond, Anker came out of the kitchen with two wooden plates piled high with bread, strips of meat, and a small cup with vegetable soup.

"Thank you, Uncle," she said in Aidish, sporting an innocent smile. Anker smiled back with less innocence, glared at Ethan, then said, "Be careful of this one. He'll be trouble. Mark my words."

"Maybe we could use some trouble around here," she called out as the man walked back to the kitchen.

She could tell Ethan was curious about the exchange, but not enough to pry. Rather polite for a soldier. Aino turned back from the kitchen and replied to his question.

"It's not technically illegal, but it is frowned upon. Many people have lost loved ones to the monsters and the church here doesn't allow them at all within their congregation, or in the orphanage. They view it as a 'corruption upon the land', thus we are corrupt if we use them."

Aino bit into a strip of meat from her plate, watching Ethan's brow furrow as he considered her words.

"It seems to me..." he began, pausing long enough to take a sip of mead, "that the land has provided people with wild plants and animals. Yet people create farms with those plants and tame the animals. The food and resources they provide are viewed as a blessing. Why would it be any different with monsters?"

Nodding in agreement, Aino continued to eat in silence. She often had the same thoughts, which had brought her and her family at odds with many people.

"What about the guards at the gate?" the man continued. "Two of the three men there had monsters with them, common monsters if I had to guess. Seems a bit hypocritical."

"Not everyone shares the same beliefs as the church. Many view monsters as a way to make life better, like yourself. Some view them as companions or part of their family, though that is not as common."

The man dipped his bread into the soup and took a bite, closing his eyes and exhaling in a way that implied he enjoyed it way more than she felt Anker's cooking deserved. She had a feeling this man fell into the latter category that viewed monsters as companions, considering he didn't seem to know much about the local culture.

What monster had he bound to himself?

"If it were up to the church," she continued, "even the guards and soldiers wouldn't use them. But the captain of the guard holds no lost love for the church. Captain Havard, and many like him throughout Aidland, insist on using monsters. Their responsibility is to protect their homes from wild monsters. Being a cardist makes that easier."

"Cardists? Haven't heart that one yet, but I like it," the man said as he pulled the rest of his bread apart, placing strips of meat between the pieces. "So Aidland is this kingdom, or country, or whatever you call it?"

He bit into the makeshift sandwich.

"Aidland is the continent we are on, yes." She looked at him with curious eyes. "Where are you from, Mr. Farris, to not know our language or even the name of this land?"

"Oh, I'm from a place called California," he waved a hand off to his left. "It's way out west."

"And it's part of this 'You-Ess' where you were a soldier?"

"Yeah, it's a state within a country. One of fifty states. And California is bigger than most of the rest of them."

"That sounds unnecessarily complicated," she replied, her upper lip curling slightly.

"You'd think so, right?" Ethan laughed, bits of crumbs escaping his mouth before he was able to stop himself. The man swallowed, then clarified, "They keep trying to split it up into smaller states, but it never happens."

Aino watched Ethan as they continued to eat, feeling as though she were reenacting the stories her father told her about her great grandfather, who was also quite strange. Apparently learning this bizarre language hadn't been a complete waste of time.

"So, back to your original question," she said, realizing

they'd gone down a rabbit trail. "While that card you tried to pay with isn't illegal, some people refuse to accept them in trades, Anker being one of them. I think he's afraid of the church, especially since they are his main suppliers of mead.

"Most people won't be so hostile, it's just uncommon to see cards out in the open. You'll be fine, so long as you don't use any bound monsters around members of the church."

The man stopped eating for a moment. From the look on his face, it might actually be worth seeing the monks try to threaten this man. Her instincts seemed to have been correct; this man was definitely bound to at least one monster.

"About a week ago," the man said, still looking at her, "I happened to be up north. I saw a boat heading south down the river toward this town."

He paused to wave down the bartender, holding up his empty cup. The boy nodded and held up a finger to say it'll be a minute.

"It looked to me," he continued, "that the woman at the front of this boat was bound to a large red bird. At least I would assume they were bound, since the bird was larger and more intelligent than what I've experienced with common or uncommon monsters."

Their conversation paused while the young bartender swapped out his pint with a fresh one.

A new perspective on Ethan began to form in Aino's mind. Observant and proving to be rather intelligent. Interesting... and dangerous, if he was capable of surviving out in the northern wilds by himself.

"Anker may be right about you being trouble," she responded with a smirk. "That was me and my crew; Aino and the Red Bird Brigade. We've gained some renown hunting down troublesome monsters, thinning hordes, and taking out bandits when the need arises."

"No one causes trouble for the red-head with a bound monster?"

"They certainly try," she chuckled. "But Aidland needs people like us."

"Well..." the man's expression turned thoughtful as he finished a bite of sandwich, "Would this 'Red Bird Brigade' be interested in letting a foreigner tag along? I could use some help getting my feet under me in unfamiliar territory. I need information and help selling some extra cards, so I'd be happy to share some of the profits."

That offer alone had its own appeal. Monster cards weren't cheap.

More than that, she'd been waiting her whole life for someone like him to show up; a foreigner who spoke the strange language passed down in her family for generations. Never thought it would actually happen.

Looking at the man now, she considered her options. He didn't look soft, but he also didn't seem violent. A straight forward sort. She had a good feeling about him, no matter what her uncle said.

"Okay, Mr. Farris. We're staying here at the tavern for a couple more days to finish trading, then we move south and east to the next town in our route. You're welcome to hitch a ride."

"Works for me," he stuck his hand out toward Aino.

She looked at his hand, met his eyes, then hooked her palm with his. A firm handshake, causing them both to smile. Anker happened to walk out of the kitchen at that moment, his arms lined with plates of food, a deep frown furrowing his brow at the sight of their grasped hands and wide smiles.

20

WENT TO MARKET

"You still haven't told me how you know my language," Ethan commented as he laid out three common monster cards on the sturdy table in front of him.

He and Aino sat behind a market stall. Beside them stood another man that seemed to be a member of Aino's crew. Like an old Norse version of a bouncer for a seedy downtown bar. Was he her security detail?

There was a lot he didn't understand yet about Aidland.

When they'd finished talking the night before, Aino convinced her "uncle" to let him have a room for the night. So long as Ethan paid the tavern owner back after they'd been to the market, all was well. So, after a medieval bath and a good night's rest, they sat in the early morning chill waiting for the rest of the town to wake up.

"I'll answer in exchange for one of those monster cards," Aino said with a smirk, like she was either joking or didn't think he could afford to pay up.

"Go ahead," he replied with a shrug. "Pick one."

Aino glared at him with narrowed eyes, but he didn't say anything else.

She snapped her hand out toward the table, like she suspected a trap, and grabbed the card with a red sparrow-sized bird. Not surprising that she'd go for that one, given her bound monster and the name of her crew.

Ethan undid the zipper of his jacket's left arm pocket, pulled out a new card, then laid it on the table where the bird had been. This one was the common fire lizard he'd tried to trade the night before. The other two were a small water turtle and a plant type cat that looked like a mix of a lynx and a bobcat.

Aino stared in shock through the whole process. Was he flaunting his wealth on purpose?

"For future reference, I'd like to have first dibs at purchasing any red birds you may come across," she said, forcing herself to look away from the fire lizard card as she put her own new card in a small pouch attached to her belt. "They're kind of my thing."

Ethan glanced at her, then nodded and turned his attention to Aino's table as a townsfolk approached to buy or trade with her. She had all the normal things you'd expect from this type of world. Furs, clothing, armor, a couple well used swords and spears, etc. Ethan expected her to do the selling, but the burly man beside her intercepted the customers and made two sales within a few minutes.

Even without understanding anything being said, Ethan could tell that the man was a natural salesman.

Townsfolk browsed the cards on Ethan's side of the table, then nodded to him and moved on without even saying hello. One woman walked back behind her own stall across the street and started laying out goods to sell.

Aino must have had them get here pretty damn early if the locals weren't even set up yet. Or maybe the townsfolk just took their time in the morning, like how Spanish cultures tended to not push urgency.

"So? Language?" he asked, remembering the trade he'd made with Aino. He watched a few people finish setting up their stalls.

"Yes, yes. A deal is a deal," she began with reluctance in her voice. "This language has been taught in my family for a few generations. So no, in case you were wondering, I am not from whatever far off land you are from. California, was it?"

Ethan tried not to look disappointed, instead choosing to be grateful to have someone to talk with at all.

"It started with my great-grandfather," she continued. "He was an eccentric foreigner, like yourself. Insisted everyone in the family learn his native language. The common theory was that he hoped someday more people like him would show up."

Ethan nodded, encouraging her to continue.

"So, I learned it," she shrugged. "Many men of the family took to it with gusto, hoping to be part of something bigger than themselves. Men tend to be like that, seeking purpose bigger than themselves. I was a more practical-minded child. To be honest, I just enjoyed having a secret language with my family. My father and I had a lot of fun with it."

A disappointed growl emanated from Ethan, causing a young girl who'd been browsing his table to squeal in fright and scurry away. He grimaced, feeling a bit guilty for scaring the girl.

"This was not the answer you were hoping for?" Aino asked, noting the exchange.

"Well..." he considered how much to share. "It was a good

answer, considering it was a truthful answer. But no, I was hoping for something more actionable."

"What do you mean?"

"When I saw you and your crew on the river, it had been as a reward for an exploration quest I had just completed."

"Really?" She raised her eyebrows, "We were a quest reward?"

"Yeah," Ethan scratched the hairline on the back of his neck. "'A clue on how to get home' was what the text box said."

They sat in silence for a while, Ethan running scenarios of what he could do next. Aino had already agreed to let him go with her, but it suddenly seemed like it wouldn't amount to more than aimless wandering. He let out a sigh. At least he'd have someone to help him learn the language and culture.

The courtyard began to get busy as Aino broke the silence.

"My family still has some of my great-grandfather's belongings. He disappeared around his fiftieth birthday. I wasn't born yet, so I don't know anything first hand, but apparently it was a big deal. He wasn't the type of man to up and disappear like that. Some in the family put him on a pedestal like a prophet, so his children split up all his belongings as relics and continued passing on his traditions."

She glanced at Ethan, a spark in her eye, "He kept detailed journals during his years in our land. My father just so happens to be the keeper of those particular relics."

"Do you think those journals mention if he planned to go home?" Ethan leaned forward, his voice filled with both hope and doubt. "Maybe a theory of how he could do it if he wanted to?"

"Who knows?" she responded with a shrug. "I've read some of them and a lot of what he wrote sounds like nonsense.

It's possible it'll mean something to you, if you really are from the same place. I do remember reading about his thoughts on 'Hidden Quests', though I'm not sure those exist. I've never completed any myself, nor has anyone else ever mentioned them."

After another hour in the market, a man walked straight up to Ethan's part of the booth, a more determined look in his eyes than most people who'd stopped by to look. He wore a chainmail shirt, carried a shield on his back, and a hatchet at his hip. Stereotypical action movie scars covered one cheek, claw marks if Ethan had to guess.

The man looked over the cards, reading each one carefully. That gave Ethan an idea.

"Is the text on these cards written in Aidish for you?" He asked Aino. "It's in English for me."

She nodded, "The cards adjust to the reader's native tongue."

A smile crossed his face. A potential loophole in the system to help him learn Aidish? They could make a dictionary or something that he could use to study! The armored man spoke while looking at the plant type cat, bringing Ethan back to the present.

It sounded like he'd asked a question, to which Aino responded in Aidish. She pointed at Ethan, then held up all ten of her fingers while she spoke. The man's face grimaced, as if in pain, then he stood straight and responded. Aino tapped a finger to her chin, calmly pointed at the man and gave a short response.

The man thought for a moment, then nodded.

Opening a pouch at his hip, he drew out a small stack of gold coins and placed them on the table. Aino then grabbed the plant cat from the table and handed it to the man.

Purchase complete.

Of course the big burly man wanted himself a little kitty, Ethan chuckled to himself. Realizing he should probably say something, Ethan made the sign for thank you and roughly spoke the words in Aidish. The man nodded in return as he took the card from Aino.

"What's he buying the card for?" Ethan asked. "Did he say?"

"He's going to have the monster watch over his daughter during the next horde attack. He's a sergeant in the town guard, so he's expected to fight at the walls. I got the impression that he lost someone important during the last horde."

Ethan glanced at her then back at the man, who was in the process of placing the card in a pouch hanging from a string around his neck. A horde attack? She said it like it was a common occurrence.

Hmm... The man was just trying to protect his child?

A small spike of panic gripped Ethan. Before he could think about what he was doing, he opened the velcro of one of his pockets and pulled out a small stack of item cards. He set one card face down on the table, put the rest back in his pocket, then slid the card toward the man.

"Please tell him to take this," he said to Aino. "No charge."

She translated, a look of suspicion on her face and confusion on the man's. The soldier looked at the card, back to Ethan, then back to the card. He picked it up and read over it, his eyebrows shooting up to his hairline and his jaw grinding like Ethan's did while processing an overwhelming emotion.

The man spoke to Aino, his voice hushed and hurried.

"He's asking if this is a joke. This card is worth more than the monster he just purchased from us," she turned to Ethan. "What card did you give him?"

"It's not a joke. If it'll help protect his daughter, I want him to have it. It's an evolution card; turn that common into an uncommon."

The man's cheeks blushed as Aino relayed what was said, water building around his eyes. He placed the card in his pouch, coughed to clear a knot building in his throat, then looked at Ethan and asked a question.

"He asked if you have any uncommon monsters for sale."

"Depends on why he's asking," Ethan raised an eyebrow. "He technically just got an uncommon for the price of a common."

Aino spoke to the man in Aidish, who then gave a wordy reply.

"He says the captain of the guard has recently been on the prowl for uncommon cards. The monsters around have been especially aggressive lately and he wants to prevent unnecessary deaths among his troops."

Ethan nodded, tapping his chin with his index finger, "Ask him if the captain favors any particular type of monster."

After translating, the man shook his head and replied, "He hasn't been picky with types." Aino turned her head to Ethan, adding information of her own, "Captain Havard's family sigil is the wolf. I'd imagine he'd be especially interested in acquiring wolves for himself, maybe even for his siblings."

"Warriors and their wolves. Classic," Ethan nodded to the man and said, "I may have some options."

Through Aino as translator, the man gave instructions to stop by the barracks when they had time after market hours. The captain would want to see the options and barter for himself, without the prying eyes of the townsfolk.

Ethan nodded, then stood and reached out to shake the man's hand. The man wore a one sided smirk, but gave a firm, painful handshake. Ethan tried not to show the pain on his face, unsure how successful he was. When they broke contact, the man walked away and continued straight out of the market without looking at any other stores.

"This is a good opportunity, Ethan," Aino said as she watched the guard. "Guardsmen often have much to trade. For an uncommon card you could equip yourself with a high quality weapon, maybe even some armor. Gathering travel supplies won't be a problem for you."

Ethan was sure he saw a glint of envy in Aino's tone.

"Well..." he considered his response as he pulled another common plant type monster from his pocket, this one a small monkey. With a wide grin he placed the new card where the plant cat had been. "I'll need you to come with me. If you need any supplies, I'm happy to add it to the trade."

"You are a strange man, Ethan Farris," Aino squinted at him again, then grunted a laugh. "And unnecessarily generous."

"Write that on my gravestone," he paused, realizing what he'd just said, "Actually, don't do that. I don't intend on dying here."

21

MARKET GAINS

BY THE END OF THE DAY, ETHAN HAD SOLD TEN OF HIS COMMON cards.

Aino made it seem like that was a lot but it hadn't put much of a dent in Ethan's somewhat bulging pockets. Not knowing what to expect when he got to town, he'd hidden the a couple hundred blank cards back at the van. Better safe than sorry. Now he realized it was definitely the right move, that he'd be fine even if someone managed to somehow rob him blind.

Some cards sold for less, while more popular cards sold for more. Classic supply and demand.

For each card purchased he'd gotten an average of five gold coins. Aino insisted it was a good average, since each gold coin was worth ten silver coins. Most laborers made a silver per day and the average person could make one gold every week and a half. So, a common monster card would be several weeks worth of pay without spending money on anything else during that time. That kind of purchase could take months to save up for.

From what he gathered from Aino, there were general amounts he could expect based on the rarity of a card. The new information was written in Ethan's notebook for future use.

- *Common Monster Card = 5 gold*
- *Uncommon Monster card = 50 gold*
- *Rare Monster Card = 500 gold*

If it took months to save up for a common monster, it would take years to save up for an uncommon monster. No wonder that sergeant had been getting choked up at the free evolution card. It was unlikely that many people would be able to afford a rare card in their lifetime. A whole family would have to pool resources and, even then, it was unlikely for a typical working class family.

Ethan realized how obnoxiously blessed his circumstances were.

Whoever brought him to this world could have left him to fend for himself. Instead, a random craft idea for his nephews had been turned into a dragon's hoard of wealth and opportunity. Clearly he had been blessed, but it was even more exaggerated than anticipated.

As it turned out, Aidland's economy used a combination of bartering and coins made from copper, silver, or gold. Classic tabletop RPG rules. Many common looking folk traded copper or silver coins for daily necessities and it was common to use hack-silver, which was silver goods literally chopped up or "hacked" into smaller pieces. But most merchants preferred to deal in coins since the weight was regulated and generally believed to be more trustworthy, making transactions quick and smooth in comparison to bulky trades.

Any break between customers, Ethan spent learning Aidish

words related to numbers and trade. The sooner he could communicate with the locals, the better, especially for meetings like the one they were currently heading toward.

"So, what should I be expecting from this 'Captain of the Guard'?" Ethan asked as they made their way to the barracks. "Is he a tough sale? Will he try to cheat us?"

"Us?" Aino asked. "I doubt he'd try to cheat me. Not unless he wants to get on the Brigade's bad side, which would be silly of him. But you? Most people would try to 'get a discount' from the foreigner. But I'm not here to barter, I'm here to translate. If you want a good deal, you'll have to work for it. Good opportunity for you to acquaint yourself with the Aidish culture."

"Yes, yes," Ethan nodded, rolling his eyes. He already assumed all that. "But what kind of man is he?"

"He's a good man, from my experience. Straight forward and his soldiers respect him," she shrugged. "He can be a little rough around the edges, like most soldiers. Yourself included."

"Little ole' me, rough around the edges? Well, I never!" Ethan held a hand to his chest, his mouth open in mock offense. He cringed at his own exaggerated impression of a southern accent, then smiled. "This is going to be fun, I think."

A snort escaped Aino's lips.

"I'm not sure 'fun' is a word I've ever heard used in reference to Captain Havard."

"I thought you said he's a good man."

"He is," she replied. "But you can be a good person and still lack a sense of humor."

Ethan's smile grew even wider.

"I like him already!"

22

AYE AYE CAPTAIN

"So this is the man with the cards?"

Havard wasn't impressed. The foreigner was dressed like he belonged hiding amongst trees, rather than standing his ground against a horde.

"This is him," Aino replied.

The captain glanced at the red-headed adventurer, whom he'd hired a few times during monster heavy seasons. He liked her, for the most part. She was honest and capable, rare qualities to see amongst adventurers and mercenaries.

"I will be translating," she continued, "as Mr. Farris is new to our land and still learning Aidish. I wouldn't underestimate him though, Havard. He can be..." she glanced at the card man, whose eyes scanned the room like he was investigating a crime scene. "...surprising."

Havard nodded, then turned to the man with the cards.

"I am Havard Havardson, captain of the guard here in the town of Trace."

Aino translated, then the man introduced himself in simple Aidish, "I am Ethan Farris."

The man held out his hand in greeting and gave a surprisingly firm handshake. It wasn't that Havard thought the man was weak, but he looked more aloof than his handshake would suggest. The captain gestured to the two chairs in front of his desk as he moved around to his chair at the other side, his back straight as a board while he waited for his guests to sit.

The card man, Mr. Farris, sat in his chair.

"I like your office," Aino translated. "Simple and efficient."

Havard gave the standard thank you gesture, though he couldn't tell if the man was speaking truth or mocking him. Appraising his office with fresh eyes, Havard couldn't help but agree with the man.

The office was sparse, just a bookshelf with several volumes of Aidland history, one of his own family's history, and message scrolls from the capital. A mess he hadn't gotten around to organizing yet. Behind his desk were a cot and two large chests, where he kept most of his personal belongings.

'A clear office is a clear mind', his father used to say.

Havard knew that many in his position flaunted their status with expensive furniture and decor, but he found it unnecessary. Better to keep it simple and save that money for more practical needs.

"I'm a simple man with simple needs," Havard agreed.

Ethan smiled, then spoke, translated to "In that case, I won't waste either of our time and get straight to the point. One of your men mentioned you were in the market for some monster cards. Is this accurate?"

"This is true. Specifically uncommon monsters. My troops are encouraged to purchase their own commons. Though, as I'm sure you're aware, they are mostly only good for distraction against stronger monsters. My scouts have seen evidence of monsters building in aggression and cooperation with each other. I suspect we will have a horde to defend against within a week."

"So soon?" Aino sat forward in interest.

"Yes," he replied, then continued to Mr. Farris. "My men are skilled, but no town is left unscathed from a horde. I aim to minimize the number of widows and orphans each horde leaves in its wake and am actively looking for ways to supplement my troops."

"Wouldn't this cause you trouble with the church?" Mr. Farris asked. "I've been told they discourage use of monsters, especially the stronger ones."

"Blegh!" Havard made a face like he'd tasted something bitter. "I don't answer to monks and priests. I'll consider their words when they start risking their necks to save their neighbors."

The card man laughed, then pointed at him while speaking to Aino. She did not immediately translate. Instead, she dropped her head, shaking it back and forth. Maybe she was embarrassed, but Havard could see a smile playing at her lips.

"What did he say? I don't appreciate being laughed at."

"He's not laughing at you," Aino looked up. "He said 'I told you this would be fun' and 'I like this man.'"

"He thinks my lack of respect for the church is fun?" Havard asked, confused.

"I think what he enjoys is how honest you are, even with a potentially touchy subject."

She looked at the card man in a way Havard looked at his men when they were a little too rowdy. The man raised his hands in front of him in surrender, saying something Havard assumed meant "Okay, Okay. I give up." Aino didn't seem to think it needed translating.

Mr. Farris reached into one of many pockets on his jacket,

pulled out three cards, then laid them on the table in front of Havard so he had a clear view of each. The captain leaned forward, noting the three uncommon wolf monster cards. A fire, a water, and a plant type. Havard raised an eyebrow and looked to Aino, who had taken in a sharp breath and was slowly releasing it to calm herself.

So she hadn't been expecting the display. Interesting.

"Am I to pick or are you willing to trade all three?"

The man rubbed the stubble on his chin, then asked Aino a question that made her bark out a laugh.

Again, Havard frowned.

~~~

The room was silent after Ethan pulled out the three wolf cards, Aino involuntarily barking a single laugh when he asked her what they were worth.

"They're worth what you're willing to trade them for. I already told you their coin value," she replied, throwing her hands up in exacerbation. "Why are you asking me, anyway? You're the one who confidently laid out three out of four cards in a set. You may as well pull out an Earth Wolf from those magic pockets of yours and trade a complete set!"

"May as well," Ethan grumbled to himself, then shrugged.

Reaching into a separate pocket, he pulled out a card and laid it in line with the other three cards. Aino leaned forward to look, already feeling a sinking sensation in her gut.

It was an Earth Wolf. A *rare* Earth Wolf, because of course it was.

Aino leaned back in her chair, a heavy sigh causing her lips to sputter. Havard's face was frozen in a deep frown, staring with intensity at the card. She couldn't tell what he was thinking. For Havard, that look could mean angry or excited. Hard to tell with that man.

"What would you be willing to trade for the set?" Ethan asked, half smirk pulling at his lips.

Havard sat up with his back straight as Aino translated, looking at Ethan with the gaze of a predator.

"What do you need?" he replied.

"I have a proposition for you. A business idea of sorts," Ethan started. "Something that could help the whole town if the right people get involved."

23

SHOCK AND AWE

"Did you stumble upon a dragon's hoard? If so, that was a strange way of using it."

Aino watched the road ahead as they walked away from the barracks, feeling an unsettling mix of frustration and admiration for the man walking beside her. Using the money he had gained from trading with Havard, he paid four year's worth of living expenses for Bjorn to be taken in as the captain's apprentice.

The idea was to train him to be a soldier so he could learn to take care of himself. Not only that, he would make the same offer for any child taken in as an apprentice, orphan or not, by anyone in town willing to train them. As a pillar of the community, Havard would be the frontman for the operation and make sure no one would take advantage of the children.

"I've been blessed," Ethan replied. "It feels wrong to hoard all of it to myself. What good is a dragon's hoard if it just sits in a pile? Besides, it's an investment"

"An investment in what? You won't make any money doing

it this way. Maybe you could if you demanded a cut of profits each child makes or something like that."

"Not all investments are meant to make money," he made a clicking sound with his mouth, like a mother to a misbehaving child. "I still have more gold than I need. It brings me joy to see the shock and awe of someone receiving unexpected generosity. It inspires hope for the future. Theirs and mine."

She knew what he meant, already seeing a lot of goodwill directed at him, a stranger and foreigner. He'd given much without expecting much in return.

"I've never been particularly generous," Aino admitted, "Definitely not to the obnoxious level you take it to."

"Oh, is that right?" He laughed. "I'm obnoxious?"

She shrugged.

"Well, this is how I choose to do it," he continued. "That doesn't mean it's the only way it's got to be done. Some people are generous with their time, which I'd say is more valuable than the gold and silver I'm offering. I don't have the time available to be generous in that way. Not if I want to get home anytime soon."

They walked in companionable silence, neither feeling the need to say more. Aino stole a glance at Ethan, whose eyes seemed distant as though lost in thought. He'd given her much to consider, like every time he spoke there was some life lesson she needed to process.

It was kind of exhausting.

The orphanage came into view, a church steeple looming behind it. Aino's experience with church folk had more often than not been lacking in generosity, both with gold and time. This was likely a foolhardy mission and she said as much to Ethan.

"They're unlikely to listen to you. Everyone knows you're

The Card Man. You're basically the antithesis of everything they believe in."

"Hmm..." Ethan pondered for a moment. "Well, it's always a no if you don't ask. If they don't want to help, we'll figure something else out."

24

SWIFT KICK

THE GROUND HIT BJORN HARD AS HE FELL, CLUTCHING HIS STOMACH, his left eye swollen. Losing his card taken hurt far more.

"Come on Bjorn, you know these things aren't allowed."

The boy looked up at Brother Thomas, who waved the Fire Bear card in the air. Behind the monk stood the orphanage, connected to the central chapel for the town.

"Please don't take it," he squeaked out. "It was a gift."

"Yes, I'm sure it was. How else would you have gotten an uncommon card? Unless..." the monk eyed Bjorn, "maybe you stole it?"

Anger welled up in Bjorn's belly, a dam ready to burst. He would never steal!

"You were seen with the foreigner who's been flaunting his cards around town," Brother Thomas looked like he had a bad taste in his mouth. "The fool can corrupt himself as he pleases, but you're under the church's care. We both are. That means we have to follow the church's rules; no cards allowed. You know this."

"Then I'll leave!" Bjorn got to his feet and held out his hand. "Give it back!"

"And where will you go?" The monk laughed, out of pity more than actual humor. "No, I can't let you run off. I'd get a beating worse than what you got. The card will be sold to provide for the church, including the children. This is the way of things, Bjorn. I promise you'll be much happier if you just accept it and more on."

A dog barked down the road, drawing the monk's attention. Bjorn registered the man's befuddled look, then glanced down the card. The distraction was a perfect opportunity to kick the monk in the balls.

The card fell to the ground as the monk collapsed in pain, hands cupped to protect his groin from further harm.

Bjorn grabbed the card and ran, not knowing where he could go. Anywhere else was better. Sure, the monks had looked after him since the last horde broke through the town. They'd provided him with food and shelter, but they also beat him and forced him to follow rules that didn't make any sense.

No, he wouldn't stay there anymore.

Turning into an alley, Bjorn stopped to catch his breath. His lungs were burning, his eye was now completely swollen shut, and his stomach felt like it was building up a massive bruise, but he felt strong enough to keep moving.

What he needed was a plan. But where could he go?

The shaded alley wall felt cool against his back as he rested, thinking through his options. The town was still relatively new to him, so he wasn't as familiar with it as his home town. His family had only been in town in the first place because they were traveling merchants caught up by a particularly large monster horde. The only people he knew were the monks at the church, the other orphans, and a few guards he'd interacted with.

Looking down at the card resting in his hands, a thought occurred to him. Well.. he did sort of know someone else.

As a plan began to form, the boy heard a sound from the rooftop above him. When he looked up, his good eye met a large one-eyed cat staring back at him. The cat jumped down to the ground beside him, its landing only audible because he'd seen it happening.

This cat looked familiar... Oh! It was with Mr. Farris in the woods!

Bjorn reached out a fist for the cat to smell, not wanting to scare it off. Turned out the cat wasn't timid at all, not hesitating to rub the side of its face with the missing eye against his knuckles like a bear scratching its back against a tree.

After a few moments the cat stepped back, meowed at him, then pitter-pattered toward the end of the alleyway. When Bjorn didn't move to follow, the cat stopped, turned its head to face him, then meowed again.

"I guess I'll just follow you. This works out better than what I had in mind anyway."

The boy stood on shaky legs, his stomach growling as he followed the cat onto the street. Hopefully it led him to some food.

25

MONSTERS AND OTHER MONSTERS

THEY WERE MONSTERS. RAVENOUS, DISGUSTING MONSTERS.

Aino sat back in her chair, the tavern now mostly empty, as she watched Ethan and the young boy tear into their second plates of food.

Then there were the animals, like the large one-eyed cat that had led the boy to them and decided her lap was the ideal spot for a nap. A dog with golden fur sat on the floor leaning against the boy's leg, watching him eat. Aino could swear the swelling in the boy's eye had gone down since they started eating, though that was likely her imagination. Then there was the small orange and white dog who sat in a chair beside Ethan, watching the room like a bodyguard.

"So... these are your... pets?" she finally asked.

"Eh," the man tilted his hand back and forth like a scale. "They're more like companions."

"Companions, right." She nodded, savoring the feel of the cat's fur between her fingers. "And they are... bound to you?"

Ethan nodded, catching her meaning. He pointed to the

small dog. "Colby-Jack was first. She's the reason I survived those wolves I traded today."

"This dog fought and survived multiple wolves?" She asked.

Colby-Jack made a "boof" sound at her, but didn't make eye contact. Ethan chuckled and scratched the dog behind the ears.

"Could have taken them all on by herself, honestly. She's a good girl," the dog gave another boof and stuck her nose up in pride, which made Ethan snort. "Yes, she's the bestest girl."

Aino was skeptical the dog could handle one wolf, let alone three, but decided not to dig further.

"What about this one-eyed cat and the golden haired dog?"

"That one is Theodore," Ethan pointed at the dog. "He's a lover, not a fighter. He has healing abilities, but he's protective, especially of children."

It was clear the dog favored the young boy, which also explained why the swelling in the boy's eye was lessening.

"Zuko there," the man continued, pointing at the cat in her lap, "is a hunter. I activated his card because I was running out of food and wasn't having much luck hunting or gathering. Had stomach pains for a few days because of some berries I thought were blueberries. They were not, in fact, blueberries."

Zuko didn't move or even acknowledge he was being spoken about at all.

"Strange, but fair enough," she said, then pointed a thumb to the boy continuing to stuff his face with food. "What's the deal with the boy?"

"I don't know," Ethan shrugged, "I haven't been able to speak to him more than a few words. Try asking him."

Apparently done answering questions, the man went back

to his eating. Aino rolled her eyes, landing her sights on the boy.

"What's your name, child?" she asked in Aidish.

"Bjorn," he replied, still food in his mouth. Seeing the look on her face, he straightened up and swallowed before introducing himself properly. "I am Bjorn Bjornson. Nice to meet you, Lady."

She noted a touch of pride in his tone.

"Your family must be fond of bears. Or they were fond of bears. I assume, since you were at the orphanage, your parents have passed?"

"Yes," the boy nodded, looking serious. He sat back, less enthusiastic about eating. "They fell to the horde last year. We aren't from here and the horde kept us from leaving. Thank you for taking me in for the night."

The boy bowed his head to her, then turned and made the gesture for thank you to Ethan. The man lifted his pint in response, then took a long drink.

"So, Bjorn, what happened? Why did the monk beat you? I assume you broke a rule of some sort," she paused for a moment, glancing at Ethan. "How do you and Ethan know each other?"

"Ethan?"

Aino gestured to the man.

"Ahh, Mr. Farris. Well..." he began, "I was kinda beaten because of meeting Mr. Farris."

Aino shot a glare at Ethan, who looked blissfully ignorant at that moment. She looked back at the boy, encouraging him to continue.

"I left town by myself yesterday. My idea was to find a small common monster I could kill by myself, then receive the blank card from the First Hunt quest. Instead, I ran for my life from two monsters that ambushed me. That's when I crashed into Mr. Farris's campsite. He and his monster friends saved me."

"So you got in trouble for leaving town unprotected?"

"No... Well yes, but that would have just gotten me yelled at. I was beat because I brought a monster card onto church property."

"And where did you get this card?" she side eyed Ethan, having a good idea of where this was leading.

"Mr. Farris was excited when he recognized my name and taught me 'bear' in his language. He pulled out this card and gave it to me."

The boy handed his card to Aino, a great sign of trust. She could almost feel Anker's glare boring into the back of her head from the kitchen door. As she glanced over the card, her cheeks flushed with a rising anger.

"You gave an orphan an uncommon monster card?!" she shouted in English, "You could have gotten him killed!"

Ethan flinched at the sudden noise, the few occupied tables around them grew quiet. He set down the food scraps in his hand, then calmly took a drink from his mead. What she saw in his eyes made her anger dim slightly. His standard jovial, fun loving expression was gone, replaced by a stern but otherwise neutral expression she couldn't quite read.

"Yeah, I gave him the card. I didn't know the boy's situation, but he'd almost gotten himself killed. He's only *not* dead because he stumbled into *my* campsite before monsters ripped him to shreds," he paused to gesture at the boy. "For whatever reason, Bjorn doesn't have anyone he trusts to protect him and he willingly walked into danger. Chances are high he would do it again. So, I gave him a means to protect himself. What would you have me do when a timid boy crosses my path, likely alone in the world and in need of someone to help him?"

"That's not how we do things here, Ethan."

Ethan's gaze drilled a hole into Aino as he slammed his palm on the table, raising the volume of his voice in a way that reminded her of her father.

"I may not be from around here or understand the customs," he seethed through gritted teeth, "but I am not a fool! Do not speak to me like one! If I see a child in trouble, I will help him! End of story!"

He pushed his chair back and stood from the table, calling Bjorn's name and gesturing for him to follow. The boy had been watching the exchange, confused by the change of mood, but got up to follow the man. Colby-Jack gave a quick low bark in Aino's direction. The cat jumped out of her lap and all three animals, as well as the boy, followed Ethan up the stairs.

"What in the world was that about?"

26

BOUND TO HAPPEN

YOU COULD TELL A LOT ABOUT A CARDIST BY THE MONSTERS THEY bound to themselves.

That's what Aino's experience told her, anyway. Take Ethan Farris, for instance. His little dog companion, Colby-Jack, was stoic and serious with glimpses of silliness. The golden dog, Theodore, prioritized healing and cared deeply about children. The one-eyed cat, Zuko, enjoyed physical affection and was a skilled hunter. A skilled hunter was both patient and relentless.

Aino sat in silence as she watched Ethan and Bjorn leave the common room, her lap empty and her chest aching. She hadn't meant to upset the man, but she'd felt like he'd done something monumentally stupid by endangering the boy. After his response, she wasn't so sure.

Clearly he wasn't as naive as she'd thought.

"I told you that one would be trouble."

Uncle Anker grunted his way into the chair where the boy had been sitting. Aino only nodded, still lost in thought.

"You want me to kick him out?" he asked, a not so subtle eagerness on his face.

"No, no," she waved a dismissive hand. "I'm just reevaluating a belief I didn't realize I had. Ethan may be trouble, but I feel like he's a good kind of trouble. We've been stuck in our ways and could benefit from a fresh perspective."

"You saying I'm stuck in my ways?"

"I said 'we', uncle. And, yes, you are."

"So what happened?" Anker grunted, changing the subject. "I was keeping an eye on your table, in case the half-starved lads needed more food. The next moment you two were shouting in that strange language."

"I thought he'd done something stupid to endanger that boy. But it seems I misunderstood the situation. He was helping the boy, it just happened to get him a beating from the monks. I blamed him instead of the ones doing the beating." Aino looked Anker in the eye, her pale cheeks flushed a light shade of red. "He's generous and cares for strangers, especially children. We could use more of that in Aidland. Hells, I could stand to be more like that."

Anker sat with his arms crossed, one hand stroking the hair of his chin. After a moment he shimmied his chair closer to hers, cupped her face in his massive hands, then kissed her forehead. He pulled back, still cupping her face.

"You'll be wanting to keep him around, then. We become the company we keep. At the very least," Anker released his grip, then stood and pushed in his chair, "don't break his trust. A good man is dangerous when trust is broken."

Giving her no time to reply, he turned and went back to work.

Hell must have frozen over for uncle Anker to speak like

that about a card collector. Turning her gaze to the top of the staircase, she wondered about the effect Ethan Farris was already having after one day in town.

27

IN A BIND

Anger itself wasn't an emotion, only a method to communicate the actual feelings that matter. Ethan had heard that somewhere. Probably a Ted Talk or podcast. But why was he so frustrated? What reasons lay underneath?

He was upset with Aino, sure, but more so with himself. His intent had been simply to give Bjorn a means to protect himself.

Instead, the boy's card was taken and he was physically abused by a monk. Thankfully, Bjorn was clever and had taken advantage of Colby-Jack's booty shake distraction, otherwise the monk would probably be dead rather than curled up in pain on the ground. Ethan's vision had gone red when he saw the man standing over the boy in the street.

There was a distinct difference between discipline and abuse. If it had been Jack... Best not to think too hard about what he'd do to protect his son.

Laying out his sleep system on the floor of his room, Ethan considered what to do next. His instincts told him what he should do, but he didn't want to rush ahead impulsively either.

Looking up, he noticed Bjorn still standing inside the doorway, absentmindedly scratching one of Theodore's golden ears.

Ethan sat cross legged on his sleeping bag, which lie on top of his thin foldable foam mattress, then gestured for Bjorn to take the bed. Zuko meowed from his perch on the headboard, one paw hanging down the side.

The boy closed the door and moved to the bed with a somber expression on his face. Ethan hadn't really thought about it, but he'd probably scared the kid. Especially considering he wouldn't have understood anything that had been said downstairs.

Once Bjorn was seated and they faced each other, Ethan closed his eyes and ran through his breathing exercise twice before he spoke.

"Bear card, please," he held out his hand to the boy, using three of the few Aidish words he'd learned so far.

The boy looked dejected, like he'd been sent to the principal's office or was waiting to see his parents' reaction to his report card full of failing grades. Still, he did as he was told and handed over the card.

Ethan took it and set it on the ground, then reached into a pocket and pulled out a stack of cards.

He hadn't had much of a need for item cards yet, other than the one he gave to the guard at the market, so he hadn't gotten around to organizing them. Sifting through the stack he saw various healing potions, a handful of revive cards of different ranks, and... ah, there they were.

Picking one card from the stack, he laid it beside the boy's bear card and returned the rest to his pocket.

Ethan pulled out his notebook, opening to a blank page, and drew two blank cards. On each card he copied word for word what he saw in English. Where the bear picture would be, he wrote "Bjorn/Bear". He drew out two more blank cards, this time leaving them blank, then handed the notebook and pen to Bjorn, who had been watching him with curiosity.

Pointing to "bear", Ethan said "English", then pointed to the word "Bjorn" and said "Aidish".

Down each line he went, voicing the word's English equivalent. When he'd finished, it was Bjorn's turn. He then pointed to the boy, to the drawings of blank cards, then mimed writing with a pen and said "Aidish".

The boy grasped the concept surprisingly quick and spent the next couple minutes writing. Looking back and forth at the cards, he filled in the blank cards, then handed back the notebook and pen. The handwriting was a bit sloppy, but Bjorn beamed at Ethan with pride. He couldn't help but smile at the boy's boost in confidence.

Ethan stared at the boy's handwriting. He wasn't sure why he expected English letters, but English letters they were not.

Instead what he saw was something akin to Viking runes. It couldn't be the same though, because Norse and Danish runes weren't an actual alphabet. Each rune had its own sound, but they represented specific concepts, usually focused on religion or nature. One rune could represent a god like Odin and another could mean rain or fertility.

Granted, how much did Ethan really know about it? Maybe runes worked perfectly for an alphabet.

This dictionary idea was going to be more difficult than he'd thought. Such is life. Either way, Ethan needed to learn this new alphabet. Maybe he should make sure he hadn't pissed off Aino, the only person he'd met who could actually understand him.

Oh well, that could be taken care of in the morning.

Dictionary project postponed, Ethan set aside the notebook then held the two cards in front of him. He hadn't done this before, so he wasn't exactly sure how it worked. Stacking the item card on top of the Fire Bear Card, he focused on its description. A text box popped into his vision.

You have initiated use of a Rare Monster Evolution Card on an Uncommon Fire Bear.

Do you wish to continue?

CONTINUE

"Ahh, there we go," Ethan smiled.

Bjorn looked confused, as usual. Ethan focused on the continue button until the text box disappeared.

In his hand, the two cards began to glow with a soft white light, melting and fusing together. Bjorn's eyes and mouth opened wide, fair to assume he'd never seen a card evolution before. Ethan hadn't either, now that he thought about it.

A minute later all that remained was a single card, the picture having changed from a young bear to an adult sized bear. Ethan's shoulders relaxed in relief, as he didn't want to waste evolution cards. But this was important. Upgrading the uncommon to a rare would make it impossible for someone to take the card from the boy.

Ethan held the card out to Bjorn, who was still in shock and didn't seem to be aware of what was happening.

"Bjorn? You there, little Bear?" he said with a gentle voice usually reserved for a toddler, not wanting to spook him.

The boy closed his eyes, like Jack used to do when he saw something scary on TV. Oof... Ethan missed his son.

After a deep breath the boy opened his eyes, looking from

Ethan to the card, then back to Ethan, but didn't reach for the card. Ethan sighed, then grabbed the boy's hand and placed the card in his palm.

He pointed to the boy, then the card, then interlocked his fingers.

"Bjorn, bear, bind."

28

FOR WHOM THE BELL TOLLS

BJORN DREAMT OF MONSTERS.

The horde that killed his parents, the monsters that chased him in the woods, the three cute but destructive companions of Mr. Farris, and the Fire Bear he'd bound himself to. His dreams were a collage of fear, love, pain, and hope.

So when he woke up to the sounds of alarm bells, he wasn't sure he was actually awake.

Alarm bells? Why would there be alarm bells? He bolted upright in bed and listened as the loud gong continued in the direction of the main gate, but nothing else happened. Mr. Farris was on the floor, his breathing heavy and slow. Bjorn jumped out of bed and tripped over his boots, only slowing him down long enough to put them on before he rushed out the door.

~~~

Aino sent her crew off to prep the boat while she stayed behind to wrangle Ethan and Bjorn. It was possible she'd have to take on the boy as well, if he refused to apprentice with Havard.

As she walked up the staircase toward Ethan's room, the boy rounded the corner and flew past her. He was already out the door before she had time to register what happened and call after him. With a sigh, she continued up the stairs.

The Red Bird Brigade's standard operating procedure had already been thrown out the window, so she may as well get on with it. The bells continued at the gate as she knocked on Ethan's door.

"It's Aino," she said when there wasn't a response.

"Come in," came a groggy and coarse version of Ethan's voice, like he could use some water. She opened the door to find him sitting on a puffy blanket made of an unfamiliar material, pulling on his boots.

"Monster horde is nearby. The Brigade is heading out before it reaches town. Pack up, we leave in five."

"Alright, thanks for letting me know," he made no rush in lacing up his boots. "Guess I'll see you around."

"Uhh..." Aino cocked her head to the side. "You'll see me right now. The boat pushed off in five minutes."

"Oh, I'm not leaving," Ethan stood, shrugging himself into his jacket with the magic pockets. Not an ounce of urgency was visible in him as he moved around the room.

"What do you mean you're not leaving? Did you not hear me?" She swung an arm out toward the sound of the bells. "There's a horde of monsters on its way to town. We'll be stuck here if we don't leave now."

"Why would I leave when I can help?" He made a face like he didn't understand why she *wouldn't* be staying.

"Aghhh!" her groan grew in volume near the end. "Hordes aren't a joke, Ethan. You're as likely to die as to be of any help.

We're not soldiers here and nobody is paying us to risk our lives."

"So... I'm only supposed to help people if I'm required to or I'm getting paid? I can't help people simply because they could use the help?" Ethan chuckled, shouldering his pack onto his back and made the face people make when they shrug. "Nah, I'll help. A lot more people will die if I don't than if I do. Unless you'd like to see more orphaned kids get beat up by monks?"

"Obnoxious," Aino huffed, stomping back out the room. "Ridiculous man."

29

FOR THE HORDE

ETHAN AND COLBY-JACK STOOD OUTSIDE THE TAVERN TOGETHER. Townsfolk were scurrying about, some nailing boards over windows. A dozen soldiers marched past toward the bells, carrying a mix of armors and weapons. As they passed, one soldier at the back stopped in front of the tavern. Ethan recognized him as the man who had bought the plant cat to help protect his daughter.

The soldier nodded at Ethan, then at Colby-Jack, which Ethan thought was nice of him. The man said a phrase Ethan recognized but didn't know the meaning of. He'd heard it around town and in the tavern when people were saying bye to each other, so he assumed it was an Aidish equivalent of "May God bless you and keep you" or "May the force be with you".

So Ethan repeated it back the best he could manage, giving a slight bow. The man nodded, then hustled to catch up to the other soldiers.

"Where do you suppose Bjorn ran off to?" Ethan scanned the area.

Colby-Jack shrugged, staring at the sky in the direction of

the bells. Following her gaze, even his poor eyesight could make out the flock of winged creatures headed toward town. For whatever reason that surprised him, expecting the horde would be a "Barbarians at the Gate" sort of situation. Instead it looked like they'd be trying to fight off Air Force bombers and fighter jets.

Ethan reached into a pocket, pulling out a stack of shimmering cards.

"Looks like we'll have to go a bit harder today," he glanced at Colby-Jack. "My knee is still giving me trouble, so I'm going to need you to watch my back more than usual. That gonna be a problem?"

The small dog somehow looked down her nose at him, even though he was taller and literally looking down at her.

"Boof," she replied sarcastically before trotting off toward the bells, her hips swaying with each step.

Ethan chuckled and limped after her.

~~~

A dark blue and red mass of flesh and feathers the size of a horse crashed to the ground in the middle of the street. The mass rolled around until the red portion separated itself from the blue, tearing off a wing from what turned out to be a very large blue bat. While the red bird worked on the second wing, Aino appeared beside them and stabbed her spear into the bat's skull.

"This was a bad idea," she muttered to herself, removing her spear from the lifeless body.

Against her better judgment, and the insistence of her crew, Aino sent the them while she stayed to "help", though her main intent was to make sure Ethan didn't get himself killed. Meeting the man was a once in a lifetime opportunity and she didn't want to see it ruined.

Clearly something bigger was going on in the background, otherwise why would she have been used as a quest reward?

Big Red cawed at her as he hopped off of the dead bat. She blew him a kiss and he took off back into the air, looking for more prey. Aino headed back toward the tavern, where she'd last seen Ethan. He'd likely already run off to the wall, but she needed to make sure. Doing her best to keep out of sight of the flying beasts, she still fought three more of the blue bats by the time they reached the tavern.

As Aino was about to cross the street to the door, a creature three times the size of a bull landed on the roof of the tavern. It bellowed a roar at something in the sky behind her, then breathed a stream of fire over her head. She dove to the ground, the heat catching the back of her neck.

"A dragon?!" She cried into the dirt. "An actual dragon?!"

The noise that followed wasn't a roar, a caw, or a squawk, but the chirp of a small bird. A bird with a deep and loud chirp, much louder than anything making that type of noise should have been. Aino looked up from the ground in time to see a giant blue and white parakeet dive directly at the dragon. It pulled up with enough time to extend its massive talons and slammed into the dragon with enough force that they both crashed through the roof.

"Uncle!" Aino got to her feet and ran, her fear of the dragon pushed to the back of her mind.

Big Red was off fighting somewhere else so she didn't know how much help she'd be, but she had to do something. The sounds of snapping furniture echoed from the building as she reached the front door. Hand stretched out for the handle, a voice rang from behind her.

"Probably best if you leave this one to me."

Aino jumped and turned in one fluid motion, the point of her spear an inch from Ethan's throat. The man took a step back, then maneuvered around her and to the door. In his hand was what looked like a solid black miniature crossbow, though Aino couldn't see any bolts or even a string to shoot a bolt. After a brief nod, he limped inside with a slight bend in his knees, both hands on the "crossbow" aimed ahead of him.

She stood there for a moment, not sure what to do.

With a firm shake her head to dispel the indecision, Aino moved through the now open door, then toward the kitchen opposite of the stairs. Where was Anker? Was he okay? The ceiling was intact, so the monsters hadn't broken through to the main floor. That was good news at least, evidence that Anker had built the place well.

"Uncle!" she called into the kitchen.

Instead of a voice in response, she heard two loud yet somehow contained explosions upstairs followed by a heavy *thwump* on the floor above her. She stopped to listen, the only sound was that of boots clomping on wood with slight hitch each step.

Good, Ethan was alive.

Relieved that the immediate danger had passed, Aino moved into the kitchen and saw Anker sprawled out on the floor, a large wooden barrel tipped over beside him. Had the barrel hit him on the head and knocked him out? She kneeled beside her uncle, holding her breath as she felt for a pulse.

A relieved exhale escaped her lips. A strong heartbeat, chest rising and falling. He was breathing, he was alive. There was no point risking moving him with a head injury, so she left him for a moment to go see what happened upstairs.

At the top of the staircase she stopped in front of the only open door and stared in awe as the giant parakeet hopped out through the hole in the roof. Ethan stood nearby reading over a card in his hand, unaware of her presence. Everything in the room was destroyed or splintered into pieces, a few blue and white feathers resting where the bird had been. Blood pooled near Ethan's boots, so red it was almost black, but there was no dragon in sight.

"Where's the dragon?" she asked.

"Huh?" Ethan looked up at her.

"Where's the dragon?" she repeated.

"What dragon?" he replied as he placed his card into his breast pocket and smirked, avoiding making eye contact. "I have no idea what you're talking about."

He walked toward her, then shimmied through the doorway when she didn't move out of the way.

"We should head back to the gate," the man's tone was casual and unconcerned as he limped down the stairs. "The flying critters are probably taken care of by now, but it looked like they'd need some help at the wall."

"This man kills and captures a dragon, fighting alongside a giant parakeet, and he has the gall to pretend that it didn't happen?" Aino grumbled, dragging her hands down her face. "Why was I even worried about him? I could be halfway to Modes by now."

She followed Ethan down the stairs, off to do whatever obnoxious thing he came up with next.

~~~

It was as beautiful and colorful as a rainbow, but as deadly as a horde of monsters. Because it was a *horde of monsters*.

Ethan logically understood what a horde was, that there

would be a lot of monsters. Once he stood on the walls and saw it with his own eyes, he realized he'd underestimated the numbers. It was less like hundreds and more like a couple thousand, at least.

Until now, he'd thought it was strange that the system called these creatures monsters. For the most part they were normal looking animals, at least most of the ones he'd encountered and caught seemed normal. Some were more mythical, like the dragon.

Ethan glanced at Little Blue perched on the wall beside him, then back at the horde. The parakeet looked majestic in comparison to the monsters of the horde.

He saw a hybrid wolf/bear that looked like only its mother would love it, maybe not even then. There were oddly mutated deer, antelope, huge rodents, alligators and crocodiles, various types of monkeys and apes, pigs and hogs, reptiles, jackals, horses, oxen, snakes, caribou... on and on and on it went.

If the strange critters hadn't been there to kill and presumably eat a bunch of people, Ethan would be fascinated by the biodiversity. His inner child was screaming with joy, like going to the zoo for the first time, except the elephants and giraffes wanted to kill everyone in sight.

He turned his eyes to the other people standing atop the stone walls. Havard was speaking to Aino who stood to his left. She did not look happy to be there, her red eagle-like bird perched beside Little Blue they'd become friends while ripping apart flying beasts together.

"Havard says thank you for your help with the wave of flyers, especially the dragon."

"What dragon?"

Aino gave him a hard glare, which he promptly ignored.

"He says it's likely a dozen soldiers would have died before being able to kill it."

"Are these numbers common for a horde?" Ethan nodded at Havard, who stood on the other side of Aino. "Or a dragon for that matter?"

"No..." she replied. "Maybe half this number is normal. I've never seen a dragon in a horde before, so maybe it was one of the horde leaders. More like an alpha than a leader, really. Dragons are smart and notorious loners, so they tend to isolate themselves from hordes like this one."

"Is there at least a theory about how this one got so big?"

"Havard believes it is because they haven't been able to send out as many hunting parties since the last horde," Aino translated the captain's response, "Many of the people that would have kept the number of monsters low had been killed."

"That's what I thought," Ethan replied with a grunt, "So, what's the plan?"

"How should I know? I just want us to not die"

"I don't expect you to know. Can you ask Havard for me?"

"Ah, right," he noticed her cheeks flush.

Aino spoke to Havard in Aidish, then switched back to English.

"He says we let them crash against the wall. They are fierce, but not particularly smart, so we should be able to whittle them down with our bows and ranged monster attacks. The main danger will come from the monsters who are able to make it up the wall."

Ethan nodded, looking up and down the wall at the soldiers lining the walkway.

Sure enough, most of them had strung bows in hand and stacks of arrows at their feet, small monsters were scattered here and there among them. He wondered how many of them were cards he'd sold the day before.

Two monks were among the soldiers, though these ones were decked out in armor and carried weapons, making them look like hardened killers rather than the religious pacifists he'd assumed them to be. This clearly wasn't their first battle. Perhaps he misunderstood the monks. Some of them, at least.

"Alright, we may as well take the time to prepare if the horde is gonna stand there for no reason."

Aino looked at Havard, who stood perfectly still other than his eyes scanning the horde.

"I think they're already prepared," she said.

"A little more couldn't hurt," Ethan chuckled in response, then pulled two cards out from his breast pocket and activated them. Out popped Zuko and Theo.

"Alright you two, your job this time around is to protect. Keep the monsters off the wall and away from the soldiers."

Colby-Jack barked and nudged Ethan's leg, pointing her nose at the stone of the wall blocking her view. He picked her up and placed her on the stone where she could watch the horde. She boofed a thanks, then stood still, like a fluffy orange/white gargoyle.

Zuko leapt up beside the dog and laid down for a nap, uninterested in the monsters. Theodore trotted along the wall, looking for anyone who may need a bit of healing. That or he was hoping someone would pet him. Ethan turned to the parakeet perched beside him.

"Little Blue, you'll be keeping monsters off the wall. If they make it up, kill them, toss them back off into the horde, or pin it down so someone can stab it in the head like we did with the... uhh... you know. And stay away from ranged attacks. Sound good?"

The large bird chirped happily in reply.

"Good."

Ethan reached into a different pocket, pulling out a large stack of cards, then a smaller stack of cards out of yet another pocket. These were his common and uncommon monster cards. He sifted through them, counting as he went. When he was done counting, he held them out toward Havard, his arm crossing in front of Aino.

Her eyes bulged at the stack of cards. The captain hadn't moved, unaware as he continued scanning the horde.

"Havard," Ethan said, getting the man's attention.

The captain looked over and grabbed the combined stack of cards as though he'd been handed a loaf of bread. He met Ethan's gaze, a questioning look in his eyes.

"These are to help protect your soldiers."

They stood in silence. Ethan looked at Aino and coughed.

"Can you translate, please?"

"Oh... Uhh yeah."

After she relayed his words, there was a flurry of activity as Havard yelled for his lieutenants. Was he a dad? Because he definitely pulled out the dad voice; those LTs came running with a quickness.

Within minutes the cards were passed around so that every squad had at least a few monsters each and Ethan could see the difference it made as he scanned the walls again. The morale had shot up, men were laughing and cheering. The two monks looked a little less stressed, even if they weren't happy about all the monsters around them. Havard spoke to Ethan, making the thank you gesture as he did.

"He says thank you," Aino relayed, "This will save many lives."

"Yeah, well it's a loan. I expect all seventy-eight cards back. Or at least all the ones that survive."

They were ready, as ready as they could be. Like a dam bursting open, the horde charged the town making all manner of awful noises. Zuko got into a sitting position, Little Blue took to the air, and Colby-Jack didn't move a muscle.

"Okay, Aino," he looked at her with a serious expression. "Stick to the plan."

"Plan? What plan?"

He smiled, pulling out his handgun, then racked the slide back to chamber a round.

"Don't die."

30

BATTLE BJORN

Bjorn was bleeding, but it was just a flesh wound. He was exhausted, yet felt invigorated. Angry, but focused.

The outer wall of the orphanage felt cool against his back as he took a moment to rest, a bloodied club grasped in his hand. It was the only weapon he could find before the horde attacked, which just so happened to be the club Brother Thomas had used to beat him the day before. The monk must have forgotten it after getting kicked in the balls.

Bjorn chuckled, reliving the blissful memory for a moment.

Surveying the courtyard in front of him, he counted a dozen monster corpses strewn about. These were only some of the ones who'd flown over or squeezed their way through the battle at the wall, a trail of bodies and body parts wrapping around to the other side of the building.

Bjorn's legs ached from circling the orphanage to make sure no monsters made it to the other kids. It wasn't only orphans there either. There were the monks, of course, but many soldiers at the wall sent their wives and children to shelter at the church during hordes.

Some monks would be there to protect everyone, but he knew from experience that they weren't much help if a monster made it inside. They cared about the children, yes, but they weren't fighters. The fighters were at the wall with the guards and soldiers. Still, their faith told them they should care, so they cared. And monks were very serious about their faith.

What Bjorn had that they didn't was a fully grown Fire Bear. In the midst of the scattered bodies sat the massive red furred beast, casually munching on a large charred rodent of some sort. Though Bjorn had fought off monsters with his club, Karhu the Fire Bear had done most of the killing.

The sounds of battle could still be heard in the distance, though he was pretty sure it was not as intense as it had been. Not a single monster had made it that far into town in several minutes.

"The Horde must have been huge for so many to make it this far."

Bjorn flinched away from the unexpected voice, turning to see Brother Thomas standing outside the large double doors of the orphanage. Somehow he hadn't heard the doors open. The monk held a mug in one hand, a tray with strips of meat and a loaf of bread in the other.

Not knowing what to say, Bjorn let his eyes browse back over the courtyard. It did seem like a lot, but he didn't have much to compare it to. He'd been hidden away during the horde attack when his parents died.

"I suppose so," he said, not looking at the monk.

"Have some food and drink," Brother Thomas said, setting the tray and mug on the ground within reach. "You've been at it for a while and need some rest. Your bear and I can keep watch."

Bjorn glanced at the monk with suspicion, then inspected the food. After a moment he decided the man didn't mean him harm, so he took a big gulp of what turned out to be mead.

Why hadn't he realized he was so thirsty? His fingers already felt a little tingly from the drink. He turned his attention to the tray and tore into the food. For a while they sat in mutual silence. The courtyard was quiet, other than Bjorn and Karhu munching away, the sounds of battle growing more faint by the minute.

The monk broke the silence.

"What'd you name it?"

Bjorn looked at the Brother Thomas, at first not understanding what he meant. He followed the man's stoic gaze, which was focused on the fire bear.

"Her name is Karhu."

The monk nodded.

"Strong name. Your twin perhaps?" He smiled at his own joke. "May I speak with her?"

"Be my guest," Bjorn shrugged, stuffing a piece of bread in his mouth. It was up to her anyway.

Brother Thomas got to his feet and walked right up to the bear. She swallowed whatever beast was in her mouth, scrutinizing him as he approached.

"Thank you for protecting the children," he held out his hand, palm up, to the bear.

She made a huffing exhale sound through her nose, which Bjorn understood as "Duh, why wouldn't I?" Karhu laid her chin in the monk's palm and he gave the chin a good scratching.

"Her fur is warm," the monk said, surprised and delighted.

"Of course. She's a fire bear."

The monk chuckled.

"I could see how that would be helpful during the cold months."

Bjorn nodded. It made sense, he just hadn't thought that far ahead yet.

"Well, I should head back to check on the children. Brother Brenn should only be left with them for so long."

It was Bjorn's turn to chuckle, despite his distrust of the man. Brother Brennen was a pushover, likely to get himself beat up if he spent much time around the orphans. The children loved him and enjoyed playing with him, but didn't respect or fear him. Hard to give orders to kids when they don't respect or fear you.

"Thank you, Bjorn," the monk said. "My assumptions about monsters have been challenged today. I have much to consider."

Bjorn looked at Karhu, who had let the monk pet her. Maybe his assumptions about monks weren't totally accurate either. That particular monk, anyway.

31
THE AFTERMATH

THE MAN LOUNGED WITH HAVARD IN HIS OFFICE, TALKING TO AINO IN that strange language of his. Havard himself was multilingual — his family prioritizing several languages in his early education — yet even he didn't recognize a single word being said.

Spread across the desk between them were twenty-five monster cards.

Fifty-three monsters had died during the battle, their cards grayed out and unusable. More had died, but a few revive cards were used before the five minute grace period had elapsed. And yet, Havard felt joy. He would put himself in debt paying the man back for those cards if it meant more of his people would live.

The card man, Mr. Farris, had not looked surprised by the lack of cards returned to him, having been at the wall and taking part in the carnage. He'd seen how much worse things could have ended up without the help of those monsters. The townsfolk were still cleaning up the dead, harvesting what they could before burning the rest.

"Your new wolves fit you well," Aino's voice broke him from his thoughts.

"Yes," he replied, clearing his throat. He looked to the floor beside his desk where Ulfa, his rare Earth Wolf, laid beside the man's strange small orange and white dog. The small dog seemed to find comfort in Ulfa's company, looking considerably more relaxed than usual.

"Yes," he heard Mr. Farris mumble in Aidish under his breath, like someone trying to memorize something.

"Don't mind him," Aino said. "He's just sick of our language barrier, so he's attempting to learn Aidish as quickly as he can. I think he's tired of needing me to translate."

"Why has he not taken his cards back?" Havard changed the subject, gesturing to the cards between them. "I've already promised to pay him for the monsters that were lost."

Aino glanced at Mr. Farris, who was writing in a small book with a strange pen, before speaking.

"All he told me was that he has a proposition for you, but needs a minute to 'process his thoughts'. I assume that's what he's doing right now."

"I'm not sure what I'll have to offer him," Havard grunted. "Especially after paying him for his help."

"I doubt he'll accept the gold, if I'm being honest. In fact, I have a feeling he won't be taking those cards back."

Havard's arched one eyebrow as he shifted his gaze from Aino back to the man. This stranger had been beyond generous already, heavily discounting the cost for the wolves, much to Aino's dismay and Havard's relief. What a rare quality to find in a man.

"What causes him to be so unnecessarily generous?"

"From what little I understand of his past, I couldn't answer with certainty. I've heard him share some mantras from his homeland; two in particular have been on my mind a lot.

"One is from a man named Luke that says 'To whom much is given, much will be required'. The other is from a legend about a man who was somehow also a spider, who said 'With great power comes great responsibility'."

Havard considered the mantras while the man focused on his little book, unaware of the conversation being had about him.

"I would argue that Mr. Farris is becoming a legend himself."

~~~

The days after the battle against the horde were busy.

Most of the townsfolk were tasked with clearing away what remained of the monsters. Some of the beasts could be salvaged for parts to use in crafting, but the majority were thrown into burn pits. The rest of town worked to prepare a feast.

Apparently, surviving a horde was a big deal. This time especially so because they lost considerably fewer people than usual.

Ethan sat at a table in the dining area of the tavern, his right leg propped up on a chair. Theo sat with his chin resting on Ethan's thigh, providing some much needed relief to the pain in his knee. They had already spent time at the medical tent for those injured during the battle; now it was their turn to rest and recover.

Ethan's chin rested on his chest, arms crossed and dozing, when a thud on the table jerked him awake. Across from him stood Anker with a plate of food in his hand and a mug of mead already set in front of Ethan. Once Anker had his attention, he set the plate down, then slid into a chair across the table.

Confused, Ethan looked up at the man. He hadn't ordered anything to eat or drink.

Anker shifted on his feet, looking uncomfortable.

"Tank yo," he said.

"Huh?" Again, Ethan was confused.

"Tank yo!" The man growled and repeated himself through gritted teeth, making the gesture for thank you. He pointed to the ceiling, then the back of his head where the barrel had hit him.

"Ohhhh," Ethan grinned wide.

Bowing his head to the tavern owner, a rush of dopamine flooding him at the man's attempt to say thank you in English. Not very good English at all, but still. It only cemented that he needed to learn Aidish, to speak to people properly and maybe teach them some English as well.

Grabbing the mug, he raised it to Anker, then took a long drink of mead. Oh Lord, that was some good mead. It probably wasn't even that great, but after the day they'd had it may as well have been liquid gold. The tavern owner nodded, stood, then walked back to the kitchen.

"Boof," Ethan glanced to his left at Colby-Jack, who sat on a chair beside him.

"Yes... that was uncharacteristically nice of him. That knock on the head must have done some good. But I'm not complaining," he glanced down at his companion. "Hey, CJ, you want some food?"

32

CLEANING AND THE FUTURE

Pieces of Ethan's strange miniature cannon were spread across a cloth of fabric on the floor.

Aino sat cross legged on the bed watching Ethan methodically wipe down each piece with a rag, some of which were as small as her pinky nail. For a few, he applied a brownish oil of some sort from a small clear bottle.

An hour passed, neither of them talking.

She was amazed by how focused he was with the task. He'd mentioned before that sometimes he gets "in the zone" and she finally understood what he meant, finding it utterly fascinating.

After he finished wiping everything down and applying the oil, he put the cannon back together piece by piece. There seemed to be an order to it, though what that order was Aino had no idea. Not after only one time seeing it, anyway. Given some time, she was sure she could figure it out.

"You know...," she started, "when we get to Modes, my father will want to meet you. And just a forewarning, I can almost guarantee he will try to convince you to marry me."

"Hah!" Ethan made a short exhale through his nose, still focused on his cannon. "Based on your tone, I assume that's common in Aidland?"

"Is it not where you come from?"

"In some places, yes, but it's not standard practice anymore," the man replied. "Do you have a say in who you marry?"

"I do," she nodded. "And I've managed to avoid marriage thus far."

"Avoid? You think marriage is something to be avoided?"

"I value my freedom," Aino shrugged. "Marriage doesn't provide more freedom than I already have."

"True enough, it can feel limiting at times," the man agreed, "though there's a kind of freedom found in limitations. A freedom to invest more of yourself in someone or something specific you love. But there's no one way to do marriage. Find someone that values what you value and make it work for you."

There was an edge to his statement. A longing that made her wonder if he spoke from experience. She found herself considering for the first time that maybe marriage wasn't a guaranteed prison. *Maybe.* Not if it was with someone like this man, she supposed. Oh no, was she actually starting to like Ethan?

"Either way," he continued, "your father is going to be disappointed."

"Oh? Am I not your type?" she asked, a playful smirk on her face.

Sweet gods, was she flirting? What was happening to her?

"My type is irrelevant," he pointed to a ring the color of polished steel on his left hand. "I'm already taken."

What did a ring had to do with marriage? Most men wore

rings and armbands, regardless of marriage, especially warriors. It was a sign of wealth and experience. That's what she had assumed when she saw his ring, even though he only wore the one. Ethan must have noticed her confusion.

"Do you guys not use wedding rings in Aidland?"

"Ahh, no," she began to understand. "There are likely some lands that use rings, but it's common practice to use wristbands and bracelets here in Aidland. The bride and groom each make one for each other and present it during the ceremony. So... you are married, then?"

Was that a hint of disappointment in her voice? Ethan either didn't notice or chose to ignore it.

"Yup," he said. "Going on five years now."

"Is it a happy marriage?"

"That's a bit personal of a question," Ethan raised one eyebrow, a slight smile tugged at his lips. "Don't you think?"

"I didn't mean to pry," she backpedaled, tumbling over her words.

Aino felt her cheeks flush, which she knew would be visible on her pale skin. Where were her manners? Had she misread the familiarity developing between them?

"Nah, I was just messing with you. I don't mind," Ethan chuckled.

Pausing the discussion for a moment, he gave his reassembled mini cannon a once over before sliding it into a sheath at his hip. His brow furrowed as though he were pondering a deep philosophical question with the scholars in Modes. It reminded her of her tutors.

"I'm not sure happiness should be the goal of a marriage," he concluded. "I think it's about being a team, having each other's backs. In that sense, it's a successful marriage. Rebecca is someone I can count on. Have we always felt happy emotionally? No. Especially not since our son was born. Having a kid puts a massive strain on relationships; a lot of couples don't survive it."

"Not only are you married, but you also have a son? How has this not come up yet? What in the world made you leave them behind?"

"It didn't seem like information I needed to share," the man's expression turned sour. "And to be clear, I didn't choose to come here."

"Huh? How did you not choose to come here? Were you kidnapped?"

"Kinda, honestly. I had just been discharged from the Army. Rebecca and I agreed it would be a good idea for me to take some time to myself before starting anything new, to get my head on straight. I was on my way to a well known hiking trail when I stopped to rest for the night. When I woke up, I was in a forest being attacked by wolves. I'm still not sure what brought me here."

"And you're eager to get back to them?"

"I wasn't at first. It seemed exciting, waking up in a new world. We don't have magic cards or monsters back home. Although this has definitely been exciting, I'm having a hard time enjoying any of it without my wife and son."

Moisture pooled in Ethan's eyes and he stared at the wall, off into the distance as if watching the sun set.

"My third night in Aidland," he continued, "I had a panic attack around the time we'd normally put my son to bed. He's almost three years old now and I had only been gone a couple days, but I already missed reading to him and making him laugh.

"Honestly, I'm blessed to have a wife that's willing to take care of our son by herself for weeks so that I could go off alone into the woods, but part of me wishes I hadn't. I don't belong here, not without them anyway. I've been ready to go home for a while."

Aino wanted to say she understood, but she'd never loved anyone the way this man loved his family. It sounded miserable, if she was being honest. A willingly painful existence. And yet, part of her longed for it. A deep longing she'd been suppressing. Why had she been so intent on avoiding it?

"If that's true, why haven't you gone home? No offense, and I'm glad to have met you, but why are you still here?"

"Oh, I've been trying," he said, throwing his hands in the air. He pointed at her, "But if you remember, you were my only real lead and that quest took me weeks to complete."

"Okay, then why did you stay to help with the horde? We could have already left and been to Modes to get the journals. Now we'll have to go by foot, unless a merchant ship passes through, which is unlikely until news of the horde spreads. It'll take much longer now."

Ethan didn't answer immediately. When he did, he sounded his usual casual self.

"I don't want to be the guy who has the ability to help but pretends like he doesn't see the people who need help. I can't help everyone, nor do I want to, but Rebecca would understand. She knows it would eat at me if I left without at least trying to help, even more so when there's a good chance people would die. I'd likely end up resenting myself and my family as the guilt ate away at me.

"Also," he added, tapping a finger to his chin, "there's no guarantee that your great-grandfather's journals will help me get home, so I may be stuck here forever."

What a strange man. Not wrong, but strange. She needed time to process everything he'd said, but for now she had a decision to make. Smacking her palms on her legs, she stood, causing Ethan to flinch at the sudden sound and movement.

"Well then, we may as well get some sleep and head out in the morning. After a good breakfast, of course. Uncle Anker was able to salvage some meat out of the hogs and javelinas from the horde, so there will be plenty of bacon."

Ethan grunted as he stood to his feet, favoring his right leg. He wiped the remaining moisture from his eyes.

"You guys eat monsters?"

"Sure, why not? It's meat. They were dead anyway. Waste not, want not."

"Huh. We have that saying back home too."

"Not wanting to be wasteful must be a universal concept," Aino shrugged. "Anyway, I'll meet you downstairs at sun up. Don't make me break in to wake you up."

"Yes ma'am," Ethan smiled as she left the room, closing the door behind her.

33
HIDDEN QUEST

A TEXT BOX POPPED INTO ETHAN'S VISION AS THE DOOR SHUT, catching him by surprise. He moved to the edge of his bed and sat down, reading the text for a hidden quest he had somehow completed.

Hidden Quest: A Change Will Do Them Good

Through your direct actions, inspire five people to reevaluate their view of the world and/or their place in it.

Reward: Go Home.

Progress: 5/5

❧

Congratulations!

You have completed this hidden quest.

Focus on the accept button to receive your reward.

ACCEPT

ETHAN WAS HALLUCINATING; he had to be. There was no way he'd completed a hidden quest to go home right after having a whole discussion about it with Aino.

Jaw locked in the open position, Ethan's right eye twitched involuntarily as he started focusing on the accept button. With immense willpower, he forced himself to pull up short.

How quickly would this play out? Maybe it would be good not to rush it. Minimizing the notification, he set about cleaning the room.

He immediately shoved all his gear into his backpack, then set it against the end table where a few candles provided the only light to the room. Next, he removed his pistol from its holster and set it on the end table, opened all his pockets, and pulled out his remaining cards. All that was left were a handful of uncommon and rare monsters he'd caught during the battle — including the dragon — as well as several item cards. There were, of course, his nine unique monster cards, only four of which he'd gotten around to activating, and the small stack of blank cards he kept with him.

Taking a deep breath, Ethan activated the four unique cards and watched as two dogs, a one-eyed cat, and a giant parakeet appeared in front of him. They all watched him, waiting, like they already knew what was about to happen.

"I'm sorry guys, I gotta go," he said, a knot forming in his throat. "But I appreciate everything you've done for me."

Colby-Jack walked up to the bed, then booped her nose against his leg. She gave him a contended "boof" before moving back in line with the others.

Ethan pulled out his notebook, tore out a blank piece of paper, scribbled out a note, then placed it on the table with a corner under the stack of cards. Before putting the notebook away, he flipped to the front and ripped out the hand drawn map he'd made on his first day in Aidland, placing it beneath his note.

Looking around the room, he tried to see if there was anything else to be done. Nothing came to mind, so he laid back on the bed, his head on the pillow.

Anxious for what was about to happen, he spent the next few minutes running through his breathing exercise. Breathe in, five count. Hold, five count. Breathe out, five count. He's nerves were fried, but at least his heart rate had slowed.

The four monsters climbed on the bed to join him. Zuko laid down across Ethan's chest, the weight providing a comforting sense of security. A living, furry, heavy blanket. Theodore settled by his feet, his warmth providing a healing effect that reminded Ethan of sitting at home with his feet in a hot bath. Little Blue perched on the headboard, somehow not blowing out the candles with the beat of his wings. Colby-jack, always steadfast, sat between his torso and his right arm, an ideal position for him to pet her. She sat still as a statue, staring at the doorway.

In that moment he felt more peace than he had since arriving in this world. He whispered another thanks to his companions again, who had been there for him when he was alone and afraid.

Bringing up the text box, Ethan took a final deep breath and focused on the accept button. His mind drifted off into sleep.

34

THE MORNING AFTER

ETHAN WOKE TO THE SOUND OF A STEADY BEEP... BEEP... BEEP.

An electronic beep. Huh, that couldn't be right. Neither his phone or watch had worked for several weeks. As he listened to the consistent beep, he found it difficult to open his eyes, like when they crusted over after a particularly heavy sleep. The battle with the horde had been exhausting, but it'd still been pretty early in the evening when Aino had left the room.

Why was he so tired?

An aching pain was in his right leg, as usual, but there were also several smaller pains across his body, many in places he didn't remember getting injured.

Rubbing the stiffness from his eyes, he noticed something hugging his index finger with a consistent pinch on the fingertip. Finally able to see, and feeling a little less groggy, Ethan took in his surroundings. This wasn't his room at the tavern. This was a hospital room. A *modern* hospital room.

A twenty-first century hospital room!

The electronic beat sped up with his excitement, but he had already tuned out the sound as he remembered the quest

notification from the night before. If he had made it home...
Why was he in a hospital? Shouldn't he have woken up in his
van, still at the rest stop in Texas?

The room was dark. A faint warm light shown from somewhere above the bed where he was reclined. To his left he saw
the equipment that wouldn't stop beeping, the heart rate
monitor. He was alive, at least. To his left was a large tinted
window taking up most of the wall and it seemed to be dark
outside. Middle of the night based on the lack of sounds from
either the room or hallway.

Below the window was a couch. Someone was lying on it,
but was turned away from him. A fleece blanket covered everything but hair, so he couldn't see the person's face. But that
hair... he knew that hair. Red, like a wildfire.

"Rebecca," he whispered, his voice hoarse and unused.

The woman didn't move.

Ethan tried to sit up and swing his legs over the side of the
bed, but he felt weak. That, and there was something weighing
down on his midsection. A strawberry-blond haired toddler
had somehow crawled onto the bed with him and lay across
his stomach, head on Ethan's chest.

The little one stirred slightly from the sudden movement
and looked up at Ethan with glazed over eyes and droopy
eyelids.

"Dice, dada?" the boy mumbled.

Ethan's chest constricted at the sound of the boy's voice,
even though he wasn't saying anything coherent. How many
nights had he fallen asleep, hoping to hear that voice again?

"No dice, Jack," he whispered. "Go back to sleep."

The boy settled back down with a sigh, head on Ethan's
chest, as though his sleep hadn't been interrupted.

Ethan brushed his fingers through the boy's hair, careful

not to wake him. Catching a whiff of his son's scent, a knot formed in his throat like a dam that could burst if the slightest crack formed. This wasn't a dream. It was real.

He was home.

35
THE END?

THE GRAVELLY SOUND OF THE FATHER'S LAUGH ECHOED THROUGHOUT the vast white chamber.

"Well..." said the Son, "that was quick. Should we have made the quest more difficult?"

The pair watched Ethan Farris waking up in his hospital room.

"No, no," the Father replied, waving a dismissive hand as he fought to stifle his laughter. "I think it worked out wonderfully. His actions have affected others who have larger spheres of influence. Highly efficient, honestly. Even if you had made it more difficult, I doubt it would have taken him much longer. A week in Modes and he would have finished that quest too."

"I'm sure you're right, Father," replied the Son, a smile stretching across his face. "The goal was to have as little direct impact as possible, so the mission was a success. I suppose now we sit back and see how it all plays out."

36
THE NOTE

THE ROOM WAS SILENT.

"Ethan?" Aino called from the hallway of the tavern as she knocked on the door. "It's well past dawn and you missed breakfast. we need to get going. Don't worry though, I saved you some monster bacon."

Silence. Not even a rustling of sheets or shuffling of feet.

"Ethan?"

She turned the handle, pushing the door open just wide enough to stick her head in. The room was empty. Strange. Had he gone somewhere already? Maybe he'd had a last minute errand to run? Unlikely, considering Aino was still acting as his interpreter. Pushing the door the rest of the way open, she stepped fully into the room. Maybe she could find a hint of where he'd gone.

Ethan's pack was gone and the bed was made, though it was slightly ruffled as though someone had been lying on it. A beam of sunlight from the window shone on the night table beside the bed, causing a glint to catch her attention. Moving to the side to get the glare out of her eye, she spotted a single piece of paper.

Aino,

Turns out I completed a hidden quest! Didn't know that was a thing. The reward says that I get to go home! Looks like I won't be needing your family's notebooks anymore, but thank you for all your help anyway.

I left my gun and my cards for you on the nightstand (we don't have magical cards where I'm from). You'll notice Colby-Jack and my other unique cards there as well. I've grown quite fond of the goofballs, so please take care of them. I've also left a map I drew from when I first arrived in Aidland. If you can find my van, I stashed a couple hundred Blank Monster Cards in the back.

I'm not great with goodbyes... so... good luck? And don't do anything I wouldn't do. Or do it anyway. Whatever works.

Cheers!

Ethan Farris

Aino sighed with relief.

So, Ethan hadn't ditched her, the system had somehow sent him home. According to the note anyway. Maybe her great grandfather finished a hidden quest and that's why he disappeared.

A hint of frustration built up in Aino's chest. Sure, she'd miss the man and his obnoxious generosity, but now her plans were shattered. What was she going to do? She wasn't eager to go back to Modes by herself and... wait a second. Did he say '*a couple hundred Blank Monster Cards*'? Of course he'd off handedly mention a hoard of wealth, the ridiculous oaf.

But what was that he'd said about unique cards? The only

thing in the room was the note and a poorly drawn map. Colby-Jack and his other companions definitely weren't there. He also said he left his gun. Was that what he called his miniature cannon? She took a brief look around the room and found no sign of that either.

Huh...

Since she no longer had a reason to go back to Modes and she'd already mentally prepared for a long walk anyway, so why not check out this 'van' he mentioned. Maybe she'd stop by to see if Havard or Bjorn would want to join her. The Captain's straightforward and honest attitude had grown on her, good traits for a traveling companion, in her opinion. Not to mention his wolves. It never hurt to have a few friendly wolves around.

Ideas began flooding her mind of how to best make use of those Blank Monster Cards. Ideas she knew would make Ethan smile if he'd been the one to come up with them. In fact, there were too many ideas. She needed to make a list.

Grabbing the note and map, she turned on her heel and walked out the door with a pep in her step.

37

THAT'S UNEXPECTED

"WELL, THAT'S... UNEXPECTED," MUSED THE SON.

"What's that?" the Father turned away from the looking glass he had been focused on, a look on his face similar to someone finally being able to hear after taking off their headphones. "I couldn't hear you over the sounds of this skirmish in *Alternate Table #444*. You'd think a modern world that loses electricity would be quieter."

"It's nothing major, for the moment anyway. Looks like the system decided to store away Ethan Farris's cards when he was transported back home. Also stored his gun and jacket, for some reason."

"Hmm..." the older voice grumbled, writing some calculations on a tablet beside the looking glass. "I suppose that means there's more he has left to do in Aidland. Does he have any hidden quests in the logs? If we do the math, I'd be willing to bet there are a few potential futures that would benefit from his return."

The Son didn't immediately respond as he scanned through hidden system messages.

"Yes, he does have one hidden quest. Though..." he winced as he read the message.

"Though what?"

"It'll be at least a few years before he even considers attempting what this quest has in mind. He'd never aim to return to Aidland without his family and his son would need to be a good bit older to undertake the quest."

"Well then, there's nothing for us to do about it now. We'll just have to keep an eye on it."

"Yes, Father. Much is changing already, the ripples of our minor interference have become waves.

"I imagine even Trace will be near unrecognizable by the time Ethan finishes his hidden quest," a knowing grin crossed the Father's face. "I look forward to his return."

The Father's set his pen beside the tablet, focusing back on the skirmish in Alternate Table #444. The hope of potential futures were his main source of joy.

PART TWO

"If we find ourselves with a desire that nothing in this world can
satisfy, the most probable explanation is that we were made for
another world."
- C.S. Lewis

~~~

"Every father should remember one day his son will follow his
example, not his advice."
- Charles Kettering

~~~

"Raising kids may be a thankless job with ridiculous hours, but at
least the pay sucks."
- Jim Gaffigan

38

PANEL/FOR REAL LIFE

THE YOUNG BOY STOOD IN THE AISLE OF THE CROWDED CONFERENCE room, staring up at Ethan from behind a microphone stand.

"Mr. Farris, what inspired you to write this book? Where did the idea come from?"

"That's a good question," Ethan spoke into his own microphone, which sat on the table in front of him. Trick of the trade: always start by saying it's a good question. Gives you a couple extra seconds to process said question. "I have an answer, but you may not like it."

Several fantasy authors sat at the table with Ethan, each with their own microphone, but many of the questions so far had been directed at him. Aidland was his debut novel and had been a pretty big hit, or so he was told. Digital copies sold online and printed copies were sold at his favorite bookstores, so it was as successful as he could ever hope for it to be.

"A car crash — one that I don't even remember being in — put me into a coma," he continued. "Everything in my book is what I experienced during the time I was in that coma. I don't know if it was real or something my brain came up with as a survival mechanism but, to me, it was as real as you standing there asking me the question."

"So, it's all real?"

"Well... some of it is exaggerated or changed in order to make it more interesting. I took my experiences and formatted them into a narrative in order to make it more readable," he admitted. "My original idea was to make it a memoir, since it did technically happen to me even if it was only in my head. But ultimately I decided sci-fi and fantasy fans would be a more receptive audience."

"Thank you," the boy replied, making the sign language gesture at the same time.

Ethan returned the gesture with a smile, causing the crowd of nerds and geeks to cheer. And group like this loved easter eggs and call backs.

This audience was already less judgmental than Ethan had feared, thank God. Many of them probably hoped they'd be pulled into another world, so why would they berate someone who wrote about it? Even with a few hundred people attending their panel, Ethan could hear the dull roar of the convention taking place outside the doors. A convention hall filled with people who spent as much of their waking hours as possible in "other worlds".

Though he wouldn't say he *belonged* here, there was a kindred spirit that brought him some comfort and peace.

Part of him wished he'd brought Jack and done some sort of family costume. Rebecca had come with him, though she was backstage waiting for him to finish so they could go to a panel for one of her favorite sci-fi authors. Fantasy wasn't really her thing, but she supported him anyway.

Oh well, maybe next time.

The next person in line was a young woman who carried

herself like a soldier, or at least like many soldiers Ethan had served with in the Army. What was it that made him think she was a soldier? Her posture? Broad shoulders and a straight back? Pushups had a way of making someone seem more confident and capable.

"Mr. Farris," she started, earning a sigh of frustration coming from the panelist beside him. "You've mentioned in previous interviews that you often feel out of place or like you don't belong, even when you were in the Army. Did it feel that way for you in Aidland? If it actually was a real place, would you want to go back?"

"Another good question. Hmm..." he extended the 'hmm' to give more time to think about how to answer. Many nights he'd sat in the dark thinking about this exact question, so he had an answer. Just because he had an answer didn't mean he had to share it all.

Tact, Rebecca would warn him.

"I did feel more like I belonged there, that my weirdness or 'out-of-place-ness' was a benefit rather than a hindrance. But it also felt incomplete. I would one hundred percent go back, but only if I could bring my family with me. I love a good solo adventure, but after a while it feels... empty. I will say, my wife is more into sci-fi and space stuff than fantasy, so it would be tough to convince her to come along."

After soldier-girl, the questions were directed toward the other authors or to the panel as a whole. Whenever he wasn't directly asked a question, his mind tended to wander toward his time in the other world. How would Rebecca handle being in Aidland, if she ever found herself there? Would she hate it?

It was almost not worth thinking about.

39
SEPARATION

"Are we sure this is the right move?"

"It's worth trying, at least. Do you want to keep spending every day at each other's throats?"

The car growled as Ethan steered left to pass the semi-truck chugging along in the right lane of the interstate. Another truck was coming down the entrance and was getting ready to merge, but there was enough time to get around.

"No, and a big part of me is excited about having a bachelor pad," he acknowledged, "I've never had a place to myself before."

"So, where's the doubt coming from?"

"Change is uncomfortable, I guess. And it'll be difficult to explain to people."

"People suck. We aren't obligated to give them an explanation," Rebecca continued to scroll through tiny house listings on her phone. "But if we have to, we keep it short and sweet."

"We love each other so much," he started, using a mock-peppy voice, "That we can't stand living together anymore."

"Sounds right to me," she replied with light hearted chuckle, causing a knot in Ethan's chest loosen.

Separation didn't have to mean an end. It didn't have to mean they stopped loving each other, couldn't continue being best friends, or stopped being a family. They wouldn't suddenly stop raising a beautiful boy together or see each other almost every day. It could work. Like she'd said, it was at least worth trying.

"I love y—" his words were cut off.

The back of the car suddenly whipped to the left as if it had been hit by a wrecking ball. The world blurred, sounds of crunching metal and shattering glass blending together. The view out the windshield turned sideways, then upside down, a splash of green visible through the windshield for a moment until they were sideways again, then right side up, only to roll once more before settling upside down.

Something warm tickled the back of Ethan's neck as he tried to settle the dizziness, finding it difficult to move his neck. The world stilled around him, blood rushing to his head causing his sight to fade and his hearing to muffle. The smell of gasoline mixed with pine needles was all he could center his attention on without feeling nausea.

His lips moved to call out for his wife, but, before he could get his voice to cooperate, his world faded to black.

40

BEEN HERE BEFORE

ETHAN WOKE TO THE SOUND OF A STEADY BEEP... BEEP... BEEP.

Something wasn't right. He'd been there before, when he woke up from his coma. This time it wasn't the day after fighting off a giant horde. This time... what had he been doing? Answering questions at the convention center, then he went with Rebecca to the sci-fi author panel...

Rebecca.

The light coming in through the window was oppressive as Ethan opened his eyes, evidence that this was a new experience. Last time he woke up in a hospital, it had been dark outside. Also his hands hadn't been wrapped in bandages, nor did he have a slight burning sensation on the back of his head.

As his eyes adjusted to the light, he took a moment to look around the room. To his right was another hospital bed. Empty. To his left was a couch, this time holding his pre-teen son. Jack was asleep, lying down with his head in someone's lap.

"Rebecca?"

Ethan's voice came out raspy, barely louder than a whisper.

"Good morning, sleepy head," the voice was deeper than he expected. Deeper and older. "You've been out of it for a while."

A series of sharp pains shot through Ethan's hands as he tried to readjust himself in the hospital bed.

"Take it easy, son. You have a lot of stitches. If you move too much, they'll have to be redone."

That sounded just like his dad. Wait, why would his dad there? Ethan blinked several times, refocusing until his eyes cleared enough to read the man's expression.

"Dad... Where's Rebecca?"

41
POST-HUMOR

Rebecca's funeral was short and sweet, thank God.

Ethan had always felt out of place at funerals, even when it was for his own wife. In his early twenties, a good friend had died suddenly in a car crash while driving to work. At the reception, he'd burst into a fit of giggles that drew glares from the other friends and family attending. They had assumed he was being disrespectful, but really he'd just remembered a funny moment he'd shared with his friend.

Funerals should represent the person it was being held for, right?

That was why, after Rebecca's funeral, Ethan and Jack sat in a now empty observatory that had been used for her reception, an urn full of her ashes in the seat between them. Looking up at the images of stars, galaxies, and the northern lights felt more like she was still with them. Rebecca loved space, was obsessed with it, even. Many late nights were spent watching meteor showers or chasing down good places to watch comets that only showed up every couple decades. It seemed like the most genuine way to celebrate her life.

Looking down at his bandaged hands, only just starting to heal over after surgeons spent hours removing shards of glass, Ethan wondered if she'd gotten the better end of this deal.

"You think we could afford to send her ashes into space?" asked Jack, his eyes glued to the Orion constellation currently above them. "She'd roll over in her urn at the chance to go to Mars."

The boy looked serious, but not how you'd imagine a preteen who just lost his mother and almost lost his dad. Instead, he was... contemplative.

"We can definitely look into it," he nodded. "If not Mars, maybe the moon? Either way, it'll be expensive with the cost of jet fuel these days."

"Oh gosh, are you going to start talking about 'the old days' again?" the boy rolled his eyes.

They both smiled as Ethan pulled Jack into a side hug, squeezing the urn between them as they kept their eyes on the display. With a sigh, Ethan stood. There was still a lot to take care of and grief didn't absolve anyone of their responsibilities.

"We should get going. You ready?"

The boy waited an extra moment, eyes scanning the domed ceiling.

"Do you think we'll ever see Mom again?"

"I don't know," Ethan admitted, "I hope so."

42

About That Time

"Compass?"

The Army compass his dad had given him sat on the table amongst an organized mess of miscellaneous camping and wilderness gear.

"Check."

"GPS?" he continued down the list on the printed paper in his hand.

"Check," Jack patted the GPS clipped to the shoulder strap of his pack.

"Bear canister with dried foods and MRE packs?"

"Check," he said as he slapped the thick plastic container, as though he were testing the quality of a watermelon at the grocery store.

"Filtration straw?"

"Check."

"First aid kit?"

"Check."

"Good good. I'll have the tent in my pack, so you don't

need to worry about that one," he made a check motion with his pen. "Sketchbook and pen?"

"Check."

"Tablet?"

"Can't go anywhere without my tablet," a hint of sarcasm in the boy's tone.

"Hey, you may not be doing traditional school, but we gotta keep learning, no matter our age. I have my e-reader too. I promise it's worth carrying a bit of extra weight."

"I know, I know," he said with exaggerated reluctance. "Check."

"Good boy. Bazooka?"

"Che–" Jack stopped short, his arm reaching toward his gear as if to confirm he owned a rocket launcher. He looked up at his dad, who had a stupid grin on his face.

"Dad, you're obnoxious."

"Don't act like you don't love it," the man stuck his tongue out at Jack who mirrored it back to him, and they both broke out into a laugh.

It felt good to laugh. Best medicine and all that.

"Alright, looks like we're good to go," his dad said as he folded up the paper and shoved it in his pocket. "Go ahead and pack your stuff the way I taught you. Heaviest stuff in the middle and up top, so keep the bear canister for last and we'll pack your puffy jacket around it to keep it from moving around."

"Too easy," replied Jack, already shoving his sleeping bag to the bottom of the pack.

He'd been looking forward to this trip for a long time, growing more and more excited as they drew close to his thirteenth birthday. Jack stole glances at his dad as they finished packing their gear, thinking about how he hadn't quite been himself over the past year. Hopefully the trip would help with that.

They were calling it a "coming of age" ceremony. A "rite of passage" could be another way to say it. Jack and his dad were big fans of the Viking Conquest Era, so these types of events felt important. The world would soon know that Jack Farris was a man.

What better way to let the world know than by doing something insanely difficult that even most adults wouldn't be able to do, like hiking two thousand, six hundred and fifty miles through the wilds of California, Oregon, and Washington. Jack always loved their hiking and camping trips, not to mention this was way better than being stuck in a classroom for eight hours a day, five days a week, like all the other kids his age.

Suck it, Todd!

This was his dad's way of doing things. Teach him something important, but in a way that worked for them. Jack was thankful for it, since he'd always had a hard time sitting still in class. He'd often heard his dad say traditional school was like sitting a child down and having them do low grade clerical work for eight hours. A life that would break anyone's spirit, but especially for a kid like Jack.

Although Jack appreciated his dad's general way of doing things, he was just happy to still have him around. The crash a year prior hadn't been kind to either of them, but his dad had been especially affected.

As Jack closed his bag, he watched his dad pack and contemplated his most recent scars. A smattering of little white marks on the backs of his hands and a few on his left cheek. Those ones were less obvious. A long jagged one ran from the back of his collar, toward his right shoulder, up the back of his head and just a bit higher than his right ear. Even the accident when Jack was a toddler hadn't left his dad scarred like this one had.

It wasn't just physical scars either. Jack wasn't dumb. He knew this hike was just as much for his dad as it was for him. They both needed something to keep them steady, to help them heal. Hiking for five to six months straight often had major impacts on thru-hikers, so it was worth a shot. Couldn't be any worse than the aimless wandering they'd been doing the past year.

"Alright, bud," his dad's voice cut through his thoughts and he looked away from the jagged scar. "It's about that time. You ready?"

"As ready as I'll ever be."

"Smart kid," the man smirked. "Wonder where you got that from."

"I think I read it in a book somewhere."

"Oh, we've got ourselves a smart ass! That's gonna be your trail name, I'll make sure of it. Everyone will be calling you Smart Ass within a week."

"No, dad! Don't do that," Jack grabbed his pack and followed his dad out the door. "That's a terrible nickname!"

"What's that, Smart Ass? I couldn't hear you over all the hard work I've done to raise you into a decent man."

"Daaaaad...."

The older man chuckled.

"Go say bye to Grandma and Grandpa. I'll pack the car."

"Yes, sir!" Jack said.

He gave his dad a crisp salute, the tips of his index and middle fingers touching the outer edge of his right eyebrow, but also stuck out his tongue like a derpy chihuahua. Solid combination of serious and goofy. Jack turned and ran back inside.

"I'm not a sir," Ethan grumbled as he moved the packs to the trunk of the car and Jack was out of earshot. "I work for a living."

43

THE SOUTHERN TERMINUS

"Mexico To Canada, 2650 miles, 1988 A.D."

Jack read the posts at the Southern Terminus of the Pacific Crest Trail, which was literally at the Mexican border. The wall was right there. He could walk a minute away and touch it if he wanted to. How was he even supposed to wrap his head around that many miles? It seemed impossible.

"Best to take it one day at a time," his dad reminded him, as though he'd read Jack's mind.

"How far are we hiking today?" he asked, trying to focus on why he'd been excited about this trip instead of considering how hard it would be.

"Somewhere around ten miles, I think. I remember your mom and I stopped for the night at a creek in a gully shortly after the eighth mile."

"You and mom hiked the PCT? How have I never heard about this?"

His dad shrugged and looked north, his eyes growing a bit distant.

"It was before you were born. We hiked the first couple

days, but I twisted my ankle pretty bad on the first day around that eight mile mark. Walked another fifteen brutal miles into town the next day and decided to call it quits. Your uncle drove out to pick us up."

Jack noted the grimace on his face people usually make when they relive a frustrating memory.

"Normally, I'd never give up on something so quickly. I would have rested up for a day or two, then gotten back on the trail. But it was spring of 2020 and most businesses had closed because of the pandemic. We weren't confident in continuing with a bum leg and limited support, so we figured we'd come back another time. You were born the following year and the timing never seemed to work out."

"Wow."

As Jack attempted to process this new information, he gazed at the trail headed north, visible through the desert shrubs.

"Yeah... I always wished we had kept going. It's been an itch in the back of my mind ever since."

"How come this is the first time we've tried?"

"Priorities rearrange themselves when you have a kid. I tried to do it a couple times since you were born, but each time I found it difficult to be away from you that long. I'd have panic attacks after a few days away. Your mom and I were used to spending time apart, since I was deployed for a lot of the beginning of our marriage. You were too young for us to feel confident about doing it together, but we'd started discussing doing it again when you turned ten. Figured you were getting old enough to pull your own weight and it started feeling more doable again."

"Hmm... I guess that makes sense. Is that why you always

hike wearing your Army boots now? Because of the ankle injury?"

Ethan looked down at his recently broken in coyote colored boots and pursed his lips together in thought.

"I suppose so. The snugness and support comforts me. I love a good pair of trail running shoes, but they don't make me feel as confident as wearing my boots."

Father and son stood together in silence for a moment, enjoying the crisp morning air.

"Well, we may as well get started," Ethan said. "You ready?"

"As ready as I'll ever be," Jack gave his dad an innocent smirk, drawing out a chuckle after such a heavy topic.

The pair started down the narrow trail single file, father in front and son following close behind.

"Oh yeah," Ethan remembered, purposefully avoiding eye contact with Jack, "Keep an eye out for rattlesnakes. I heard a big one was spotted recently somewhere in the first few miles."

"A what?!"

44

UNAWARES

"THE APP HAS A BUNCH OF COMMENTS ABOUT A LARGE RATTLESNAKE'S territory around here. It covers the first ten or so miles of the trail, so we need to keep our eyes and ears open."

"What do we do if one of us gets bit?" asked a small humped creature.

"I... uhh... I'm not sure," replied a larger humped creature. "Do you know?"

"Me? You're the grown up! You're supposed to know this kind of stuff *before* risking six months of exposure to snakes."

"Hey, I may not know exactly what to do, but I know how to get help. We use our gps—" the larger one tapped a small orange and black thing attached to its shoulder, "—to get rescue people out here."

"Okay," a small amount of relief in the small one's voice. "That's better than no plan at all, I guess."

"It'll cost us, like, three grand if they have to come get us though. So, let's do our best to not get bit."

"Excuse me, what?"

The voices of the strange humped creatures faded around

the next corner, no longer concealing the light clack of the cautious snake's deformed rattle. It hadn't felt particularly threatened, but it had stayed coiled and ready, in case they were more aggressive than the last humped creatures to pass by.

Sunlight warmed the snake's leathery skin as it settled back to rest. A bit more sun to warm the blood and it'd be time to move again.

Lots of territory to cover.

45
TRAIL MAGIC

"Is this trail magic?" asked Jack.

Ethan watched him open the off-brand ice chest stationed at the end of a small bridge they'd just crossed. A stream was flowing below the bridge, a family with young children having a picnic on a small sandy area beside the water. Above the chest was a sign stapled to the wood.

> **PCT Thru/Section Hikers - Enjoy a free ice cold water or sports drink. One per person. Drop trash in the bag and we'll haul it out when we're done hanging out at Aztec Falls. Or come hang out with us and we can give you a ride into town afterward.**
>
> **- Buck & Doe**

They'd just been talking about needing to head into town to resupply, after deciding to bypass Big Bear Lake. Lake Arrowhead was a smaller town, but had everything they would need and probably had fewer people stopping in.

"Happening upon something right when we needed it?

Sounds like trail magic to me," Ethan shrugged, then held out a hand. "Pass me a water, please."

"That's awesome. Are we taking a zero day or just resupplying?"

Ethan smiled as the boy handed him a water bottle. They'd been on the trail for a few weeks and he could already see a resilience developing in his son. A sturdiness from doing something difficult and physically demanding for an extended period of time.

"We made good time this week. There's a hotel near the lake we could stay at for a night. How about we head to Aztec Falls and see what Buck and Doe think?"

"Sounds good to me," replied Jack, grabbing himself a blue sports drink. "Is it just a waterfall? Must be more to it if they're hanging out there."

Ethan nodded. He'd actually been there once before Jack was born. It had taken him at least an hour to build up the courage to jump from the tall rocks into the pools below.

"You'll see when we get there. It's a bit off trail, but there should be a painted rock pointing out where to climb down. There used to be, anyway. Let's toss our trash and head that way."

46
HILL CLIMBERS

WHEN WAS THIS STUPID MOUNTAIN GONNA END?

Jack strained to steady his breathing as he followed his dad up another switchback. Stupid switchbacks, making you feel like you're making progress when you're just walking back and forth. But his dad... the man seemed to have no difficulty with the climb, while Jack was on constant lookout for a good rock to rest on.

They finally came to a stop at the top of the next switchback where a gloriously flat rock stood overlooking the valley down below. Jack had never been so happy to see a rock. Before he had a moment to shrug off his pack, his dad pointed up the trail.

"Let's keep going. We're almost to the top, which will be a better place to eat lunch and take a longer break," he pulled out his map app on his phone. "That sets us up to reach a couple nice camp spots at the bottom of the mountain before nightfall."

The trail seemed to find humor at Jack's misfortune, if it

were somehow capable of laughter. Was the slight wind rustling the bushes nearby its way of laughing? More like a chuckle. The mountain was mocking him! Stupid mountain!

"I think we can make it. What do you think?" his dad asked.

Tearing his eyes from the flat rock, Jack took a long drink from his bottle. He gave a simple thumbs up, not trusting himself to say anything out loud without sounding like he was whining. How on Earth was the old man handling this better than him? Didn't he have a bad knee? Had he been faking a knee injury Jack's whole life?

~~~

Every step downhill felt like falling, the entire weight of his body and pack crashing ruthlessly into his aging knees. The best ultralight gear money could buy wasn't enough to ease his struggle.

Ethan had fallen behind Jack as they hiked down the other side of the mountain. His knees felt every impact, screaming at him to stop and stretch or give up, while his son was jumping around like a spry billy goat. This was exactly why he'd pushed so hard to get to the top quickly, knowing he'd need a long rest before going downhill. Getting down this mountain was going to take him a while.

Stupid, high maintenance knees.

Taking another moment to stretch his calves and hamstrings against thin tree trunk, he kept an eye on Jack. It was nice to see the him get a second wind. The combination of lunch, rest, and a nice view had recharged the boy, as though he hadn't just been huffing and puffing all the way uphill.

Must be nice. Ethan shouldered his pack and turned downhill toward his son. Giving him a thumbs up, he started down the next switchback.

Stupid switchbacks.

47
TRAIL NAMES

"YOU READY?"

"As ready as I'll ever be."

The question and answer had become a routine of theirs over the past month. They'd put on their packs, do the call and response, then start walking. They did it every morning and after every break throughout the day.

"Hey, Leak."

Ethan turned to look at a trio of twenty-somethings, a woman and two men, who'd stopped to fill their water at the same stream.

The woman, who was maybe mid to late twenties and couldn't be more than ten years younger than him, seemed intent on ignoring the younger guys as she called out to Ethan. She had the look and demeanor of someone who'd been a college athlete, he'd guess volleyball if she were a bit taller. Maybe some sort of track team? Pole vault?

"Yeah?"

"That's Jack's trail name now," the woman stated. "I've decided."

"What is?" He asked.

"Ready. You always ask him if he's ready and he always says he's as ready as he'll ever be. So that's his name now."

The two young guys with her paused from filling their Smart Water liter bottles and looked at Jack, who blushed from the unexpected attention.

"I like it," one of them said. "It suits him."

The other simply nodded and went back to filling his water. For the life of him, Ethan couldn't remember the names of the young men.

"What do you think?" He looked at his son.

"Best one I've heard so far." Jack shrugged. "Way better than 'Leak'."

"Listen here, you turd, you're the one that suggested that name."

Jack placed his hand on his chest and gaped in mock offense, "All I did was mention to some people that you're always saying you gotta take a leak!"

"Hey, I can't help that I have a bladder the size of a thimble," Ethan laughed. "Besides, peeing outside is the epitome of freedom. I experience more freedom in a day than most people do in a week."

"If you say so," replied Jack, unconvinced, as he turned back to the young woman. "Thanks for the trail name, Pax. I wasn't sure I'd ever get one."

Pax gave him an award winning smile, which caused an even deeper blush on his half-ginger complexion. "It's my pleasure, Ready."

"Alright, best we get going before you become one of her passengers," Ethan nudged his son on the shoulder. "You ready?"

"I'm Ready," Jack nodded, his back straight as an arrow.

Pax chuckled as the pair started back on the trail. When they had walked a good distance away from the trio, Jack pulled up beside Ethan on a wide stretch of trail.

"How'd she get her trail name?"

"You don't remember? You were sitting right there when she and I were talking a few nights ago."

"Huh... no, I must have been reading or something."

"Probably. Well, I gave her the trail name that night."

"Okay, but why Pax? I don't know what that means."

"In the airline industry, it refers to passengers or passenger flights, as opposed to cargo shipments," Ethan scratched at the growing facial hair on his cheek. "At least that's how it worked when I was deployed in the Army, catching passenger flights on C-130s or C-17s between countries."

"Huh," Jack did some internal calculations. "But what does that have to do with her?"

"Oh, well it's pretty obvious once you've noticed all the young male hikers hang around her, trying to catch a ride," he grinned at his own classic dad humor, then gestured toward his son, "If you weren't hiking with me, I imagine you'd be trying to stay near her too."

The boy's face flushed a bit, but talking about girls wasn't a new thing between the father and son. Ethan tried to have honest conversations about typically uncomfortable or taboo topics many parents avoid. Finances, politics, religion, sex, etc etc.

"Yeah... probably. I mean, she's gorgeous!" he exclaimed and they both burst into laughter.

"True enough. That's why the young guys hover or hang around for longer than they should."

"So, you agree that she's gorgeous? How come you're not hovering around her too?"

Ethan shrugged, waiting a moment to take in the scenery before responding.

"It's not really what I came out here for. Sure, she's cute and it's fun to have her around from time to time, but I dunno. My libido hasn't been particularly active these days. I guess it's not as urgent for me now as when I was younger. If someone were to initiate something, I'd consider it, but I'm not looking to change things up right now."

"Do you miss mom?"

"Every day."

"Me too," Jack nodded, looking off into some nearby trees as they continued walking. "She was the best."

"Yeah," Ethan released a heavy sigh as he absentmindedly reached his hand up and traced the jagged scar on the back of his neck. "Neither of us would be the men we are today without her."

Ethan and Jack felt a mutual desire to leave it at that for the time being, so they just kept walking. There was a lot of ground still to cover before they stopped for the night.

48

RESUPPLY BLUES

"If it has more than five ingredients, put it back. I don't want us to get thru-hiker's gut."

"I know, dad," Jack replied as they walked straight toward the aisle with nuts and jerky. "You say this every time we resupply, at least a dozen times now. I know what I'm doing."

Jack noticed his dad looked less peppy than usual, his cheeks drooping a bit and bags under his eyes.

"Hmm... I guess it just helps me to say it out loud. Helps me focus," pausing for a moment, Ethan looked down at his boots, then continued. "Grab what you want and meet me at the produce. I'm gonna grab some bananas and see what kinds of dried fruit they have."

His dad pushed the cart down the aisle and turned left before Jack could apologize for giving him a hard time.

They were both struggling today. Jack was handling it by being kind of a turd and his dad was handling it by sticking to the routine as best as he could. Maybe there was something Jack could do to help them both.

"Hey, Ready."

"Biscuits!" Jack jumped and turned at the same time toward the voice behind him.

Pax stood nearby with a bag of turkey jerky and a tin of toasted coconut almonds in her hands. Her brow was raised like his reaction had caught her off guard too.

"You alright, bud?"

"Uhh, sure. Sorry about that, you just surprised me."

Jack tried not to stare at the woman as she nodded and turned to continue browsing the snacks in front of her. She looked... smaller than usual. Maybe he'd grown some since they last saw her? His dad had mentioned this was the age when he'd sprouted up. Oh, the wonders of puberty.

"I see you haven't quit yet," he said in an offhand, innocent tone.

She glanced up at him from the list of ingredients she was reading and smiled.

"I'm not particularly fond of giving up."

"Neither are we," Jack agreed, straightening his back a little.

"So I've noticed," Pax chuckled. "How's your dad holding up? I saw you guys talking before he walked away. He seemed a little... off, I guess."

"Yeah..." Jack looked back at the end of the aisle where his dad had walked out of view. "Today is my mom's birthday."

"Oh, I see. I was curious why it was just the two of you hiking. Are they still married?"

"They were, but not anymore. They got into a bad car wreck last year, the car rolled and landed upside down. My dad was able to get himself out first, then pulled my mom away from the wreck, but she died in the ambulance on the way to the hospital."

Jack felt the back of his neck where his dad's jagged scar would be.

"That's how my dad got all those scars," he continued. "The ones on his hands are from all the broken glass and the one on his neck happened when he pulled my mom out, nicked it on some metal."

"Damn... I would never have guessed. You both seem so stoic all the time, like nothing bothers you."

"That's who he is," Jack nodded. "Me too, I guess. Every once in a while he hits a slump, says it's when the feelings overwhelm him. I try to find ways to help, if I can."

"That's a lot of responsibility for a teenager."

"We're a team," Jack shrugged. "He's there for me and I'm there for him,

He'd gotten used to helping carry the burden, like how your pack starts to become a part of you after hiking a while.

"Alright," Pax clapped her hands and rubbed them together like a scheming rat. "Tonight I'm making myself part of the team. We're gonna celebrate you two and your mom the best way I know how: pizza, cake, ice-cream, alcohol, and good company."

Pax hooked her arm into Jack's and turned them to face the end of the aisle.

"You ready?" she asked.

Jack smiled.

"I'm Ready."

"Good. Now, what's your dad's favorite kind of alcohol?"

49

THE BEST KIND OF THERAPY

"Are you sure it's alright for me to crash here with you guys tonight? I don't want to impose."

Pax, Ethan, and Jack had spent the past couple of hours eating, drinking mead, and telling stories. How they'd found mead in the small town was a mystery to Ethan, but he was thankful they had.

Memories of his time in Aidland and his monster companions had recently flooded his dreams. He hadn't thought much about Aidland for years, really only when Jack asked to tell him the stories or when doing press for his book.

Had it even been real? The doctors insisted that it was a side effect of the medically induced coma they put him in after his van had been hit by a semi truck. Ethan wasn't so sure, but he also didn't have any proof it was real. It wouldn't, as the saying goes, hold up in a court of law.

But now he was sitting on a motel floor somewhere in Oregon, side by side with an attractive young woman, leaning back against a bed as they passed a bottle back and forth. Jack had succumbed to the bit of drink he'd been given and crashed in the other bed an hour prior. Since then, Ethan and Pax sat together, talking.

"Of course you can stay with us. You can have this bed and I'll share the other with Jack. He won't even flinch when I push him out of the way. The boy sleeps hard even without any alcohol."

"True," she chuckled. "He really liked the taste of mead. I'm surprised you let him have any."

"Eh, I figure he'll try alcohol eventually. His maiden voyage may as well be with his dad nearby to make sure he's okay."

"He's a good kid," Pax took a sip from the bottle and handed it to Ethan. "And you're a good dad, Leak."

Ethan's eyes unfocused as a memory of Rebecca on a swingset with Jack washed over him. Feeling a bit of panic, he took a deep breath and went through his breathing exercise.

"I do what I can," he said, pausing to finish off the bottle and set it on the floor beside him. "Doesn't always feel like enough, but, like you said, he's a good kid."

They sat in companionable silence, just close enough that their shoulders were touching. Ethan was barely aware of it, lost in his own thoughts, and neither felt the need to say anything as Jack snored lightly in the background.

Pax eventually broke the silence.

"Are you familiar with the term 'cuddle therapy'?"

"I've heard of it," Ethan turned his head toward her, a slight smirk on his lips. "I remember reading about a woman in Seattle who had a 'cuddle therapy' business that did quite well. Haven't stayed updated on it though."

"Mhm," she turned her eyes to look into his. "Let's do that."

"What, right now?"

"Yup," she stood to her feet and held out her hand. "Come on, we're sharing the bed. I call little spoon."

"Alright, but only cuddles. I don't want to risk trauma-tizing Jack."

50

BREAKFAST

"Don't look at me like that."

Ethan nudged Jack to try and get that stupid grin off his face, looking just like Colby-Jack had years before. Smug, creepy little dork.

"You slept together," Jack replied, continuing to look smug.

The father and son sat in a booth at a diner near the motel. The plan was to have a good breakfast and get a slow start to the day in order to compensate for the unnecessary amount of food and drink from the night before. Ethan was impressed by his son's complete lack of a hangover, even though he'd had a decent amount of mead for his age. Pax joined them for breakfast, but she'd just gotten up to use the restroom, so of course Jack took the opportunity to tease his dear old dad.

"Yeah, we slept together," he admitted with a sigh. "But that's all it was. She called it 'Cuddle Therapy'."

"Well, dear father of mine, cuddle therapy looks good on you," Jack paused, bit into his last piece of bacon, then pointed the bit he still held at Ethan. "You look lighter. A hint of happiness peaks through the mask."

"Eww, stop acting so mature. Who are you and what have you done with my teenage son?" Ethan sighed, resolving to be honest with Jack. "But yes, my shoulders and back do feel less tense than usual. I know you probably instigated that whole evening somehow, even if you didn't do it on purpose. Thank you."

The boy nodded and finished his bacon, then stabbed his fork into his pancakes as though they hadn't just had a special father-son bonding moment. Little turd.

"I'm gonna have to get myself some of that 'Cuddle Therapy'. I bet it felt real nice," he winked at Ethan, who laughed, happy that his son was comfortable making these kinds of jokes with him. "Do you think she'll want to keep hiking with us? Be one of our passengers for a change?"

Ethan shrugged and took a sip from his mug of tea before responding.

"Maybe. It's up to her. She's under no obligation to come with us just because we cuddled."

"You guys talking about how we slept together last night?"

The pair looked up as Pax arrived back at the booth and slid in to sit beside Ethan, elbowing him in the side before resting her hand on his leg. His heartbeat stuttered for a moment.

"We were, as a matter of fact. Jack here was hoping you'd keep hiking with us so he'll have a chance to get some cuddle therapy."

Jack's face turned beet red as he stared daggers at his sweet, innocent father. Pax laughed at the exchange.

"I'd be honored, Ready, but unfortunately you're a bit young for me. You're quite handsome though, like your father," she squeezed his leg. "I'm sure you'll be getting plenty of cuddle therapy sooner than you think. But don't rush it. A good cuddle should be savored. Right, Leak?"

Ethan nodded, his cheeks feeling warm.

"As for hiking together, I'll have to pass this time around. I'm taking another zero day in town. I have some work I need to catch up on, then I'll get back on the trail."

That surprised Ethan, "You work while hiking?"

"Eh, it's mostly maintenance. I can access everything I need from my phone, as long as I have decent reception or wifi available," she glanced back and forth at the father and son. "What? Is that unusual? How do you guys afford the hike?"

"Dad gets disability from when he was in the Army," Jack said, shoving more pancakes into his mouth.

Ethan reached across the table and flicked him in the forehead.

"That's not the whole story, dork," he clarified for Pax. "I do get disability, which eases a lot of the urgency. But I also get some passive income from a few books I've written. It's plenty for us, especially considering we don't have to pay rent while we hike."

"I guess we're all doubly blessed. I know a lot of people had to save up for a long time to be able to take six months off to hike. So, you're a writer? What do you write? Anything I would have read?"

"Science fiction and fantasy, mostly, though I also wrote a couple non-fiction books. They could be considered 'self-help', but I'd label them under perspective pieces myself. That or psychology/philosophy."

"Dad's really proud of those ones. Gets hyper focused on his novels, but he won't shut up about his 'perspective pieces'. Personally, I prefer his novels. Especially 'Aidland', which I think needs to become a series. You should check that one out."

"I definitely will, if they're available on e-book?" she ended her sentence as if it was a question, looking at Ethan. He nodded, then she continued. "Cool. I'll buy the first one and tell you what I think next time I meet up with you guys. Writing isn't really my cup of tea, but I read excessively when I'm not hiking."

Pax pulled out her phone and ran a quick search for 'Aidland' in her browser.

"Ethan Farris? Ooooh, that's a good name. It suits you," she looked at Jack. "So that must mean you're Jack Farris?"

"The one and only, baybay!"

51

A BOOK OF CONTEXT

"That book was not at all what I expected it to be."

Pax had caught up with father and son by the time they'd reached the Bridge of the Gods, right at the border of Oregon and Washington.

"Well, what were you expecting?" Ethan asked.

"I don't know!" she threw her hands up, exacerbated. "It's a fantasy novel. I expected it to be crazy and fantastical or something. Instead, it felt... normal? Like real life, but with a bit of magic thrown in."

Ethan laughed. He'd heard this many times since he decided to write the book and had his own response prepared.

"People are people, regardless of the setting. If a man suddenly finds himself in a fantasy setting, does he just become a different, more exaggerated version of himself? A caricature? Or does he continue being himself, just in a different environment? Sure, the new environment will affect the types of decisions he'll need to make, but it doesn't change the life he lived up to that point. The man he had become."

Ethan finished speaking as they reached the middle of the

bridge, pausing to look out over the Columbia River. The day was overcast, which he felt was the perfect welcome into the state of Washington.

"Geez. I didn't expect to get so philosophical," replied Pax. "Where did you even get the idea from? Pokémon and Vikings seem to be a strange combination, but Aidland felt like a real place."

"Good luck getting a straight answer on that one..." Jack muttered to himself.

Ethan didn't respond immediately, his brow furrowed over his eyes, blocking the light and making them look darker than actually were. Pax stood on his right and Jack had moved to his left, all three of them taking in the beauty around them. It'd become routine after hiking for so long, stopping to look around and appreciate where they were walking. It would otherwise be easy to miss it all, watching the trail right in front of them.

Jack rested against the railing, looking sour. He'd tried to get his dad to answer that question many times, but he'd always avoided giving a real answer.

"When Jack was very little," Ethan started, "I was in a car accident that put me in a coma. That's what everyone tells me anyway. I don't remember any of it.

"Do you not believe that's what happened?" Pax wasn't sure what this had to do with the book, but she figured it was leading somewhere.

"I don't really know," he turned and continued across the bridge. Pax made a questioning look at Jack, who shrugged and followed after his dad.

"If that is what happened, then I had an incredibly vivid dream while in the coma. The Aidland book isn't fiction to me. It's more of a memoir or autobiography, but as a narrative retelling of the couple months I spent there. It's why I only ever wrote one book and didn't turn it into a series. There wasn't anything else for me to write."

"How come you're talking about this now?" Jack's voice held a hint of hurt in it, "I've seen the video of you answering it, but that's it. Since mom died you won't talk about it with me anymore. Now Pax is here and suddenly you want to talk about it?"

A chuckled exhale escaped the Ethan's nose as he saw Pax stiffen as she walked behind them, so he stopped and turned to his son.

"This has nothing to do with her, Jack. It's just... every time it comes up, I feel myself start to panic. So I've been avoiding it. That's not fair to you, but I didn't know how to deal with the possibility that I might be crazy for thinking it was real. I don't want you to think I'm crazy. The thought that I may be losing my mind is terrifying. Your mom matched my crazy, which I realize I'd taken for granted."

Ethan paused, hesitant if he should share the next bit.

"You're old enough now for us to talk about it and this hike has forced me to work through some of my fears. I've actually been thinking about talking to you about it. The closer we get to the end of this hike, the more I feel my mind wandering toward thoughts about Aidland. My gut is telling me that something important is happening, but I'm afraid of what that could mean."

Jack threw his arms around his dad in a bear hug, their packs making it an awkward ordeal, the top of his head a couple inches taller than his dad's shoulders. Damn, the boy had grown up. When did that happen?

"Well, I, for one, hope it's real," Pax interjected, barely loud enough for them to hear.

The father and son broke their embrace and turned to Pax, who'd been quietly watching them. The pair broke into laughter, like two kids sharing an inside joke.

"What?" she asked. "Was that rude to say?"

"I say that I hope it's real all the time," replied Jack. "But what makes you say it?"

She turned her head to the side, embarrassed that she thought they'd been laughing at her expense.

"I guess it just feels better than what I've got going on here. Magical companions, monsters, adventure. I dunno. It's not like my life is bad. I don't need to worry about money much anymore, but I don't have close friends and my family are either off doing their own thing or don't particularly like me. I'm tired of living in a high tech world that makes connecting easier, yet somehow more difficult to actually connect with anyone."

Pax made an exacerbated motion with her hand toward Ethan, then finished her thought.

"Reading your book felt more of an escape than most of this hike has been."

"You connected with us!" Jack interjected, toothy grin on his face. It made Pax snort, easing a bit of the tension in her shoulders.

"Yeah, and I like you guys. You don't try to get anything from me, unlike the kinds of people that tend to hang around me. They don't really see me, they just see something they want."

That was the most Ethan had heard her talk about herself, especially being so vulnerable. He thought she was much better at connecting than she gave herself credit for.

"You're good company, Pax," he said.

They smiled at each other and Jack could swear he saw a

twinkle in their eyes. Jack glanced back and forth at the pair, who were holding eye contact for an uncomfortable amount of time. He rolled his eyes and broke the silence with a couple loud claps.

"Alright, we're burning daylight here! This trail isn't going to hike itself."

Ethan gave his son a light, playful smack on the back of his head, throwing him off balance enough that he almost fell over.

"You're a turd, you know that?"

"Oh? I wonder where I get it from."

52

NORTHERN TERMINUS

THE GROUND RUMBLED BENEATH THE NORTHERN TERMINUS AS THE three hikers reached the end of the Pacific Crest Trail. The rumble was low, the rustling of trees and shifting of dirt drowned out by their excitement.

It looked just like the Southern Terminus, except it was surrounded by lush, green trees instead of dusty desert brush and a wall that stretched into infinity. Who knew that Canada and Mexico looked so different? Everyone, probably.

The main difference for the three hikers resting their hands on the posts was that being at this terminus meant the hike was complete. Finished. After five months, they'd walked the full two thousand, six hundred and fifty miles of the trail. They hadn't even been hit by any crazy weather or wildfires that year, so each mile was actually on the trail instead of having to find detours.

That in itself was rare. The thru-hiking purists would be salivating with envy.

"What do we do now?" asked Jack, removing his hand from the post.

"I guess we head back to civilization." replied Pax. "Maybe get something to eat?"

"Well, duh. But what are we going to *do*? I'm supposed to start high school, something I am not at all looking forward to. Weird social atmosphere that doesn't make sense to me... I mean, who even cares about prom or picking a college or being popular? The trail made sense. I walk, eat, sleep, poop, and then walk some more."

"I agree. I'm not sure what to do now either. I had a rough plan in mind before the hike, but I'm not super confident about it anymore," Pax turned to Ethan to get his opinion, finding him staring off into space. "Ethan, what do you think?"

"Silence.

Ethan didn't respond. Didn't even move an inch, other than his eyes flitting back and forth, like he was reading from an invisible bulletin board with the day's water reports. Pax nudged Jack and gestured for him to look at his dad.

The boy watched for a moment, knowing that his dad was prone to get lost in thought from time to time. That was usually where his best ideas came from. But this was different. He was focused on something, not zoned out. Jack followed his line of sight, but only saw trees, rocks, and the terminus posts.

"Dad?"

Without breaking his gaze, Ethan turned his head slightly and spoke, but not in reply to their questions.

"Jack, do you have a floating symbol in the upper right hand corner of your vision?"

"Huh?"

"It would be almost transparent until you focus on it," Ethan continued. "Looks like a tiny, blank trading card."

"Dad, what are you talking about? I don't see anything."

A chuckle escaped the man's lips, relieving some of the

tension Jack hadn't realized had been building in his shoulders and neck.

"Bud, you haven't even looked yet."

"I see it!" shouted Pax. Jack flinched back, not expecting the outburst, and watched her flinch back in surprise. She stood up straight and her eyes began flitting back and forth like his dad's. "Whoa... is this... real?"

Not understanding what was happening, but not wanting to be left out, Jack focused on the spot in his vision his dad had mentioned. Once he knew where to look, and actually attempted to look, the symbol was immediately visible.

Great, now he felt dumb for saying he couldn't find it.

As soon as he brought his full attention to what looked like a blank Pokémon card, Jack was assaulted by a pixelated text box floating in front of him. He instinctively took a step back, but the weight of his pack caused him to lose his balance and he fell hard onto his backside.

"Ow..." he muttered as he closed his eyes. The text box was still visible.

Congratulations!
You've completed the Hidden Quest: Quadzilla, Your Legs Must Be Tired

Requirement: Hike all 2,650 miles of the Pacific Crest Trail
Reward: Transport/Transfer to last location in Aidland

Progress: 2,650/2,650

To Accept or Decline your reward, focus on the desired button.

ACCEPT
DECLINE

"Do you see it, Jack?" Ethan asked, unconcerned or unaware that his son had fallen on the ground.

"Dad, is this what I think it is?"

"Yes, but don't hit accept yet."

Jack looked at his dad, but the text box followed his movement, still blocking his vision.

"Huh? You don't want to go back to Aidland?"

"Of course I do, but we're not ready for it yet. We're almost out of food and have nothing to defend ourselves with except pocket knives." Ethan's voice trailed off and paused, like he was remembering something. "We don't have any cards either and I don't know if Colby-Jack and the others are still bound to me."

"Okay, I understand, although I actually do have some cards on me," Jack muttered to himself as he moved his head around, the text box never leaving his sight. "This thing is so cool, but is there a way to minimize it? I can't see a thing."

The boy focused on where he would expect a minimize button to be on a computer program and the box shrank back to the upper right symbol it had sprung from. Oh wow, that was a relief. Jack looked around the terminus clearing, which was empty except for the father and son.

"Hey dad?"

"Yeah, bud?"

"Where's Pax?"

53
THE DONE THING

"DAD, WE NEED TO GO AFTER HER."

Ethan's mind raced as his son stared daggers at him. He wanted to go after Pax too, but he also didn't want to risk his son's safety by mindlessly following her underprepared into a dangerous world filled with monsters.

What had she been thinking?

"We need to prepare," he answered, unsure of his own words.

"Are you kidding me?" Jack replied. Ethan's heart broke hearing the disappointment in his son's voice. "There are monsters there. You're willing to risk letting Pax die alone?"

What a simple way to view the world. Didn't he used to see the world that way? When had he stopped? Probably since the accident, if he had to guess. Ethan closed his eyes and took a deep breath before responding.

"I want to protect her, but I need to protect you. She chose to go without any sort of preparation or protection. She made an impulsive decision, but that doesn't mean we have to as well."

"Well, then," the boy's voice took on a particularly defiant tone. "Come protect me."

Ethan snapped his eyes open to an empty clearing, already knowing what Jack had done. The little goober forced his hand. Though he was angry with Jack, he couldn't help but be proud of him. A decade ago, he would have made the same choice.

Cursing himself for not having prepared more, Ethan decided instead to be grateful for all the training he'd put himself and Jack through over the years.

"That boy is going to give me an aneurysm," he muttered to himself, but couldn't hold back the smile of a proud father.

Terror may have slithered its way into his heart these past couple of years, but months of hiking in nature had taught him a lot. Put one foot in front of the other and soon you'll get where you need to be. It had helped him rebuild some of his resilience.

Pulling out his phone, Ethan unlocked his screen to see a photo of Rebecca. Tears threatened his eyes as he gave her a silent farewell before stuffing it back in his pocket. Shaking off the rising panic from his hands, he took a deep breath in, held it for five seconds, then released it.

Without further ado, the text box appeared back in his vision and he focused on:

ACCEPT

54
THE BLIZZ

A ROAR ASSAULTED ETHAN'S EARS, FREEZING WIND NEARLY PUSHING him off his feet. He opened his eyes to a white and gray landscape, snow coming in sideways, barely able to see ten feet in front of him.

Spinning in place, the cold not yet registering in his mind, Ethan looked for any sign of Jack. Had they not been sent to the same place? A long buried panic bubbled up in his chest, causing him to take shorter, more frantic breaths. His hands were shaking, only partially due to the cold.

"Jack!" Ethan shouted, desperation clear in his voice.

The sound of a car door sliding shut reached him through the wind, though it was faint.

A car? Here? The only car likely to be here was his van, although that didn't seem likely since the van had been totaled when it was hit during his coma-inducing semi-truck collision. The photos had been convincing, though he had to admit that he hadn't seen the wreck in person. Maybe it was duplicated? Would that mean he was a duplicate?

Ethan shook the thoughts from his mind. No time or point thinking about it now.

Looking in the direction where he thought the sound came from, he saw a small flicker of light, almost like a blackish orange ghost dancing in mid air. Not knowing where else to go, Ethan moved toward the light, his well worn coyote brown boots and tactical hiking pants already damp as he trudged through half a foot of snow.

Drawing closer to the ghost light, Ethan's heart skipped a beat. It *was* his van! The outline of the its body was clear though the falling snow and a flickering candle was visible through what he knew was the window of the sliding door on the passenger's side. The tint of the window gave the flame its blackish orange color.

Continuing forward, he crashed into the side door, now realizing he was still only wearing his t-shirt from the clear fall day in Washington. In his panic, he hadn't thought to pull out his cold weather clothes, gloves, and beanie from his pack.

Desperate to make sure Jack was safe, and to prevent frostbite, Ethan grabbed the handle and slid the door open with the creak of cold metal.

Inside the van were three people: Jack, Pax, and a young man in leather armor, cotton pants, boots, and what looked like a large fur cloak across his shoulders. Though... the redtinged fur seemed to take up the entire back half of the van. A rumbling growl came from the left side of the wall of fur, drawing Ethan's attention to a massive snout with a pair of beady eyes staring back at him.

"Hello again, Mr. Farris." The young man smiled a big, toothy grin at Ethan, speaking in English with a rough Scandinavian accent. "Shut the door before we all freeze."

55

WELCOME WAGON

"Bjorn? You've gotten older."

"Hah! You're one to talk."

The man looked more worn and weathered than Bjorn expected. Not unhealthy or weak, in fact he looked quite fit, but... not as all powerful as he remembered. Bjorn was just a kid last they'd seen each other, so his memory was likely askew. Still, though Mr. Farris looked strong and capable, as the carriage door slid closed Bjorn noticed a multitude of scars on the man's hands. If he wasn't mistaken, he also glimpsed a jagged scar on the back of the man's neck before he turned around and sat down beside the young boy.

There hadn't been much time to speak with the boy or the woman before Mr. Farris appeared, but it was clear he and the boy were related. They had the same prominent brow and observant look in their eyes. Doubtless they were analyzing him as he was them.

"This is Bjorn?" The boy, who was about the age Bjorn had been when Mr. Farris had upended his dreary life as an orphan, appraised him with a hint of skepticism in his voice. "He looks... older than I expected. And he's all scarred up."

Laughter boomed in the small carriage, causing the boy and woman to flinch away from Bjorn and Karhu. The large red tinged bear grumbled at the noise. Mr. Farris didn't flinch, but did raise his eyebrows.

"My apologies, I forget how loud it can be in this strange steel carriage. It echoes as though we were surrounded by sheer cliffs. I only laugh because I had literally just been thinking those same words about Mr. Farris here," Bjorn explained. Looking the man over again, he continued, "You look like you've seen many battles since I last saw you."

"Something like that," the man responded after a longer pause than seemed necessary, followed afterward by more silence.

Glancing between his three guests, Bjorn tried to discern the story behind the silence. He was clearly missing something important. Oh well, it was not his place to pry and the man had always been a mystery. Both the boy and woman shivered slightly, reminding Bjorn of the blizzard outside.

"Oh, ravens! Where are my manners? You are cold from the blizzard. Karhu," he turned his head slightly behind him, "would you warm up the carriage a bit more, please?"

The bear grumbled again, not moving, but the air did feel slightly warmer already. Bjorn reached over and scratched behind her ear, her preferred method of expressing gratitude. As she gave a more contented grumble, Mr. Farris seemed to remember something, as though a candle was suddenly lit in the darkness, and began unbuckling the strange looking pack resting at his feet.

"We may want to put on our camp gear," the man said as he pulled out a coat that looked both impossibly smooth and luxuriously puffy, like a cloud had been captured from the sky. All three of his guests put on similar coats, with a variety of colors, before anyone spoke again.

"So, you're really Bjorn? The boy my dad met in Aidland?"

Ahh, so this was the man's son. The boy must have been two or three years old when Bjorn had first met his father. No wonder the man had been eager to find his way home. And yet, here they both were. And was this woman his wife? She seemed a bit young. Closer to the age Mr. Farris had been when he'd last been in Aidland.

Interesting.

"Yes, though I haven't been a mere boy for some time. Now *you're* the boy *I* met in Aidland," he and the boy shared a chuckle, "So, your father has spoken of me, uh... I'm sorry, what's your name, lad?"

"I'm Jack. He didn't talk about you much, but he wrote a book about his time in Aidland."

"A book?"

Now that was a surprise. Both a warrior and a scholar? That was a diverse skill set in Aidland. Most people focused their attention on one or the other. Bjorn let his gaze fall on the man again, analyzing him in a new light. He supposed it made a certain amount of sense, the man had been regularly writing in his small book before he'd vanished.

"I gotta ask," the voice coming this time from the woman. "How is it that you speak English? My understanding was that only Aino and her family knew how to speak it."

"Well, Mrs..."

"Pax. Just Pax."

Bjorn smiled, excited to answer, "Well, Pax, it's become quite popular around our region. Mostly because of Aino and

The Farris Wheel. Everyone is required to be fluent in English before they can be a full fledged member."

Mr. Farris silently placed his face in his hands, covering an odd expression, but with an obvious shake of his head. The woman wore a smirk that seemed to be stifling a laugh. And the boy stared at him, mouth slightly agape, speaking in almost a whisper.

"Did you say 'The Farris Wheel'?"

Bjorn looked between the trio, not sure what the issue was. Was he not honored that they'd chosen to use his name? He replied slowly, making sure his confusion was clear.

"Yes... Our company is named 'The Farris Wheel'. We train new cardists around the town of Trace, using a cyclical method for both masters and apprentices. Aino is considering spreading further out toward Modes, but there's been push back from her father. I don't understand what's so funny. Ms. Pax, please keep your laughter down, the echo will agitate Karhu. Don't look at me like that, Jack Farrisson! Mr. Farris, will you please explain to me what is going on?"

56

THE FARRIS WHEEL

"A FERRIS WHEEL IS A MECHANICAL RIDE AT FESTIVALS," ETHAN explained, "Imagine a giant carriage wheel with seats at the end of the spokes that lifts people up into the air as it rotates."

"That sounds... terrifying."

The expression on Bjorn's face, scrunched up as he tried to imagine it, made Ethan chuckle.

"It can be, if you're afraid of heights. What made you guys decide to call it 'The Farris Wheel'?"

The young warrior's expression switched back to a full-faced grin, clearly proud of what he'd helped build.

"Aino named it after you because she designed it based on the agreement you set up with Captain Havard to train me."

"Ahh, right. I almost forgot about that," replied Ethan. "And how's this membership work, exactly?"

"Basically, one member takes on a younger apprentice and teaches them their trade or craft. Blacksmith trains a black-smith, gardener trains a gardener, etc. After they've learned the basics, a group of members will take the apprentice out to find and capture their first monster, ideally one that would mesh well with their new trade."

"Hmm, I see," Ethan stewed on the concept, thinking through the implications of their system. "I imagine when the apprentice becomes a full member, they train the next generation of hopeful members?"

"Ehh, mostly," Bjorn shrugged. "It depends on how skilled they've become. Sometimes it depends on their age, but many new members prefer to give back by helping with monster hunts. Not everyone is meant to be a teacher."

"That's true," Pax agreed with a chuckle, then turned her skeptical business mind onto the warrior. "So this is free? The members do this out of the kindness of their hearts?"

That was a good question, actually. In Ethan's experience, few people did anything without some sort of personal motive or incentive. Bjorn burst into laughter, a growl of frustration rising from the bear behind him.

"No, no," the warrior replied, his laughter settling into a light chuckle. "Does anyone really ever do anything out of the kindness of their hearts? Each new member owes their first two blank monster cards from quest rewards. The first goes to The Farris Wheel, which is used for future apprentices and horde prep, while the second is payment to the member who trains, houses, and feeds them."

Seemed like a good deal to Ethan. Must work pretty well too, considering they'd been at it for a decade. Turning to Jack and Pax, he decided to turn this into a teachable moment.

"That explains why most of them help with monster hunts instead of training new recruits. Monster killing quests are a surefire way to get blank cards. It's dangerous, but would be the quickest way to pay off the debt."

The pair nodded their understanding. They'd both read his book, so they already knew about the quests he'd completed.

"Dad, will I have to be a recruit?"

The look in Jack's eyes was difficult for Ethan to read. Was he wanting to be a recruit or was he hoping he wouldn't have to?

"If you'd like, I suppose. That's up to you, though. I can train you, at least in reference to the cards. I don't have a trade to teach, beyond general handyman type stuff, and I'm not much of a fighter without a gun. Actually, that reminds me," he snapped his fingers. "I wonder what the system did with all my stuff back in the day. Did you two get any notifications?"

A ripple of excitement passed through the van as their eyes simultaneously glazed over and they exclaimed.

"I do!"

"Hell yeah!"

"Bjorn, do you mind if we put our convo on hold for a minute so we can look through our notifications?"

"Take your time," Bjorn said as he stretched, folded his hands behind his head, and leaned back into the warmth of his bear companion. "Not much we can do until the blizzard passes anyway."

Ethan nodded, a knot in his chest loosening. Had he really missed the boy so much? They barely knew each other. Hell, they had only exchanged a few words a decade ago. Even hearing Aino and Havard's names had brought some feelings of longing bubbling to the surface. Were they doing well? Did Aino ever warm up to the idea of marriage? Was Havard still Captain of the town guard?

Man, Ethan was looking forward to catching up with them. *'Soon enough,'* he thought to himself as he turned his attention to his notifications, eager to see what the system had in store for him.

57
FOUR KINDS OF PEOPLE

WELCOME: OLIVIA PRESTON (aka PAX)

You've been chosen to participate in a once in a lifetime opportunity. Prove yourself worthy and continue down the path of a Cardist.

None of your equipment has been deemed compatible with the local system. Oopsies.
Adaptation to local guidelines unnecessary.

Congratulations and welcome to your new world!

PAX READ THE NOTIFICATION THREE TIMES BEFORE MOVING ON TO THE next, a heavy sigh escaping her nostrils.

What did she expect? She hadn't had any cards on her while backpacking like the ones Ethan had described in his book. Still, it was disappointing.

Moving on, she recognized the notifications for the two starting quests: **The Very Best** and **Collect Them All**. Again, she read each three times before closing them. The last notification was unexpected, but brought a small giggle bubbling to the surface. Oof... hopefully nobody heard that. Pretending not to care if anyone heard her giggle, she read the text two more times, then moved on.

Hidden Quest: A Whole New World

Requirements: Jump headfirst into a new world without a single adaptable item.

Reward: 1x Blank Monster Card

Progress: Complete

Congratulations!
You've completed the Hidden Quest: A Whole New World

You're either incredibly brave or lacked the foresight to prepare. Either way, you did it!

To receive your reward, hold out your hand and focus on the ACCEPT button.

ACCEPT

Wow... Snarky system in charge here.

'Though, it isn't wrong,' she admitted to herself.

It hadn't even occurred to her that she could take her time to prepare, on instinct assuming the offer to go to a new world would time out if she didn't immediately accept it.

After focusing her attention on the "Accept" button, she turned her gaze to Jack and Ethan. The card appeared out of thin air and dropped in her hand, but the giddiness she'd felt a moment prior dissolved as a pile of less fun feelings erupted to the surface, like Mentos in Diet Coke. They likely only arrived so quickly because they cared about her safety.

Ethan had an intense expression, his prominent brow furrowed as he read through whatever the system was telling him. Now that she thought about it, had he looked at her even once since he got in the van? Why would he be avoiding her? Oh no... She had put his son in danger! Stupid! What had she been thinking?!

Feeling overwhelmed, Pax turned her eyes away from them, only to notice the young warrior peering at her from his reclined position. His body looked relaxed, but his eyes drilled straight through her, like he knew what she'd done. Shifting her gaze again, she gripped the new blank card in her hand.

She didn't know how, but she'd find a way to make it up to them; weigh the scales of trust back in her favor.

Somehow.

~~~

WELCOME: JACK FARRIS

You've been chosen to participate in a once in a lifetime opportunity. Prove yourself worthy and continue down the path of a Cardist.

Some of your equipment has been deemed compatible with the local system. At least one of you had some forethought. Adaptation to local guidelines has been initiated.

Congratulations and welcome to your new world!

"Whoa, it worked."

Jack's voice came out breathy, barely loud enough to be considered a whisper. Definitely quieter than the noises Pax was making.

He knew it! The Aidland stories were really real!

He knew his dad too well to think he'd made it all up. Fiction was never his style. Metaphors and analogies, sure, but writing non-fiction had always seemed more up his alley. Jack's chest puffed out a bit at the system's compliment of his forethought, proud of himself for taking the time to prepare some cards after the conversation they'd had back at the Bridge of the Gods.

It hadn't been easy, using a motel computer and printer while his dad went out for a rare solo meal, but he'd made it work.

Having never been one for hefty muscles and brute forcing his problems away, Jack had sketched out a sheet of cards that focused more on subtlety and day to day practicality, rather than strength and power. Sure, he was in good shape for a thirteen year old, especially after months of hiking, but his brain was and always would be his strongest muscle. If he'd actually cared about school, he'd already be graduating instead of preparing to enter High School. But school was dumb, the most boring way to go about learning things. Life outside classrooms was way more interesting.

Dozens of strategies for thriving in this type of world had

been bouncing back and forth in his brain for months, but Jack knew he'd have to adapt once he actually got here and interacted with the world.

Excited to learn more first-hand from the system, he pulled up the next notification, a quest called **"The Very Best"**. After that was **"Collect Them All"**, which he'd completed, then **"Collect Them All II"**, which had a progress of three out of five completed.

This had been strategic as well. Create three monster cards, even though it meant only completing one quest. The idea was to take his time acclimating to a new world and not draw too much attention to himself, like his dad had done by accident.

On to the next notification!

Adaptation Complete

Your Monster Cards have finished adapting to the local system.

Cards Adapted:
3x - Unique Monster Cards
3x - Unique Item Cards
3x - Blank Monster Cards

Maybe he should have brought more blank template sheets with him, rather than just one, but he didn't want extra weight in his pack if it had all turned out to not be real. Oh well, nothing to do about it now.

Jack closed the last notification, readjusting his eyes to the low light inside the van. Pax was done as well, but she looked defeated for some reason. The warrior across from them was watching her the same way he'd seen people concentrating on a difficult math problem. His dad was still focused, though, a glazed over look in his eyes. Probably still angry with Pax for being impulsive, and Jack for putting himself in danger.

Meh, he'd do it again if he had to. She was his friend now, or like an older sister. Although he didn't really know what it was like to have a sibling, so that was a guess. Besides, how much more could they have prepared without being completely obnoxious?

That's how he saw it anyway. You can't be prepared for everything. *'Improvise, adapt, overcome'* had been a family motto of sorts for years.

Eager to show his dad the cards he'd made, Jack waited for him to finish. Without anything else to do, he grabbed Pax's hand and gave it a comforting squeeze, causing her to glance at him with an uncharacteristically timid smile, squeezing his hand in return.

The van remained like that for a while, only sounds of the rumbling breaths of the bear in the back of the van and the blizzard outside to occupy them. Jack didn't have much experience with snow, but it sounded to him like the winds were dying down. Hopefully they would be able to get out and explore soon.

~~~

WELCOME: ETHAN FARRIS

This is normally where we say "You've been chosen... once in a lifetime opportunity..." etc. Since this isn't your first time here, we're gonna skip it.

Instead, we'll say "Welcome Back!"

None of your equipment has been deemed compatible with the local system.
Adaptation to local guidelines is unnecessary.

However, all personal effects, to include all bound and non-bound monster cards, item cards, and any foreign equipment, were put in timeless storage at the moment of your previous transfer.

Note: All bound monsters remain bound until death.

To retrieve the aforementioned items from storage, hold out both hands and focus on the ACCEPT button.

ACCEPT

Oh, Lord. That was a lot to unpack in one notification

Ethan re-read it again, allowing himself to feel some relief, especially in his bunched-up shoulders. You know you're stressed when your shoulders start creating a cave out of your chest. And, of course, the fear that his lack of preparation would get them killed turned out to be a waste of brain power.

Typical.

Taking a deep breath, Ethan mentally hit ACCEPT.

Out of whatever timeless storage they'd been held, stacks of cards appeared in Ethan's hands and spilled to the floor. One stack, which looked like it was entirely Blank Monster Cards, stood tall in his hands before finally toppling over, slapping the floor between him and Jack. Huh. The system must have considered the blank sheets he'd left in the van as belonging to him and, for some reason, separated them from their sheets into individual cards.

Yikes, that probably meant that at some point Aino came all the way out here after reading his note, only to find an empty van.

Ethan glanced at Jack, whose eyes were wide as a pair of UFOs spotted by some old coot in an Arizona desert. Pax's eyebrows were raised, less in surprise and more in the soft look of relief. Bjorn sat forward, elbows on his knees, eyes drilling into Ethan.

To be fair, it was an awful lot of cards.

Slowly setting the remaining cards down, Ethan's fingers brushed against a familiar fabric. Below his hands lay his Army jacket and pants, both clean and neatly folded. Lying on the jacket was Ethan's handgun, slid into its holster, full magazine resting beside it.

"Well…" he mumbled to no one in particular, "that went better than I expected."

~~~

Wow. Just… wow. So. Many. Cards.

Bjorn watched his guests with a mixture of fascination and suspicion.

The woman, Pax, had at first looked giddy, then distraught, maybe even on the verge of tears, as she read through her notifications. The boy, Jack, wore a mischievous grin as his eyes readjusted to the dim light of the van after reading his. Definitely up to something clever, at least by the standards of young men.

Both had received cards as they accepted whatever rewards the system offered, but the amount was negligible to Bjorn. He could earn the same amount of cards within a couple weeks of hunting while scouting for signs for hordes, which happened to be exactly why he was out here in the first place.

Several days from Trace, there wasn't much other reason to go out this way. Reports of larger concentrations of monsters had been coming in from hunters north of town, so Bjorn had been sent to check it out.

But Ethan... The man analyzed his excessive amount of cards, most of which seemed to be Blanks, with a neutral expression.

There had to be over a hundred of what Bjorn considered to be the most valuable cards a Cardist could have, especially for those in The Farris Wheel. It had taken them the better part of a decade to build the community into what it was today, yet he could start a dozen more branches in other towns with the wealth of cards casually scattered on the floor in front of him. Aino would not be happy if he let this opportunity slip through his fingers.

Opening his mouth to suggest the trio come back to town with him, he was interrupted by a cacophony of roars and animalistic noises in the distance only slightly muffled by snow. That was not the sound of the blizzard, which had settled at some point in the last few minutes. No, that was the sound of something alive.

Monsters.

Plural. Hundreds, at least, based on the volume and variety of noises.

Shoving aside any thoughts of wealth, Bjorn packed up his gear and pulled Karhu back into her card to make space in the van.

"Is that what I think it is?" asked Ethan, a slight chill in his voice from the drop in temperature.

Not looking at the man as he snuffed out the candle sitting on the black box, Bjorn replied, "They must have kept moving during the blizzard. Rare ice types leading the charge, I'd guess. We'll be fine, but we need to move. Now."

"I'm sorry," the woman interrupted. "What's happening?"

The boy answered before Bjorn even registered the question.

"It's a monster horde."

58

HOLD THE HORDE

"I WANT TO HELP."

The van was a flurry of movement around Jack, more frantic than he felt was necessary. His dad, on the other hand, sat quietly sifting through his cards after telling Bjorn to take Jack and Pax back to town. He'd stay back to stall the horde, which Jack thought was strategically a poor choice.

"Not this time, Jack," his dad shook his head as they looked each other in the eyes. "Hordes are dangerous. Their entire purpose is to kill and destroy."

"But... but," Jack stuttered. "But I prepared for this. I had cards in my pack that the system adapted."

He pulled out a handful of cards from his pocket as proof. He'd been so excited to show his dad, but now the man was so focused that he wasn't listening. A knot tightened in Jack's chest, thinking that if he left with Bjorn, it'd be the last time he'd see his dad.

A hand rested on Jack's shoulder as he watched his dad step out of the van, wearing his old Army jacket. It looked... incorrect. Jack had never seen his dad as a soldier before, being too young to remember when he'd gotten out of the Army.

"I wouldn't worry about your father, Jack Farrisson," said Bjorn, the hand still on his shoulder. Jack looked up at Bjorn, only slightly taller than him. The warrior clearly admired his dad, eyes carrying a look of pride. "If I were a horde, I wouldn't want him standing in my way. Especially not when his son's safety is on the line."

The warrior gave his shoulder two encouraging pats before turning away from the van and the man preparing for battle. He didn't wait for Jack and Pax, didn't ask if they were ready. Pax quietly accepted a card his dad held out to her, then turned and followed after Bjorn. Jack turned as well, wondering again if today was the day he'd become an orphan.

~~~

"This is probably a terrible idea."

Ethan muttered to himself, glancing back for a moment to see his son walking away. His hands shook, the beginnings of panic constricting his breathing. The only thing keeping a meltdown at bay was the cold air filling his lungs, which had always seemed to help in the past. Bracing, invigorating.

Still, should he be splitting away from his son right now? Things were about to get crazy violent, sure, but even the idea of Jack being out of his sight scared the hell out of Ethan. It had taken a couple weeks on the trail for him to not feel anxious about Jack sleeping in his own separate tent.

Fortunately, or unfortunately, there wasn't time to second guess himself. If Bjorn was correct, the horde was only minutes away from the van.

Ethan's nerves turned to steel as a memory popped front

and center in his mind. He'd been at the mall with Jack and Rebecca, looking around one of those stores full of nerdy clothes and tchotchkes from cartoons, anime, and other popular TV shows and movies, when people burst into the store screaming that somebody was shooting.

For a split second, Ethan had thought the person was excited about a movie being filmed in the mall or something like that.

Quickly realizing that his family was in danger, it was like a switch flipped in his mind. There was no hesitation as he led his wife and son out the back of the store, down the outside staircase, and into the parking lot to put as many cars as possible between them and the danger.

Once they were safe, all he could think about was whoever this shooter was. How dare they cause the fear he had seen on their faces?

Never again. Not if he could help it. Tamping down his rising anger, Ethan dug out a stack of cards from one of his jacket pockets.

"Sorry guys. This is going to be a rough reunion."

59

CHANGE OF PLANS

THE GENERAL SOUND OF BATTLE, AND MONSTERS TEARING EACH OTHER apart, was not at all what Jack expected.

Admittedly, he was somewhat grateful his dad sent him away. Imagine, your first battle in a new world being against hundreds of terrifying elemental animals.

No thanks. Actually... Yes, that sounded kinda awesome. Like the perfect way to test out some of the strategies he'd been working on.

Lungs burning from keeping up with Pax and Bjorn at a constant jog, he was thankful for the months of hiking his legs had just gotten accustomed to, as well as the training his dad had let him do for PE. Krav Maga conditioning had been miserable while he was going through it. Like that time he'd gotten super nauseous after a session and had to sit against the gym wall, eating pixie sticks until his body settled.

He hadn't thought much of it at the time, but the training, rock climbing, and live action roleplaying with dulled versions of actual viking style weapons had all been to prepare Jack to thrive in Aidland. What he'd assumed were just shared special interests with his dad turned out to be way more important.

What he wasn't thankful for was his dad's overprotectiveness now. He hadn't seemed worried at all during the hike, even during the wildlife encounters. That one huge rattler near the trail on the first day had scared Jack enough that he almost tried to quit the trip right then and there. His dad had instead encouraged him to pretend it wasn't there, act non-threatening and move past out of reach of the snake, which fortunately had been several feet away. But still... rattlesnakes were scary.

So why did he give a card to Pax and not him? Had he actually heard Jack say he'd prepared some cards? It didn't seem like he had been listening at all.

"So, Pax," Jack started, breaking their silent trudge through the snow. "What card did my dad give you?"

"I'm not sure. I haven't looked at it yet," she replied, her breathing still a bit labored. "We've been in kind of a hurry."

"Knowing Mr. Farris, it was probably something obnoxious," Bjorn said without turning his head, chuckling to himself.

"Now that I think about it, your dad never mentioned in his book what the unique cards were that he didn't bind to himself," Pax turned her head just enough to make sure Jack knew she was talking to him. "Do you know what the other five were?"

"Other five?!"

Bjorn stopped abruptly and turned, Pax almost running into him.

"He already had four monsters bound to him when we met, not to mention the dragon he captured from a horde, which was at least a rare. You're telling me he had five more of those beasts, and they were all *unique?*"

Jack thought that was an interesting reaction for the warrior to have.

"Uhh... yeah?" Pax responded. "Is that not common?"

"Hah! No, it's not common. Does the word 'unique' mean something else where you come from?"

When Pax shook her head, the warrior threw his hands in the air and turned around, muttering to himself as he stomped off.

"I wonder why he never bound the others," Pax pondered aloud.

"My guess is there's a limit to the number of unique monsters a person can bind to themselves..." Jack responded, his gaze shifting off into the distance toward the disturbing sounds of the horde. There was a muffled response from the woman's direction, but he was only half aware of it.

"What are you planning?" Pax said, poking him in the side to get his attention.

Jack flinched, not realizing he'd stopped paying attention to his surroundings, causing his cheeks to burn. Oops, probably bot smart to zone out with a bunch of dangerous monsters nearby. Pax didn't follow after Bjorn, waiting for Jack to answer.

Smirking and turning his head to the side in order to hide his blush, he did his best to sound innocent.

"What makes you think I'm planning something?"

"Are you two coming, or what?"

The pair looked at Bjorn, who'd finally noticed they hadn't followed, then looked at each other. With a smirk to match Jack's, curling up one side of her mouth, Pax repeated her question. This time with a conspiratorial tone.

"So, what *are* you planning?"

60

OUCH

"CJ, BLOCK!"

A fluffy blur of white and orange slammed into a bat-like creature as Ethan ducked out of the way of its swooping attack. Experience had taught him that even an uncommon monster wouldn't survive one of Colby-Jack's body slams, so he turned his attention to survey the battle.

Little Blue, the giant parakeet, and Drake Von Scaley-Boy, the rare dragon he'd caught a decade ago, kept the skies clear, swooping this way and that. Every few seconds a flying creature fell into the mass of monsters on the ground just outside the defensive line Ethan had established. The perimeter was really just a smattering of monsters they'd managed to kill and catch before the main body of the horde arrived, but it worked well enough.

Zuko, the one-eyed unusually large house cat, hunted from amongst the trees behind enemy lines. The uncommon and rare monsters never even had a chance to defend themselves. Goldy, the cleric-like golden retriever, and Colby-Jack, the booty shaking body guard, remained near Ethan to keep him safe. Because they were bound to him, they each instinctively knew their lives depended on him staying alive.

His strategy had been simple: kill a monster and immediately capture it with one of his many blank monster cards. It had worked well initially, but became near impossible as the bulk of the horde arrived. The field was so crowded, Ethan had spent most of the battle avoiding attacks while attempting to get to fallen monsters.

While he worked out a new plan, a large white mass of beast advanced slowly into his peripherals. He turned to see Zuko dragging a white bear toward him, somehow avoiding attacks from the common monsters of the horde. The cat stopped beside him, dropping the weird grizzly/polar bear looking thing, then gave a curt nod before bounding back into the trees.

Silly cat.

Ethan couldn't help but smile. With the bear, probably a rare, they'd get a lot more breathing room.

Grabbing a blank card from the small stack he held in his left hand, he bent down and touched it to the bear. While he waited for the activate button to appear, a bark of warning sounded behind him. Before he had time to turn, something heavy hammered the back of Ethan's head. Stumbling forward, he thought it strange that he didn't feel any pain. There was a dull pressure though, which was concerning. The sounds of monsters battling faded from his ears and he grew dizzy.

Uh oh, that wasn't a good sign.

Unable to keep his legs under him, Ethan collapsed forward, face down in the dirt.

~~~

Zuko cringed at the thought of the lifeless mass of white fur he'd delivered as he stalked the back of the horde for his next target. The creepy, feral looking bear had been harder to kill than the other monsters so far. Did that mean it was a Rare?

The thought of Ethan binding himself to this thing made Zuko feel sick, his one good eye squinting to keep a hairball, and a round of nausea, at bay. Still... It was a powerful monster and they were in dire need of strong monsters at the moment.

Whatever. It wasn't his responsibility to make those decisions anyway; his role was to hunt and deliver his kills to his Cardist. Colby-Jack would take care of the rest.

~~~

Goldy did his best to relieve the swelling in Ethan's skull, but it was slow going. A whimper escaped his snout as he tried to drown out the noises of battle nearby.

'*No, not your job,*' he reminded himself. '*Let Colby-Jack take care of that.*'

Arguably, Goldy's role was more urgent, the whole battle being pointless if their Cardist died. Not only was Mr. Ethan the most bestest Cardist ever, but none of The Bound knew what would happen to them when a Cardist with unique monsters died. The group had already unanimously decided they were not interested in finding out anytime soon.

~~~

High above the horde, a pair of sharp talons released a thrashing beaver-like creature. It thrashed all the way to the ground, where it landed on three other monsters. None of them got back up.

Bullseye!

From his literal bird's eye view, Little Blue took stock of the battlefield. His role was simple: provide intel to their leader and tactician, Colby-Jack, while picking apart any packs of monsters working together. Fortunately for the giant parakeet, most wild monsters didn't have any range attacks, leaving him free to scout and deal with the few remaining flyers of the horde.

Time to report.

Pulling his wings into his body, Little Blue dove directly toward the center of their battle line, then spread them out again to pull at the air for a quick stop directly beside Colby-Jack. The parakeet gave two short chirps and a trill before taking back to the sky.

It was going to be a long day.

~~~

Ouch!

Drake Von Scaley-Boy used his long tail to smack away another monster that had reached his domed wings. Why did the overgrown feathery house pet get to fly free, while he, a powerful and vicious dragon, was put on shield duty?

The fight had been going well until their Cardist got himself bonked on the head like a hammer to an anvil. The dragon longed to be set loose to rip apart the fools who dared to challenge him and his Cardist. Instead, he was stuck in his role as a living shield, keeping back any wretched creature that found its way through their front line.

It was an important role, protecting their Cardist, even if it was embarrassing. What really frustrated him was that now he was going to lose a bet with his blue feathered rival, that a Rare dragon could kill more than that precious snowflake of a house pet. Unique bird, his scaly red backside! He had no way to prove it, but Drake suspected the small she-wolf-in-charge was interfering on purpose, the little cheat was probably in on the bet somehow.

Sparing a glance at the she-wolf leading the captured commons and uncommons, a shiver ran up Drake's scaled back as he realized Colby-Jack was staring at him. To openly accuse the she-wolf of cheating was a death sentence.

That cute bundle of fur was terrifying.

6I

REINFORCEMENTS

"He's surrounded."

No way, thanks Mr. Obvious! Jack frowned at Bjorn's observation as he scanned the field in front of them. The snow had turned to slush and the meadow was filled to the brim with monsters, many of them tall enough to block his line of sight. From their position within the nearby trees, he could really only make out an impossibly large parakeet, as big as a teenage boy, flying above the center of the battle.

If nothing else, the bird's presence confirmed his dad was alive.

Still... it was strange that none of the monsters broke off to continue on toward the town. It's like they found a person and became hyper focused on him until he was dead.

"How many do you think there are?" Jack asked Bjorn, whose eyes analyzed a nearby tree.

"Not sure. A typical horde is formed by a few hundred monsters. This one—" he gestured at the field, then focused back at the tree, "is hard to gauge. I've never seen a horde attack a single person before. Their behavior is strange."

Before Jack could ask a follow up question, Bjorn was moving toward the tree, staying crouched and out of sight.

"What's he doing?" Pax whispered beside him, a card clutched firmly in her hand, hard enough that her knuckles had gone white.

The man was a scout, so it was safe to assume he was looking for a better view. Information is power and all that jazz. It didn't seem helpful to tell her any of that though. She was just scared and unsure of what to do.

"He'll be right back." Jack said instead, then grabbed one of her hands and did his best impression of his dad's reassuring expressions.

Sure enough, the warrior scampered up the tree, stayed long enough to grimace, then hurried back down. Barely rustled a leaf. Wow, he was good.

"How's it look? Does my dad need help?"

"I couldn't even see him. His companions are still fighting, but his dragon is on the ground, using its body and wings to shield something like a dome. I didn't see the golden dog with the healing abilities, so I'm guessing your dad is wounded and recovering under the dragon," the warrior sighed. "I'm not sure what we should do. He told me to keep you safe, but he also needs help."

Jack's cheeks flushed, anger welling up in his chest. Anger at so many things. The monsters for attacking, himself for not staying back to help, and his dad for sending him away in the first place. Regardless of where the anger stemmed from, it needed an outlet. Fortunately there was a screeching mass of creatures that would do nicely.

Turning to Pax, fire in his eyes, Jack held out his hand.

"Let me see the card my dad gave you."

Like a piece of driftwood in the middle of an ocean, she clung to that card.

Wow, Pax is not great in an emergency.

"Look, I'll give it back. I have a plan, but I need to know what we're working with."

Reluctantly, she loosened her grip on the card and let him take it. Looking it over for a few seconds, Jack smiled and handed it back.

"Activate that card. Bind it to you when the prompt comes up." He turned to Bjorn, speaking before the man had an opportunity to stop him. "We're gonna need enough power to break through the horde and get to my dad. Our best bet is the giant stack of blank cards, which are probably with him under the dragon."

The warrior listened, a grin building as Jack laid out his plan. Bjorn pulled his sword from its sheath, which was quieter than in the movies he'd seen. A large red tinged bear appeared behind the man.

"Hell yeah, kid. I like your style."

62

SOUNDS UNLIKE SILENCE

IT WAS A COMMON TRAIT AMONG MEN TO OVERESTIMATE THEIR OWN capabilities, to think that they don't need help.

That was how Ethan consoled himself as he lay huddled under the dragon's wings. If he was being honest with himself, he hadn't really thought through staying to fight an entire horde alone. Jack said he'd prepared for this to happen, but it hadn't clicked in Ethan's brain right away. If he'd stopped to think for even a second, he would have realized that likely meant Jack had at least one unique monster card in his pack during the system adaptation.

His son could have helped. Wanted to help, even.

Ethan generally considered himself to be clever, but Jack was a real strategist. Every strategy game they played together had been brutal more the moment Jack had turned ten. Chess, Risk, Monopoly, Stratego and other similar board games had become more and more difficult to win. He'd quickly learned to dominate video games, whether they were multiplayer first person shooters like Counter-Strike and Call of Duty, or single player tactical games like Fire Emblem and Battle Brothers.

Anything that required quick thinking or pattern recognition, really.

The boy was a natural.

So why had Ethan sent him off with Bjorn and Pax? Fear, probably. These things usually boiled down to fear. He wasn't sure he could handle losing his son after losing his wife. Fathers aren't meant to bury sons. That's backwards. But, in sending him away, he'd put him at risk of losing both parents. Now Ethan wished he'd kept him close, so they could win or lose together.

A frustrated growl rumbled in his throat. Stupid! Stupid dad move, Ethan!

He smacked an open palm into his forehead, immediately remembering the reason he was lying down instead of fighting. A wave of nausea crashed over him as he held back the urge to vomit. The feeling was miserable, but it did have the benefit of getting him out of his catastrophizing spiral.

This wasn't where he would die. But to survive, he needed a plan.

Keeping his eyes closed, he drew his attention to the overwhelming sounds on the other side of his leathery panic room. What did he have available that he could make use of? Pockets full of cards. Most were blanks, which would be effective if some stupid monkey thing hadn't thrown a rock at him. What item cards did he have? He should look through those.

As he undid the velcro for the pocket that held his item cards, the sounds outside suddenly changed. The yips, roars, and screeches of the wild monsters moved away from his hiding spot.

A roar ripped through the noise, followed by the strangest howl Ethan had ever heard, more like a dozen howls all perfectly synced together. Bjorn's bear? That didn't seem right, it was just a fire type bear. Had they come back for him? But what did that howl come from? One of Jack's cards?

His thoughts remained muddled, even as the nausea settled.

Goldy whimpered as Ethan wiggled his way toward a tiny opening in the wings, ears assaulted by what could only be described as two eighteen-wheeled trucks plowing through a road filled with hundreds of bodies. It was disgusting and brought the taste of acid up from his throat. He settled back down, deciding it'd be better to let Goldy's healing do its thing.

The grizzly noises grew louder as they drew closer, then came to an abrupt halt as the sounds of the horde took back over. As Ethan considered what to do next, one of the dragon's wings slid aside, allowing a blurry figure into the space. It was difficult to look at, causing some pain in his eyes, until the blur fell away to reveal a Jack crouched in front of him with a small multicolored lizard holding tight to his shoulder.

"Hey, dad," the boy said, a wide grin on his face.

"Hey, Jack."

Oof. It even hurt to talk. Ethan gestured at the lizard, a questioning look on his face.

"Oh, this is Pedro. He's a chameleon."

Pedro stuck his tongue out an almost imperceptible amount, then withdrew it. Interesting way to say hello.

Jack looked Ethan over, stopping for a moment at Goldy, then back again until they made eye contact. Feeling a complete lack of energy to explain what happened, he tapped the back of his head lightly, then gave his son a thumbs up. The boy nodded in return.

"Alright, well we can take it from here. Zuko has a bunch of monsters lined up, so I'll need your blank cards. Also, here —"

Jack handed him a card. "— Give this to Goldy. It should help get you on your feet.

Ethan took the card, at the same time handed one back to his son.

"Oh, is this a pizzly? Cool."

"Pizzly?" Ethan managed to grunt.

"Yeah, aggressive hybrid of a polar bear and a grizzly bear."

"Ahh."

Barely managing a nod, Ethan tapped the pockets that held his blank monster cards. Without hesitation, Jack fished out a deck's worth. With another nauseating flutter, the boy and lizard switched back to their translucent blurry form, then left the safety of the dragon.

Alone again, Ethan tried to wrap his head around what was happening, but found it difficult to think through a building headache. No more help in the fight, he looked over the card his son handed him.

Unique Item Card: Power Up

Permanently increase efficiency of one bound monster's ability by a twenty to forty percent.
NOTE: Effectiveness determined by the target monster's rarity.

Single Use Card. Hold to the bound monster's card to active.

Did Jack say to use it on Goldy? Ahh, his healing ability; of course.

"Clever boy," Ethan gestured for Goldy to move closer. He needed to get back out there to help his son.

63

DOG, BEAR, WHAT'S THE DIFFERENCE?

"THAT... IS A BIG DOG."

Sitting beside Karhu, the rather large flame bear, was a dog of almost the same height and width. Its face kind of looked like a bear, covered with smooth black fur, while the rest of its body was a mismatch of natural toned fluffy, yet coarse, fur. Bjorn gawked at it. The only thing he could think to compare it to was a dire wolf... but this was clearly not a wolf.

Spread around the meadow were hundreds of corpses, monsters they hadn't been able to capture before their timers ran out. The area was blissfully silent, in a way Bjorn had only experienced after an excessive amount of death had occurred. Even then, there were usually sounds of people barely clinging to life or the wails of loved ones tending to their dead.

Off to the right, Ethan and Jack sat side by side talking quietly to each other. The little orange and white dog sat in front of them, watching for danger, occasionally stealing a curious glance at the large bear dog. The third dog lay beside Ethan with its head in his lap, its golden fur looking especially wavy and beautiful for some reason. In Jack's lap was a lizard, no bigger than Bjorn's hand, who seemed to change colors as the boy stroked its back.

Scanning the area, Bjorn shook his head. The day had not gone at all how he'd expected.

Stopping at the metal carriage had meant to be a time to rest before returning with his scouting report. Now... so strange. How had a simple scouting mission turned into four people destroying an entire medium sized horde?

Glancing again at the father and son, all of their cards hidden from view, he wondered how many monsters they'd caught. He thought again of the people that could be helped with that wealth of cards. Orphans, like him, who could have a real chance at life.

"Would you like to pet him?"

"Huh?"

Bjorn realized he had been staring at the large bear-dog. Pax was scratching behind one of its ears, looking at him with a smirk.

"Would you like to pet him?" she repeated.

"Uhh, yeah. Sure," Bjorn stammered, then composed himself. "What's his name?"

He stepped forward, keeping a wary eye on Pax. She was more calm and confident than he had seen since meeting her. A drastic change. Perhaps she'd been out of sorts and made a poor first impression. He'd need to observe her more closely.

"His name is Big Ben," she replied as he arrived at the bear-dog.

That wasn't a surprise. It was common for Cardists to add adjectives like "big" to their companion's name. Like Aino's bird companion, Big Red. Bjorn casually scratched where the dog's jaw and neck met, both palms facing up. Pax's expression softened somewhat as the creature grumbled with pleasure in an odd twelve toned voice.

"How'd you know he'd like that?"

"I didn't really think about it," he shrugged, continuing to scratch. "This is what Karhu likes, so I just kinda... did it."

Seeing her smile at that, he felt a light flutter in his chest. Wow, she was really pretty. How had he not noticed before? Huh. After a minute of scratches, an annoyed grunt sounded from Karhu.

"Come here, Mama Bear," Bjorn chuckled. "You're next."

64

A FIRST

"Well, that was certainly one way to go about it."

The Father and Son watched the four Cardists amidst a sea of crushed, burnt, ripped, torn, and otherwise mutilated bodies of monsters. The Father scratched at the hair of his chin for a moment. No bellowing laughter, as there often was, but neither was there any sign of anger in his eyes.

"The boy has a keen strategic mind," the Son remarked, nodding toward Jack.

They'd both been impressed with the boy's custom chameleon card and how he'd made use of it. Slinking through the fray to capture the stronger monsters Ethan's cat, Zuko, had been singling out was a strategy they had not seen before. It was considerably more efficient use of time than the cat dragging each one back into their defensive circle.

Every once in a while the boy would appear beside Pax and drop a stack of cards before disappearing back into the horde. From what The Son could tell, the group only activated uncommon monsters, keeping the rares in reserve. No point binding monsters to yourself for the sake of a single battle unless it was absolutely necessary.

Clever. Long-sighted.

"A warlord in the making, that one," replied the Father.

The Son nodded. It didn't happen often with the Alternates, but he felt an immense amount of respect for the father-son duo. If only there was a way to... hmm... actually, it was technically possible, wasn't it? But should he? Just because he *could*, didn't mean he *should*.

There could be unexpected consequences, but there was always some risk when Alternates were involved.

"Father, this was a first in Aidland. Will they be rewarded?"

"Hmm? Oh, yes," he waved a dismissive hand, turning his attention to Alternate Table #444. "The System is working on it, though I get the impression you have something specific in mind."

His Father knew him well.

The Son understood they still had other Alternates vying for their attention, but these ones had grown on him. The future looked more hopeful with those two involved, making him reluctant to move onto the next task.

He hesitated for a moment, taking one last look at the father and son sitting together. The gamble may not work out in the long run, but it was worth a shot. He'd only ever put in a handful of requests with The System, each time being certain it would be worth the risk.

This was one of those times.

65

UPGRADE

"How am I both overpowered and incredibly frail?"

A slight tremor remained in Ethan's hands as Goldy's healing ability spread warmth across his body. The blizzard had stopped, but trampled snow covered everywhere outside the ring of death, so there was still a decent chill in the air.

"I'm sorry I sent you away," Ethan dropped his chin to his chest, heart aching with regret, then glanced over at Jack. A knot of pride stuck in his throat, overshadowing the ache. "Thank you for coming back for me. You know, you're a natural at this."

"I know it," Jack blushed. "To be fair, I've spent a lot of time thinking about it."

The chameleon sitting in Jack's lap rumbled a slight purring sound as the boy continued to stroke its leathery skin. They sat like that for a few minutes, enjoying the silence together.

A squeal of delight broke the serene moment as Pax jumped up and down beside her new massive dog companion.

Ethan smiled as he remembered drawing out that card a

decade earlier. It was based on one of the dogs his family had when he was a little boy, a German Shepherd/Chow Chow mix who howled whenever his dad played a harmonica. The dog's twelve tone howl had been terrifying to the horde and would have been to Ethan as well if it hadn't held so much nostalgia.

"Guys, I finished a bunch of quests!" shouted Pax, waving around a handful of reward cards and packs. "I even beat a hidden quest and got a unique card!"

A unique reward? That was new.

Ethan looked down at Jack, whose eyes were already glazed over. Curious if he'd completed a hidden quest too, he pulled up his notifications.

The first couple were for the standard kill and capture quests. He'd already done several iterations of those, so he wouldn't get as many rewards as Pax or Jack would. The last notification was not at all what he'd expected.

<u>Hidden Quest: For the Horde!</u>

Requirement: Destroy an entire horde as part of a group with five or less members (bound and unbound monsters not included in the count)

Reward: 1x Legendary Monster Evolution Card
Progress: Complete

Congratulations!

You've completed the Hidden Quest: For the Horde!

NOTE: This quest has never been completed in Aidland. Your reward will be upgraded from Legendary to Unique quality.

To receive your reward, hold out your hand and focus on the ACCEPT button.

ACCEPT

Very interesting...

The wheels in Ethan's mind turned as he reread the text. How could he make the best use of a Unique Monster Evolution Card?

An idea began to form, something he'd need help to make happen. Something Aino and Havard would probably be interested in. Ooooo, now he was feeling excited for the future! They should get going and get to town!

Ethan stood to his feet, steadying himself for a moment as Goldy's warmth dissipated. He turned to Bjorn, intending on telling him they should get going. Instead, he paused as a single card appeared in Bjorn's hand.

The young warrior gaped for a full fifteen seconds before looking up at the others. His eyes searched theirs as though he was waking up from a dream, not sure what was real. Ethan smiled as he looked around the group, seeing the excitement in each of their faces.

"Maybe we should talk through how to go about using these cards while we head back toward Trace," he suggested.

"I have a few ideas," came the mischievous voice of his son, who was standing up beside him.

"Hah! You're always ready, aren't you?"

66

Q'S AND A'S

"How are the preparations going?"

Across the desk from where Aino sat, Captain Havard eyes never strayed from the stack of papers he was studying. She scratched the ear of the large tan wolf lying beside her as she considered his question. The fact that Havard's wolf preferred to sit with her said a lot about how close the pair had become over the years, spending more and more time together as they developed The Farris Wheel.

She had to admit, she was quite fond of Havard. He was steadfast, reliable, had a calming presence, and was relatively easy on the eyes. But most of all, he made her feel part of a team.

"Aino?"

As she looked up, she realized his gaze no longer on the papers, instead observing her. Reading her. Did he know what was on her mind? Possibly, but he would never assume. He'd wait for her to share.

"How come you've never asked me to marry you?" she asked, still scratching the wolf's ear.

Oof, where did that come from? Judging by the slight turn of his head, like a curious wolf, he also didn't know where it came from. But was it really out of nowhere? Her dad visited recently and there was no way he hadn't tried to convince Havard to propose. 'Make an honest woman of her.' A man in his position was exactly what her father looked for in potential husbands for his daughters.

So why hadn't Havard asked?

"Is that something you want?" he replied. "My understanding was that marriage is not something you're interested in. You've outright stated it on at least five occasions."

"That's true," she chuckled, "I'm just curious why you've never asked."

Havard's expression softened in a way that would only be detectable by someone who knew him well. His head cocked slightly to the other side, like a dog hoping for a bite of whatever scrap of food you were holding.

"Did I not just explain why I haven't?"

A good man. More proof. Doesn't say more than he needs to. Said what he meant and meant what he said. Aino admired him even more as he went back to studying his papers, as though the conversation hadn't put him off at all. Like it'd never happened. Just another Tuesday.

Actually, what day was it? She'd lost track of the original question. Oh, right, the incoming horde.

"Well then, to answer *your* question," she started, deciding to follow his lead and move on, "preparations are going as well as they can without a scouting report. Standard defense measures, with specialists on reserve ready to mobilize once we know what we're dealing with."

"Hmm," Havard sat back from his desk, looking up to the ceiling in thought. "Bjorn doesn't usually take this long. He should have been back already, right? Any reason to be concerned?"

"Well, the blizzard may have slowed him down a bit, though Karhu's fire would mitigate much of the danger," she continued to scratch behind the wolf's ear, not worried. "I'm sure we'll hear from him soon."

Havard nodded. They sat in comfortable silence for a few minutes, each lost down their own personal thought trail, when a knock at the door snapped them back to reality.

"Come in," Havard called.

The door opened to reveal one of his lieutenants, a former orphan like Bjorn, who also happened to be a member of The Farris Wheel.

"Ma'am," he nodded to Aino, then to Havard, "Sir."

"Hey Nils," she replied. "What can we help you with?"

Having grown used to her and the captain working together, it didn't seem to bother him that she'd been the one to speak first.

"Our scout has just returned from the north."

"Bjorn is back?" Havard asked.

"Yes sir."

"Good. Have him report here. We need to know what we're dealing with."

The lieutenant hesitated, not immediately saying he'd carry out the order. That was odd for Nils, who Aino knew to be diligent in his work, annoyingly so at times.

"What's the problem, Nils?" Havard asked, coming to the same conclusion.

"Well, that's the thing sir. If Bjorn is to be believed, there is no problem."

"As in, the horde has changed direction? Do we need to warn Modes?"

"No sir. As in, the horde has been destroyed."

"Destroyed?" Taking longer to process that than she'd care to admit, Aino simply stared at the lieutenant. "Entirely? No monsters heading this way?"

The lieutenant nodded.

"If they are to be believed, yes."

"They?" Aino's eyes narrowed. "Who is 'they'?"

"Bjorn arrived with three strangers, or at least I've never seen them before. A young boy of apprenticing age, a woman maybe a little older than Bjorn, and a man roughly the captain's age."

"Did these three have any active monsters with them?" Aino glanced at Havard, curious if he was following her train of thought. "Was there a small, orange and white dog with them?"

"Yes ma'am," confusion clouded the lieutenant's face, "How did you know that?"

"It's Ethan," she stated, sitting heavily back into her chair, struggling to believe her own words. "He's back."

"So it seems," replied a serious looking Havard. "And he's brought some friends. Friends strong enough to destroy an entire horde."

67

OVER A PINT

"We tell you that the people of Trace are in your debt, that you could basically ask anything of us, and you respond with... wanting to start a boot camp?"

"Basic Cardist Training, or BCT if you prefer," the man nodded, taking a drink from his cup of mead.

"Okay... and you want us to help?" Aino shouldn't be surprised by any of this, and yet she was. "But you just got here."

Aino took in the strangeness surrounding the new arrivals as Uncle Anker brought over a tray filled with pints of mead. Bjorn had taken the young woman off for a tour of the town, so there was a pint for Aino, Havard, Ethan, and even the boy, whose eyes went wide and jerked over to Ethan, as if to say "Can I?"

"Go ahead, Jack. You earned it," he chuckled.

The boy immediately chugging the mead with gusto, wincing at the bittersweet taste.

They were an interesting trio. The woman was at least a decade younger than Ethan, but they didn't seem to be more than friends. If the boy was his son, and this wasn't his wife, something must have happened to her.

Eyeing Ethan closely, she could see how life had worn him down, yet he retained some of that optimistic relentlessness she remembered. His skin showed a considerable number of new scars, but there hadn't been even a hint of his old limp when they walked together to the tavern.

With an internal sigh, she refocused her attention back to his training idea. There'd be plenty of time to catch up later, she supposed, considering the threat of a horde had vanished. The group had done the town a huge service, the least she could do was humor the man.

"The Farris Wheel already kind of does what you're talking about, but with a focus on community and learning a trade, rather than creating battle ready soldiers. I admit though, both are essential."

"I find the idea agreeable," added Havard, to her surprise. "We do something similar with the town guards, but only with martial skills. We don't have dedicated Cardist training."

"But what would that even look like?"

She wasn't against the idea, but she was having a hard time imagining the difference between this "BCT" and The Farris Wheel, a community she'd spent years building. There'd be hell to pay if this made all her work worthless. Why not just add a new Cardist training branch to The Farris Wheel?

"The idea is based on my personal military experience. Ten weeks of training split into three phases: Red, White, and Blue.

"Red Phase is all about breaking the recruit down physically and mentally, which will allow us to re-create a more solid foundation.

"White Phase is about building them back up with the perspectives and mentalities that an effective Cardist needs. At that point we could lend them a common monster card to practice with while they learn self-defense and everything we know about how the cards work.

"Blue Phase would focus on preparing them for whatever they will do next, whether that's The Farris Wheel, the town guard, or whatever else they want to do."

With a more clear vision of the idea in her mind, that in would precede joining The Farris Wheel or the town guard, Aino had to admit it be a great boon to have new members already be trained and capable Cardists. Havard remained silent, so it was safe to assume he was in the same boat. The idea was solid, no use denying that, and it could help the entire town prosper.

They could use it as a test run for people that are hesitant about committing to a community like The Farris Wheel. Give people a taste of being a Cardist — not just the monetary value of cards — without making huge life changes in the process. Everyone around the table took a drink while they thought it over.

"How would this be funded?" she asked. "We're doing well, but not well enough to make it available for free."

"Oh... uhhh," Ethan scratched the back of his neck, "I just figured I'd pay for it."

"Ethan..." she sighed. sweet, innocent Ethan. "I remember and am thankful for your obnoxious generosity, but if we're going to do this, we need to do it right. It needs to be self-sustaining. What if you were to die or vanish again? It would fall apart within months if we don't set it up to succeed on its own."

"Just offer to sell them cards after they've graduated," everyone turned to look at Jack, who was staring hard at a point on the table, his cheeks flushed red. "Trainees will become attached to the monsters they train with, especially if we let them pick, and will be willing to pay to keep them. If they are poor locals who can't afford a common card, they'd probably be willing to join The Farris Wheel or the Town Guard to pay for it. Win, win, win."

"The lad makes a good point," Havard admitted. "Simple. Effective."

"Good idea, Jack!" Ethan cheered as he smacked Jack in the center of his back, causing the boy to turn and vomit. Moving his boots just enough to avoid the mess, the man laughed.

"He takes after his mother!"

PART THREE

"To improve is to change; to be perfect is to change often."
- Winston Churchill

~~~

"Some people don't like change, but you need to embrace change if the alternative is disaster."
- Elon Musk

~~~

"Keep the change, ya filthy animal."
- Angels with Dirty Faces, as seen in Home Alone

68

READINESS EXERCISE

"They came out of nowhere sir. We're surrounded, but have it well in hand."

Brother Thomas analyzed their situation. As the lead instructor for this group of trainees, their safety was his responsibility. He was, however, also assigned as observer and was not meant to intervene unless absolutely necessary.

Having spent the better part of a decade as a member of The Farris Wheel, he'd fought plenty of monsters, especially standing with others against hordes. This was different. They were out in the open, exposed and surrounded. Most of the trainees were teenagers without any experience beyond their lessons at the Basic Cardist Training course.

His instinct was to protect the students, but ultimately his worry was for nothing. They'd spent the last several weeks learning about monsters, getting comfortable around their companions. Not only that, they spent time fighting monsters, both during group hunts and regular sparring sessions against their peers. Each student knew their own capabilities and that of their assigned teams.

Which was why, at that moment, there were monster bodies scattered beyond the encircled recruits, spears held facing outward like the quills of a porcupine.

Brother Thomas had been impressed by how quickly they'd adapted to being attacked. Sure, there was an initial hesitation, but the young woman currently reporting to him, Mette, had immediately began barking orders and simple commands for battle formations. The individual wedge formations arranged themselves based on melee or ranged capabilities.

They had meant for this to be a training exercise, learning how to live outside the safety of walled towns, not as a full test of their development. He had to hand it to them, they were handling it like professionals.

"Very good, Mette. You've done well. Let me know if you need assistance. Otherwise, I'll continue as observer."

She nodded, already shouting to a nearby recruit holding a bow to keep the flyers from entering the perimeter.

Confident he wouldn't be needed right away, Brother Thomas activated his own monster card. Appearing at his right shoulder was a bumble bee the size of a fully grown watermelon.

"Brother Bee, see if you can't bring me a few monsters worth catching."

The bee gave two lackadaisical buzzes before lumbering off toward the perimeter. The trainees were all familiar with their instructor's companion, so Brother Thomas wasn't concerned about letting him buzz around the battle. This was as good a time as any to make use of the Blank Monster Cards Mr. Farris had given him before they'd set out into the woods.

A horde could be both dangerous and profitable, especially

with the commission he earned for each monster caught and sold using Mr. Farris' cards. If he could turn a profit from this horde, maybe he and Anker could finally afford to spend some time perfecting their Monster Mead recipe.

69

FIRST CLASS - GRADUATION

Shouts and whistles rang over the crowd gathered outside the northern gate of Trace.

From the nearest tree-line an epic display of elements shot into the air. The light and heat from a hidden dragon's flame collided with a misty shower from another instructor's water type tortoise, creating a mixture of different colored steam, like a contained rainbow, blocking the crowd from seeing those gathered on the other side of the mist.

Battle drums echoed from amongst the trees as a synchronized line of graduates marched through the mist toward their friends and families.

A small child near the front of the crowd was the first to see them and shouted, clapping her hands as she jumped up and down in excitement. As though the little girl opened a valve in a dam, the crowd went wild, cheering as the graduates drew closer. Names were shouted, drowned out by general whoops and hollers.

The graduating class split in half as they reached the speaker's platform, coming back into formation on the other side, like a river around a boulder. The drums came to an abrupt halt as the two dozen fresh graduates stopped in front of the platform, facing the crowd.

Looking over the graduates from atop the platform, Ethan's chest welled up with a strange mixture of pride and loss. Pride at the accomplishment of those standing before him, as well as everyone who'd made it possible. Loss at knowing there would never be another first class to graduate. If he was honest with himself, he was also grieving his own Army Basic Combat Training graduation. He'd never felt more like he belonged than that day, standing beside others who'd done something ninety-nine percent of the population would never dream of doing.

A cough sounded from beside him on the platform, as well as a simultaneous boof from Colby-Jack to his left, reminding Ethan it was time to address the crowd.

The gathered crowd went silent as the drums stopped, other than a few children giggling and one random dude whistling in the back. Ethan looked over those gathered, drawing inspiration from their faces.

One particularly familiar face stood out, a sergeant holding a long-haired green cat, one that he'd purchased in the market when Ethan had first come to Aidland. The man's eyes were ringed with red, barely holding back tears as he turned his eyes from one of the teenage girls within the line of graduates. Ethan met eyes with the man and nodded before speaking.

"People of Trace," he addressed the crowd. "Thank you for coming out to greet your returning family and friends. I know it's never easy sending off loved ones, especially when there's a lot of work to be done at home this time of year—" a smattering of chuckles came from some of the gathered families, "—But it was worth it. You should know, they aren't the same people they were when you last saw them, almost four months ago. A couple weeks of travel and a few months of intense training has helped them grow in ways that are hard to explain.

"They've become more physically and mentally resilient, quite an accomplishment for an already resilient town," a round of cheers broke from a group of the Town Guard, which brought a smile to Ethan's face. "They've learned the ins and outs of being a Cardist. They've also learned basic self-defense, which will help them regardless of what life they decide to live. More importantly, they learned to work together, melding the powers of their companions in unexpected ways. You may be surprised to learn that the graduates went on several monster hunts up north and even defeated a small horde that ambushed them, allowing every graduate to complete several quests."

Gasps broke from the crowd, which turned to cheers. Whether it was excitement that their loved ones earned cards or the lessened danger of another horde, Ethan didn't know. After a moment, he held up his hands to quiet the cheering.

"As I'm sure many of you know, each graduate was given a common monster card to train with. Because it's not sustainable for us to let them keep the cards for free, each new Cardist has been given a few options to pay us back for their training and new companions. Some have already agreed to join The Farris Wheel, led by Aino," Ethan gestured to the woman standing beside him, then to the Captain standing beside her, "or the Town Guard, led by Captain Havard. Whatever they've decided to do, it will be to the benefit of the community.

"Before we release them back to you, we at the BCT have decided that, because this was our first official class, we wanted to do something special. Each graduate will receive an extra gift. Jack, if you would please start passing them out. Graduates, wait to open them until I give the go ahead."

From the side of the platform, Jack and two other instructors moved down the line, shaking each graduate's hand and giving them a single card wrapped similar to how The System rewarded packs of cards.

"Ethan, what are you doing?" whispered Aino, confusion in her voice as they waited for the gifts to be passed out. "You didn't tell us about this."

"It wouldn't be a very good surprise if we'd told you about it," he whispered in reply, a smirk on his face. "Also, how's my Aidish? Is it coming across naturally?"

Aino only shook her head, obviously thrown off by his continued obnoxious way of doing things. She looked at Havard, seemingly pleading for his help. The captain instead just nodded as he followed the progress down the line of graduates.

"Your grasp of the language is impressive, honestly," he said, Aino sighing beside him. "The crowd doesn't seem to have any trouble understanding."

"Nice," Ethan did a mental fist pump and turned his attention back to the gathered people as Jack handed out the last card.

"What each Cardist has been given is called a 'Monster Upgrade Card'," gasps and murmurs came from the crowd, many wouldn't have much experience with upgrade cards. Aino just shook her head and Havard chuckled. Once the noise to lessened, Ethan continued. "This card will increase their common monster to uncommon, or uncommon to rare for those that may have already upgraded their monsters during training."

A few graduates started turning to look at him in disbelief, but caught themselves and stayed facing forward. A few shouts and questions from the crowd spoke the disbelief for them. Many immediately understood the wealth being gifted to their loved ones, potentially benefiting their families for generations.

"This is a gift for those who decided to trust us and be a part of our first class. In no way will it be added to any debt they may already owe, since this is from the BCT and not The Farris Wheel or the Town Guard."

Jack smiled up at Ethan as half of the crowd went ballistic, the other half having more of a slack-jawed silent expression. Quieting them down again, mostly, Ethan continued.

"We have one more card to give out," he raised his voice to cut through the excited chatter. It was honestly impressive that the graduates were keeping their composure through this. "About a week ago, we surveyed each graduate to see who they believed should be considered 'Distinguished Honor Graduate'. The person they respected most during training and who was most crucial during our monster hunts."

The crowd grew silent in anticipation, hoping to hear their loved ones' names.

"Sergeant Bori, please step forward."

Those near the sergeant turned to look at him as he set down the green cat and stepped forward. He looked up at Ethan, a look of hope on his face.

"Mette, daughter of Bori, Sergeant of the Town Guard, has earned the respect of her fellow recruits and of her instructors. Though she was one of the younger recruits, Mette and her companion were the main reason the group survived when they were unexpectedly attacked during a monster hunt. Because of this, she has earned an additional upgrade card.

Sergeant, we thought it fitting for you to be the one to present it to her."

Jack walked up to the sergeant and handed him a card, shook his hand, then ran back to his position beside the platform. The sergeant no longer held back his tears, marching straight to his daughter and embracing her in a massive hug.

Ethan had to look away to keep himself from breaking into tears as well, causing him to notice a flashing symbol in his peripherals. He decided to ignore it and turned to address the rest of the crowd. There'd be time for notifications later.

"Ladies and gentlemen, boys and girls, put your hands together for Aidland's first graduating class of Basic Cardist Training!"

70

A YEAR OF PROGRESS

THE YEAR THAT FOLLOWED THEIR ARRIVAL FLEW BY.

It had to be one of the fastest and busiest years Ethan had ever experienced, at times feeling like a snail's pace. Especially the tedious administrative work. Boring stuff was still boring, after all. But they finally did it; the Basic Cardist Training was up and running.

Months had been spent planning and creating a curriculum, while simultaneously cleaning up the old abandoned town north of Trace. Training with potentially destructive monsters seemed like something to keep away from more populated areas.

Within that time, Pax and Bjorn spent a lot of time together, scouting and clearing the area. They were married before the BCT really started to take shape.

No one was surprised.

Ethan was happy to see her find somewhere she felt she belonged, though it was a bummer how little they saw of each other. Everyone around him seemed to be finding their place in the world, or at least someone to share it with.

Sure, there had been a few people who'd tried to court Ethan throughout the year. There had been a couple fun flings, he just wasn't interested enough to go beyond that. He wasn't afraid of remarrying, though Jack teased him about it relentlessly, and he felt he'd already gotten through the worst of his grief.

Still, he felt a bit empty. Instead of dealing with it directly, Ethan put his focus and energy into creating the new training program.

While Aino and Havard spread the word that they'd be opening by summer, Jack helped Ethan with the curriculum. Several drafts were thrown out before they were confident enough to start some small trial runs, when they'd had the flexibility to make edits before the first official cycle of recruits. Ideas they thought would be great ended up being overcomplicated for people who had zero experience with cards, while the simplest training tools turned out to be the most effective.

Keep it simple, smartypants.

By the end of that first year, Ethan had become mostly fluent in Aidish and had only burned through the monsters he'd caught during the last horde. The goal of creating a self-sustaining organization left him with about a hundred or so Blank Monster Cards to work with. As interest in the program grew, he'd even hired on veteran cardists from Trace and some of the trial run students to lead more cycles.

If he wanted to, he could walk away and be confident that it would continue to succeed. Probably a good thing too, because he'd become unbearably restless.

Though he enjoyed the area, not to mention his new friends and colleagues, Ethan felt an itch in his mind and legs. An itch that only ever subsided when he was on the move, like during their hike of the Pacific Crest Trail. It was fortunate timing, then, that he had received quest notifications during their first graduation ceremony.

Hidden Quest: A Company of Belonging

Requirement: Using the wealth and experience you've been blessed with, create a place that draws people together and encourages community.
Reward: A new, personalized quest.

Progress: Complete

Reward received automatically. See notification for details.

~

Personalized Quest: Home, Home on the Road

Requirements: Walk/Travel to the southernmost tip of Aidland, where the idea of opening a branch of the Basic Cardist Training would likely be well received.

Progress: 0/3,533 Miles

Reward: Besides spending more time on the road with your son? It's a surprise, but we promise it'll be worth it.

"Dad, you okay?"

Ethan turned to see his son standing next to their backpacks, wearing a mix of modern and Aidish styles of clothing.

Little Pedro, still perched on the boy's shoulder, also had a concerned look on its face.

What a strange situation he found himself in. His son and a sentient chameleon both being concerned for his well being.

It had actually been Jack who first suggested it was time for them to go somewhere new, before Ethan had a chance to mention his new quest. The boy had struggled to make friends his own age in the area and wanted to see what the rest of Aidland was like.

Like father, like son.

"Yeah, I'm good," he finally replied.

"Hi Good, I'm Ready," the boy said in a decent Aidish accent, chuckling to himself.

Could a dad ever be more proud of his son?

"Boof!"

"We all know you're ready," Ethan bent into a squat and scratched Colby-Jack behind both ears. "You're the goodest girl ever!"

The dog responded with a satisfied grunt, then turned and walked out the door, booty sashaying as she went.

71

BOOKS-A-DOZEN

"The fact that there's even coffee in a fantasy world continues to amaze me."

"A good book and a cup of coffee transcends worlds. Am I right or am I right?"

The cafe portion of the book store had finally emptied of all but one customer after the morning rush, the owner and her only employee busy cleaning and resetting the tables for lunch.

"When you're right, you're right," replied the owner, a warm feeling in her chest as she surveyed the shop.

Finding coffee in this world had been a game changer. It was more common than back in her own world, if that were even possible.

A few years ago, she'd never thought she'd own a business, let alone own one in a world filled with monsters and magical trading cards. It was strange that she'd come to enjoy her time in the southern reaches of Aidland, considering it had been forced upon her without her consent. She'd lost everything and everyone who had meant anything to her, but she'd still attained a semblance of peace and purpose.

The whole first year had been one giant dark cloud in her mind, probably would have gone comatose from depression if she hadn't needed to keep moving to survive.

The men of the town tried to flirt with her, some of them directly asking her to marry them. She knew now it was just the Aidland way of helping widows and unmarried immigrants, but it only made her feel worse, even if she did appreciate the attention.

Still, she'd made the best of it, turning her interest in books and coffee into a thriving beachside hotspot for the locals.

The project had been difficult at first. The locals didn't speak English, which meant the few books that the System transferred with her weren't particularly helpful.

With the help of Ella, a teenage daughter of the family who'd taken her in, she was able to pick up Aidish in a few months. Several people became rather obsessed with reading and wanted more. But not everyone in Aidland could read, so she hosted a weekly class led by the scholar she purchased writing supplies from.

Not having a huge selection of books available, the shop owner used those supplies to write her own short stories, basing them on her life before coming to Aidland. The stories were a big hit and a new "Science Fiction" shelf was born.

The shop owner gathered the few books customers had left on their tables, walking back to the shelves and putting them back in order. It wasn't much of a book shop, but at least it was hers.

"I can finish cleaning up, if you'd like to get some fresh air," came Ella's voice. "Just don't forget to take Tortie with you. It's been a while, but sometimes monsters come up on the beach."

At the sound of its name, a maine coon sized cat with tortoiseshell fur jumped down from the top of a bookshelf, sauntering toward the front door, not waiting to see if she would follow. With a chuckle, she thanked Ella and followed after the cat down to the beach.

The shop owner breathed in the smell of salt water as she reached the shore, then settled herself onto the sand. The sounds of crashing waves relaxed her as Tortie climbed into her lap.

The cat curled up and meowed for pets, but kept a casual awareness of the water, in case she was needed. Half an hour they sat, enjoying the calming sensations of the ocean, when the shop owner remembered she hadn't looked through her notifications since before last week's monster hunt.

Would she ever get used to that part of this world? She'd never paid much attention to role playing games in her past life.

The shop owner pulled up her notifications, happy to see she'd completed another tier of **"The Very Best"** quest. Her smile curved up on one side into a smirk as she thought about how the reward would help keep her shop open for another few months, at least. There was another notification, which was surprising. What else had she accomplished recently?

<u>Congratulations!</u>
You've completed the Hidden Quest: Books-A-Dozen

Requirements: Create a place that encourages learning, community, and a good cup of joe. Bonus points if it's near a beach.

Reward: It's a surprise. Head back to the shop to see what it is.

Progress: Complete

Reward will be received automatically when circumstances permit.

"Hidden quest? Huh, that's weird," she wondered aloud. How come no one had told her about hidden quests? "I'll have to ask Ella."

Curious to see what the reward would be a hidden quest, she stood up from the sand, fast enough to draw an annoyed meow from Tortie.

"Oh shush, you'll be fine," she said, a flutter of excitement in her chest. "I wonder what my reward will be!"

72

SMELLS LIKE POTENTIAL

There wasn't much of a book selection, if Ethan was being honest. At least in comparison to the bookstores back home.

Thinking back over his time in Aidland, he'd only ever seen Havard reading and those were mostly scrolls or messages having to do with logistics. The more he thought about it, the more he realized how impressive this small collection actually was.

While continuing to browse the titles on the shelves, occasionally picking one up to flip through, Ethan eavesdropped on Jack talking with the teenaged woman working in the cafe. She had said they weren't serving any more food until lunch, so they got to chatting instead.

"Yeah, we call it 'Basic Cardist Training'."

"And you just... teach people? For free?"

"Yup. Though, they have to pay for the card they learn with if they want to keep it afterward."

"That's pretty cool," there was an obvious teenage girl lower lip pout in her voice as she continued. "We don't have anything like that around here. Our family has one uncommon monster card that gets passed down to the oldest child. I'm the middle of three... so I doubt I'll ever get one."

"Well..." Jack started, "Maybe we could start a branch of BCT out here. What do you think, dad?"

Ethan stood from the shelf he had been squatting beside and considered the location. Beachside town with a cafe/bookstore. He and Rebecca used to talk about opening something just like it, the whole vibe was very much up his alley. Not to mention the quest notification sending him out here for that specific purpose.

"We can look into it, for sure. Talk to whoever leads the town, since it's more than a two man job. It would take a while to get started, though," he could see the excitement drop from the young woman's face. "But I'm sure Jack here would be happy to teach you the basics until then. We have spare common monster cards and he's something of a Cardist expert."

"Oh wow! That would be amazing! I could be your first student!"

The girl grabbed Jack's hands from across the counter, making zero attempt to hide her excitement. Jack's cheeks flushed bright red. Oh no, his boy was developing a crush already!

"You should definitely talk to Miss Rebecca about getting it started."

The smile on Ethan's face dropped, Jack dropped some piece of wood he'd been fiddling with. Had he heard her right? That wasn't a common name used here in Aidland, as far as he could tell.

"Did you say 'Miss Rebecca'?

"Yes! The owner of the cafe!" she replied, unaware of the change in his expression. "She's not from here, but she's super cool and a great boss. If you're wanting to work with the Elders to start something, she's the expert."

As the girl finished speaking, the door to the shop opened with a tiny chime of a bell attached at the top. Standing in the doorway was a beautiful red-headed woman wearing a mixture of Aidish clothing and a vintage gray NASA shirt. Ethan knew that shirt. He'd bought her that shirt for Christmas while he was deployed overseas.

"Rebecca?"

"Ethan?"

"Mom?"

The woman turned to Jack, tears welling up in her eyes. She looked like she was deciding between a dozen different things to say, settling on simply holding out her arms.

"Come here, my little warrior."

73

A REUNION OF SORTS

"So... I died?"

"Yup. Or my Rebecca died, at least. So..." Ethan hesitated, "Your Ethan and Jack died too?"

"Car accident on the way home from a convention," she stated simply, lost in contemplation. There was a moment of pause between them. Ethan could feel a particular question forming in her eyes. "What'd you do with my body?"

Yup. He knew that's what she'd care about.

No need for an existential crisis for Rebecca, lover of the infinite void that is outer space. Why had he even been worried about how she'd react? Rebecca, the sci-fi nerd who didn't even like stereotypical fantasy stories, just spent the last three years in a monster riddled, medieval/viking era world. Not only had she survived, she'd thrived.

"We had you cremated and put into one of those tree pod things," Ethan replied, "So you'd help a tree grow nice and healthy. We planted it at your parents' house, since they're the least likely to move away."

"I'm sure they appreciated that."

She didn't seem particularly thrown off by mentioning her family either. Huh. Maybe she'd already gone through the stages of grief.

"They do, though it wasn't our first choice. Jack wanted to send your ashes to Mars, which felt more like something you'd want. We even looked into it."

"Too expensive?"

I nodded.

"Pretty sure it's meant for people who have more money than they know what to do with."

Rebecca shrugged her shoulders in response, eyes turned away and looking off into the corner.

Was she imagining her body in a tree pod, planted underground? He'd thought about it a lot. Like, what if you put somebody's body in the pod, but it turned out they weren't dead? Terrifying. Fortunately, she'd been cremated first, so there was no chance of that happening.

Looking at her, it struck him how surreal this was. Sitting in a cafe in Aidland, catching up with his dead wife. He'd imagined seeing Rebecca again, sure, but he never actually expected it to happen. There wasn't exactly evidence supporting the possibility of reuniting with dead people in a fantasy world. Based on the extended silence between them, he guessed she was thinking something similar.

"So, the evidence suggests we're from alternate realities. I died in yours, you died in mine," she theorized, breaking the silence. "Assuming life with your Rebecca was similar to mine... did you ever tell Jack about our plan to separate?"

There it was. Ethan knew the conversation would lead there eventually. He breathed in a chest and stomach full of air, then nodded as he slowly exhaled.

"How'd he take it?"

"Better than you'd expect from someone his age. He's an observant kid, so he could tell something was up."

"That's not surprising," she bit her bottom lip, then continued, "And how has our time apart been for you?"

Ethan laughed.

"I wouldn't call it 'time apart', Rebecca. We didn't split, you were taken from me," he took another deep breath in, held it for a few seconds, and released it before continuing to breathe normally, "I'd be lying if I said I didn't feel some relief. But, mostly, I went on autopilot to make sure we didn't fall apart."

Conflicting emotions fought for dominance over Rebecca's face. She'd never been great at hiding how she felt. The saying is that people wear their heart on their sleeve. Well, Rebecca wore it on her face.

"And how about you? You seem to be doing well," Ethan waved a hand at the shop, knowing that encouraging her to talk would better help her process, then added, "You look like you're happy here."

"I am," she admitted. "The last three years have shown me how capable I am. I feel more like myself than I've ever felt in my life, more confident. I'm happy you and Jack are here..."

"But?"

"How do you know there's a but?"

"Because I know you, Rebecca. Just say what you're feeling. I can handle it."

"But... I'm afraid that I'll go back to being the timid, unsure version of myself who feels like I can't do anything on my own."

Her face fell into her hands as she leaned forward, elbows resting on her knees.

This was why they'd decided to live separately. They loved each other and didn't want a divorce, but something hadn't been working for a while. They'd needed space to figure it out, but she died before they were able to give it a shot.

It had been years since then and they weren't the same people anymore, so... he supposed they did get the time apart that they needed. But also, she wasn't even his Rebecca. She'd married some other version of Ethan. That was a can of worms that he wasn't sure they should open.

"Well, we don't have to figure everything out yet. For now, we can just enjoy getting to know each other again."

"True," she replied, voice muffled through her hands.

"How about a three phase plan?" He held up a finger for each item as he listed them. "One: we go for a walk along the beach so I can catch you up on what brought us out here. Two: we find Jack and – what was the girl's name again?"

"Ella," she replied, hands combing her hair back as she sat up straight in her chair.

"Right. Two: we find Jack and Ella, then grab something to eat. Three: we enjoy each other's company, have some cuddle therapy, and get a good night's sleep."

"I do like a good three phase plan," she pondered aloud. "Cuddle therapy, eh?"

"Yup."

"I feel like there's a story there."

Ethan spent a few extra moments taking in his wife's freckles and wavy red hair, which she'd grown to her shoulders. He felt at home, a knot growing in his chest as he stood up.

"I'll fill you in while we walk," he offered her his hand. "You ready?"

She took his hand, stood up beside him, and pulled him into a hug. She nestled into his neck, allowing him to rest his chin on her head. That was a feeling he'd been missing.

Someone to come home to.

74

LIKE A DOG WITH FLEAS

"You're leaving soon, aren't you?"

"Huh? What makes you say that?"

"Well, you've been acting like a dog with fleas, antsy and ready to run straight into the ocean. At least since my class graduated last month."

Jack sighed as he lay on his back, scanning the night sky showcasing the most stars he'd ever seen with his own two eyes. If he squinted, he could see the hazy beginnings of the Northern Lights. Or this world's equivalent, anyway.

Ella was right, of course.

The last year had been amazing, something out of his dreams. Jack and his dad had finished building another branch of the BCT, he could spend time at the beach every day, he'd made a new best friend who appreciated the way his mind worked, and he had his mom back.

Somehow.

He still didn't understand how that worked, at some point deciding figuring it out wasn't worth the risk of losing her again.

"I get restless when I'm in one place for too long," he replied. "I get it from my dad. He's ready to leave too, I think. My parents get easily irritated at small things when they need to change things up, and it seems to be that way for me too."

"Sure. But aren't you going to miss m— uhh, your mom?"

Jack turned his head to the side just enough to read Ella's expression. Her eyes, ringed in red and on the cusp of tears, also scanned the sky. What she was looking for, he could only guess.

"Of course I'll miss my mom. I'll miss a lot of things, and people," he nudged her with his elbow. "But the longer I stay still, the less enjoyable I am to be around. I get cranky and stop enjoying things I usually can't get enough of. Sand between my toes becomes grating instead of comforting, the sounds of the ocean become nails on a chalkboard rather than soothing background noise."

"Hmm," her eyes continued their scanning. "I suppose it makes sense. Better to leave before something you love becomes insufferable and you're no longer excited to come back."

"Exactly," Jack inched his hand close to hers, then intertwined their fingers, neither of them breaking their gaze from the stars. "And I have many reasons to be excited to come back."

Ella gave his hand a light squeeze, cementing his conflicting feelings. Excitement to follow his newest quest, yet also a longing to stay in this moment forever. Why did life have to feel like constant contradictions? He belonged here, but also on the road.

"What's a chalkboard?" asked Ella, a playful confusion in her tone. "And why would nails on them be unpleasant?"

Jack laughed, a blessed detour from the downward spiral he was headed toward.

Oh well. There was plenty of time to have an existential crisis when he was his dad's age. For now, he'd just have to make the most of his contradictions and apply the scientific method like his life depended on it.

75

MIND CLOUDS

"You need to leave."

It wasn't a question, not a discussion. There was no room for argument. She stated it as a fact.

Not that Ethan was likely to argue anyway. He'd felt the dark clouds rolling in over his mind for some time, not to mention the quest he'd gotten to check on the BCT branch back in Trace, a pack of rare item cards as incentive. The System and Rebecca were obviously in cahoots against him, both telling him to leave. They both knew he'd go crazy if he stayed in one place for too long.

Still, he was reluctant to leave. Losing Rebecca again terrified him, even knowing time apart would be good for both of them. His body felt unwilling to cooperate, so he stayed silent.

Ethan clutched a small book Rebecca had written sometime in the last year about the time they'd driven through Utah in the middle of a Mormon cricket swarm. The road was bathed in cricket blood. The locals in Aidland really seemed to like that story, maybe because of their own experience with hordes. Ethan, however, was having trouble focusing on the words.

"Do you want to come with me?" he asked, finally finding his voice. Please say yes. Also, please don't say yes.

In response, she laughed. A full belly laugh. Of course she did. How rude. At least, it would be if Rebecca had a single rude bone in her body.

Ethan frowned.

"I don't think either of us would enjoy that after a few days," she replied as her laughter settled.

"What about Jack?"

"I'm eternally grateful to get to know Jack," she was smiling, a single tear trailing down her cheek, "but we need to accept that he's not my son. He's yours. I had my chance and I'm happy to have him in my life, but he needs his dad right now more than he needs a strange mirror image of his mom."

"That's true, I guess."

A pause hung between them as Ethan searched for any solution to grab hold of, like a free climber halfway up a cliff-side. The panic never one hundred percent goes away, it seemed. After a deep breath, he managed to squeak out what he was really struggling with.

"I'm afraid of losing you again."

Small waves crashed at their feet, the cold water keeping him from crawling too far into the deep dark cave in his mind. Oof, he really did need to get moving again. Rebecca moved to stand between him and the ocean, cupping his head in her hands.

"You'll be back," she said, certainty in her eyes.

A dam in Ethan's chest cracked, tears gathering in his eyes. A hearty full body sob was building up, ready to break, when Colby-Jack barked from her perch as guardian on the sand dunes. She rarely actually barked, which meant she really needed his attention.

Emergency? The pair looked at each other and moved toward the dunes where they found Jack and Ella were running toward them from the direction of town.

"How much you wanna bet it's a monster hunt? There've been rumors of a horde gathering east of us."

"No bet," he smiled. There wouldn't be anything else this urgent, so he'd lose that bet.

The gloom in his mind and tightness in his chest receded almost as if they'd never been there at all. There was nothing quite like a potential emergency to get Ethan out of a funk.

He looked back to Rebecca, who smiled at him.

"Go on. I'll be here when you get back."

EPILOGUE

Pax stepped over a root jutting into the trail.

"How do you even come up with this stuff? I mean, I'm honored that you wrote me into the sequel, but you didn't have to make me out to be so reckless and impulsive... even if it is kinda true."

A chuckle and a grunt were all Ethan was able to give in response as he continued down the trail. Who knew where his ideas came from or where they would go? His style of writing was akin to putting one foot in front of the other, just like with hiking.

This particular hike marked the third backpacking trip he had been on with Pax in the two years since they'd finished the Pacific Crest Trail together, though this was their first time without Jack. With just the two of them, it was only a matter of time before the conversations became more personal.

Ethan's now sixteen year old son had recently bought his first car, an old, gray 2000 PT Cruiser they'd found for a thousand dollars. He'd agreed to match whatever money Jack put into it and the boy had still bought a cheap car.

Honestly, it made him even more proud of his son, if that was possible.

Everyone's first car should be old and never one hundred percent likely to get you to your destination.

So Jack went to spend the summer with his friends, driving up and then back down the Pacific Coast Highway, camping on or near as many beaches as possible.

It was terrifying, as a parent, to let him go. How do you not worry about your son going on an adventure without you? In the end Pax had helped convince him it would be good for both of them, mostly by promising a few weeks worth of "Cuddle Therapy" while they hiked the John Muir Trail in Northern California.

"Do you ever wish Aidland was real?" asked Pax after another hundred steps down the trail. "Not just stories you'd imagined?"

"I mean... it's kinda real. The fans won't stop asking about it, so, if nothing else, it exists in their heads."

"Sure," replied Pax. "But I didn't ask if it was 'kinda real'. I asked if you ever wish it was real."

It wasn't an unexpected question. When he'd finally gotten around to writing a sequel to Aidland, the question had been asked during almost every interview. He'd come up with witty responses, but always to kind of shield himself from thinking too hard about it.

Ethan stopped walking, deciding to focus on how he really felt about it, rather than where his next steps would land. Twist your ankle once on a small rock and you'll become paranoid forever.

He took in the scenery around him, what he'd missed by staring so hard at the trail. Yosemite really was beautiful. No less beautiful than Aidland had been.

As Pax stopped beside him on his left, he felt a nudge against his right hand. Next to him stood an all white dog, some mix of Cocker Spaniel and Sheltie. Maybe some other breeds thrown in.

The shelter he'd adopted Mozzarella from didn't know for certain, nor did the previous owner. Supposedly the man had gone through a nasty divorce and wasn't able to take care of her anymore. You never know if those stories are true, but Ethan had immediately connected with her and the stupid cheese name felt like it had been a sign.

A reminder that the magic of companionship can come in all shapes and sizes.

"I dunno," he started. "Sometimes, I wish it were real. But I have no control over it, so is it really worth thinking about? I'm content with my life, with all its peaks and valleys."

"Which peaks and valleys are we talking about here?"

One side of Pax's mouth pulled up into a smirk as she pulled her shoulders back and chest forward.

She grabbed his hand, intertwining their fingers. Pax wasn't his wife and might not ever be, since Ethan couldn't really imagine recreating the intensity of marriage. Still, they were very close. A kind of casual intimacy that his sensitive heart appreciated.

And there it was, a feeling almost like belonging. Peace, maybe? It was just a flicker, a moment in time where his heart felt full.

It wasn't something he felt often, usually only as he watched Jack grow up. The lack of that feeling elsewhere in his life made Ethan hyper aware of it any time he did feel it. Each flicker gave him renewed hope that there would be more to come.

A flicker of peace was enough for him.

EPI-EPILOGUE

"Do you think he knows?"

"Do I think who knows what?"

"This Alternate of Ethan Farris," replied the Son.

Sitting in a translucent chair similar in style to an Adirondack, the Son held up a paperback book, the front more of a simple title page than a proper cover. The Father didn't look, but the Son continued speaking anyway.

"He wrote a surprisingly accurate sequel to the usual standalone after finishing the hike, even though he never made it back to Aidland. There's a general lack of big picture context, but still... strangely accurate."

"Do we know why this Alternate didn't make it back to Aidland?" the Father asked.

"The System says he never finished the hidden quest because they bypassed a section of trail in Northern California. Apparently, a twisted ankle slowed them down earlier in the hike and they got stuck behind a snowstorm that the other Alternate's group didn't."

"Hmm... Well, unless he's developed more than a passing

understanding of String Theory, he can't know anything for certain. I suppose it's possible for an Alternate to experience Deja Vu-like visions or dreams, assuming their life was similar to that of the original."

The Father stood from the Alternate Table he'd been bent over all day and scratched his chin, as though something had just occurred to him.

"Unless he got a System message of some kind, but the System wouldn't do that."

"Well, it hasn't done it before," the Son pondered allowed, his attention slowly drawing back to the chapter he was reading. "That doesn't mean it isn't capable of doing it."

"Valid point. If it did, there'd be a reason that lines up with our overall goals. Maybe the System did it to help the man process his grief? It's been known to provide comfort like that before."

The Father let out a long suffering sigh, his eyes widening as they rested on the book in his Son's hands.

"How'd you get an advanced reader copy?"

"I'm subscribed to the newsletter," the Son replied, not looking up from the book. "First one hundred replies were sent ARCs. You can read it when I'm done, if you'd like."

The Father nodded, thankful for his son's forethought. None of the other Alternates had written a sequel, so it was a rare find. He turned back to the table, already distracted.

"Nothing to do about it all now, anyway. I suppose we'll just keep an eye on the Alternate and see what happens."

AFTERWORD

I have a personal goal of reaching 1,000 reviews of my book. This is for no other reason than having an arbitrary goal to achieve that will make this project feel like a success.

So, even if you thought the book was mediocre at best, please consider leaving a review. Doesn't even have to be long. I like short reviews.

Some examples:

- Ehh, it was alright.
- Mediocre at best.
- I'm just here so I don't get fined.
- What did I even read? Was any of it even real? My chest hurts for some reason.
- Ten out of ten, would recommend.
- Seven out of ten, would recommend.
- My eyes, dear God, my eyes!
- Why do I have a sudden urge to adopt a corgi?

You get the idea. Thanks for reading!

Acknowledgments

People I want to thank, bullet point style:

Britt - My Wildfire. Honestly, I don't know if I ever would have given this a real shot if it weren't for you. Switching up our family dynamic, you as financial provider and me as stay-at-home dad, allowed me the opportunity to put dedicated time and effort into my need to write. Neither of us know anyone who's pursued something like this, which can make it seem impossible and a waste of time. You still never tried to convince me it was a bad idea or not worth doing. No matter where life takes us, I've got your back and I know you have mine.

Finn - My little wildfire. I thought that the landscape of my life had changed when I met your mom, but you take the metaphor to a whole other level. Since you were born, I've had to seriously evaluate what in my life was worth saving and what I needed to let go of. Writing helps keep me sane, which I need being your dad, so I decided to focus my limited free energy there instead of all the less important hobbies I used to have. Thank you for your giggles, your *hugs, your kisses, and for allowing me to vicariously experience things for the first time again. This acknowledgment won't mean much to you until you're older, but I wanted to say it anyway.*

Mom - When I was a kid, a teacher brought in a bunch of those blank hard cover books for us students to write and illustrate our own stories. I don't remember what I wrote about, but I remember loving it and bringing them home to show you. I remember you saying something like, "This is good. You could do this." I took it to mean I could be a writer, if I wanted. Core memory.

Dad - My first reader. Probably the only person I trust to have as a beta reader, knowing I'll get thoughtful and helpful feedback. I don't trust people easily, so that's a big deal for me. It wasn't until after you read it that I thought anyone other than me would enjoy my writing.

Kyle - Growing up together playing card games like Pokémon and Yu-gi-oh were a big inspiration for this story. I often think about how skilled we were at Yu-gi-oh, playing 2v2 against the other kids at the bowling alley. We'd bet super rare cards and win every time. It never felt like a gamble though; that's how well we meshed our strategies together. I know you don't need my thanks, but you get it anyway.

Hans and Heidin - Your passion for Pokémon and the hand drawn cards you create for fun are what inspired the opening scenes of this story, so thanks for just being excited about something and wanting to share it with your dear ole' uncle.

Thomas, that Irish dude I met on Reddit - The first non-family member to read the book. Your excited feedback as you read through the chapters on your lunch breaks brought me life and joy in a time when I was afraid to share my work with anyone. Your reactions were exactly what I was hoping for in a reader. Cheers, mate!

You, Whoever you are - Are you a friend or member of my family who read this because you wanted to support my work? Are you a friend of a friend? Do you have no relation to me whatsoever and somehow found my book? Whoever you are, thank you for taking the time to read it and I hope you enjoyed it. If you didn't enjoy it but still somehow made it to the acknowledgments, that's alright too. I'm not everyone's cup of tea.

Author Recommendations

Every book is built upon the shoulders of other authors.

The following are some of my favorite fiction authors who have influenced me in one way or another, in no particular order. I know none of them, nor did they ask in any way to be listed. I just love their work.

- Nicholas Eames - The Kings of the Wild Series. 1970's/80's style rockstar mercenaries in a fantasy world. Need I say more?
- John Scalzi - Old Man's War Series and pretty much everything else he's ever written. His style and humor definitely influenced my willingness to let myself be silly in my writing.
- Douglas Adams - Hitch Hiker's Guide to the Galaxy. Any time I thought "Maybe my writing is too sporadic or all over the place", I remember how he took a whole scene to describe a whale and a pot of petunias popping into existence and falling to their deaths.
- Casey Hollingshead - His work on the Battle Brothers game, as well as the Battle Brothers series of books.
- Peter Clines - 14 and The Fold are brilliant books. His "Ex" series is also phenomenal. I don't know how his work isn't more well known.

- Andy Weir - The Martian is one of my all time favorite books. The movie was great, but the book really draws you in and makes you feel how long he's been alone. Project Hail Mary is a masterpiece.
- Bernard Cornwell - The Last Kingdom series is something else. The Netflix show is great, but I really got sucked into the books.
- Blake Crouch - We constantly look up to see if he has anything new out or in the works, then giggle like school girls when we see he released something. They're all great books.
- Cliff Graham - King David, but as an actual violent warlord. Having been a soldier myself, it's incredibly refreshing to read his "Lion of War" series.
- Ted Dekker - My childhood was filled with Ted Dekker books. The Circle Series specifically will always hold a special place in my heart.
- Donita K. Paul - Dragon Keeper Chronicles. Again, I don't know how her work isn't more well known. Beautiful stories.
- Bryan Davis - Dragons in our Midst series. Dragons meet the Knight's of the Round Table. I love when two stories collide to make a new one.
- Xavier P. Hunter - The Metagamer Chronicles. One of the first LitRPG type books I ever read that actually ends, rather than the author never finishing it.
- Shirtaloon - He Who Fights With Monsters. Ongoing series than I never get tired of. LitRPG at its finest.

- Matt Dinniman - Dungeon Crawler Carl, initially self published, recently got a book deal. I lost my mind when I saw hard cover copies of the first three books in stores. Gives me hope for my own stories.
- J.R. Matthews - Portal to Nova Roma series, an AI creates himself a body and a portal to another world that has magic. Can't wait for the next book. Jake's Magical Market series, definitely an inspiration for creating my own story that involved cards.

And now, a less verbose list of some non-fiction that have been instrumental in becoming the person I want to be. In no particular order:

- Simon Sinek - Start with Why and The Infinite Game
- Chris Gethard - Lose Well
- Mason Currey - Daily Rituals: How Artists Work
- Timothy Ferris - Tribe of Mentors
- James Clear - Atomic Habits
- Cheryl Strayed - Wild
- Chris Guillebeau - The Happiness of Pursuit
- Derek Sivers - Anything You Want
- Chuck Wendig - Gentle Writing Advice

About the Author

Derek Kenney is just a man. He puts on his pants one leg at a time, like any other. He traveled the United States in his early twenties, served in the US Army in his late twenties, and is focusing his thirties on writing and his family. He grew up in Tracy, California, but lives wherever makes sense for him and his family at each stage of life.

This is Derek's first book.